Look for these titles by *Shiloh Walker*

Now Available:

The Hunters Series
The Huntress
Hunter's Pride
Malachi
Hunter's Edge

Grimm's Circle Series
Candy Houses
No Prince Charming
I Thought It Was You
Crazed Hearts
Tarnished Knight

Always Yours
Talking with the Dead
Playing for Keeps
For the Love of Jazz
Beautiful Girl
Vicious Vixen
My Lady
The Redeeming
No Longer Mine
A Forever Kind of Love

Print Collection
Legends: Hunters and Heroes

No Longer Mine

Shiloh Walker

Samhain Publishing, Ltd.
577 Mulberry Street, Suite 1520
Macon, GA 31201
www.samhainpublishing.com

No Longer Mine
Copyright © 2011 by Shiloh Walker
Print ISBN: 978-1-60928-016-1
Digital ISBN: 978-1-60504-991-5

Editing by Heidi Moore
Cover by Kanaxa

This book has been previously published and has been revised from its original release.
First Samhain Publishing, Ltd. electronic publication: April 2010
First Samhain Publishing, Ltd. print publication: February 2011

Dedication

This book went out of print sometime in 2005 or 2006.

Since it's been out of print I've had a number of readers ask me if I'd ever release it again. My initial response was ***NO***—capital letters, italics, bold font and all. :o)

It was my first attempt at a full-length romance. It's not one of my better attempts either. It's rough, the characters are a little over dramatic, a little overdone, and sometimes, I didn't like either of them very much.

But, like many writers' "first" attempts, it does have a special place in my heart, and part of what makes it special is the story itself.

It's rough, although I revised and smoothed it out.

It's a little full of angst and drama, although I'm trying to work on that too.

So while I know some of the flaws with this story, and I know I can fix some of them, fixing a lot of them would actually be changing the story. There is also something that happens in the course of the story that was a little too painful for me to deal with after a personal loss of mine that happened in 2005.

Because of that loss, because of the work that would be needed to get this book a little more...reader ready, I was hesitant to think about putting it back out there. But so many people have asked, and I hate to keep saying NO—capital letters or otherwise.

For those who kept asking...I hope you enjoy.

And always, always, always for my family. I thank God for you every day of my life.

Chapter One

It was hot—the kind of heat that wrapped around a person, threatened to suffocate, threatened to choke. Hot, with leaden, overcast skies that seemed to promise rain, but it had been overcast for days and they hadn't seen a drop.

Nicole Kline was just outside of town when she flipped on the radio and heard the weather report. A storm was coming.

Great.

Not the ideal day for a run into town, but it was either suffer the heat or suffer the frustration when all she found for dinner was Cheetos and frozen ground beef. If she had paid attention to the weather before they had left home she would have suffered the Cheetos, the frozen ground beef—and her younger brother's griping.

Yum.

Instead of trying to make the thirty-minute drive back to her home in the hills, she decided to grab her groceries then go to her dad's and wait it out there.

She made it in and out of the store in under twenty minutes. As she walked outside with her infant son, Jason, perched on her hip, she glanced up at the sky. The sight of the thunderheads piling up overhead made her wince.

Her brother, Shawn, bumped her shoulder with his. "Come on," he said. "We're going to get soaked if we wait around too long."

She made a face. "We're going to get soaked anyway." She chucked her son under his chin and smiled at him. Not that he was at all worried about those clouds.

The scent of rain hung heavy on the air.

Looks like the farmers are going to get the rain they want and then some, Nikki mused as she secured the straps on the baby's car seat. After she finished securing Jason in his seat, she went around to help her brother finish loading the groceries into the back of the SUV.

Flattened drops of rain splattered the hood of the car as she slid into the driver's seat. Then Nikki glared at the skies as the clouds burst, dousing the parking lot under a deluge of water.

"Don't sweat it, Nik," Shawn advised. "We can just wait it out at Dad's."

She sighed. That had been the plan anyway, not that she had told Shawn. Her brother and her father were on the outs for some reason, which was why Shawn had been spending the past few weeks at her place.

She could hear Jason jabbering to himself from the backseat.

"Dogs, dogs, dogs," he chanted over and over while he played with a tattered stuffed mouse and chewed busily on the remaining ear.

At least that was what she *thought* he was saying.

Flicking Shawn a glance, she ordered, "Put your seatbelt on, will ya?"

Rolling his eyes, he fastened the lap belt and drawled, "Yes'm." He gave Jason a look in the mirror, circling his finger at his temple. The baby laughed and clapped his hands before launching into a long and detailed jabbering monologue with his friend, Mouse.

Hazel eyes squinted, Nikki stared through the windshield, blocking out the noise of the rain and her son's jabbering. Even though she drove with the lights on, she couldn't see much more than fifteen or twenty feet in front of her.

Twenty minutes passed and she still wasn't at her dad's. The store wasn't even ten minutes from there, but that was under normal driving conditions.

Growling with frustration, she snapped, "I can't see a damn thing in this!"

The rumble of thunder edged closer. Lightning flashed.

"You're almost there, sis. It's just up there."

She spotted the turn off as Shawn spoke. "Almost there, fella," she said as Jason started shrieking, "Eat! Momma, eat!"

"Just a few minutes, Jas—"

Neither Shawn nor Nikki saw the other car. It came flying around a curve fast—so fast—and hit them from behind. She was thrown forward. Blinding pain sliced through her head and a loud, thunderous crash filled her ears.

A blaring noise rent the air, but above it she heard a baby's panicked, startled cry.

From the passenger seat next to her, Shawn swore viciously, grabbing for the door handle.

"Jason!" Her voice was garbled, choked. Blood filled her mouth and a red haze clouded her vision.

Instinctively she slammed on the brakes, wrenched the steering wheel to the right towards safety. Off to their left was a steep drop off—

Another jolt struck her SUV, throwing her back. She was pinned against the seat by her safety restraint as the world started to spin before her. Above the roaring in her ears she heard thunder and the screeching sound of metal against metal. Then all was silent.

Chapter Two

May.

Three Years Later.

The house was silent save for the monotonous clacking of fingers hitting the keyboard. The woman sitting at the desk worked in silence. Almost in a trance.

She had been up since before dawn, lingering in the kitchen only long enough for a cup of coffee. She had drank half of it but that had been hours ago. A need to visit the bathroom and a painfully dry mouth had made her leave her office twice and two half-empty diet Cokes sat on her desk next to the forgotten coffee.

She hadn't eaten, but that wasn't unusual. Even at the best of times her appetite was sketchy. When she was nearing the end of a story everything that wasn't absolutely vital was forgotten.

That meant she drank a little, got up long enough to pee and fell asleep when her eyes would no longer stay open.

Keying in one final sentence, Nicole Kline heaved out a sigh and leaned back in her chair.

Her daze left her, and as it did she grew startlingly aware of one thing.

She *hurt*. The headache had been brewing for some time, but she'd ignored it in favor of the story.

The headache was only part of it though. Her wrists and the backs of her hands alternated between numb and excruciatingly painful. Her back and shoulders were stiff and she knew when she stood she was going to be really, really sorry.

Nikki hit save, her mouth stretching wide with a yawn. She backed up the story to a flash drive and shut down before giving into the urge to bury her head in her hands.

Okay, maybe the headache *was* the worst of it. The demon throbbed behind her eyes and nausea churned in her belly. Her hands were shaking. "Idiot," she mumbled. "Deserve what you get for trying to ignore it."

She fumbled in the drawer for a familiar bottle and downed a pill dry before she stumbled over to the couch in the corner. She buried her face in her arms to cut off the fading light and prayed for oblivion.

She awoke at ten.

If it hadn't for the alarm going off on the simple wristwatch she wore, she might have slept another five or six hours easy.

The headache had subsided but a million little aches remained. Her shoulders were stiff, her back a line of fire and when she first sat up, she could barely move her arms.

A marathon writing session and sleeping that way on the couch was not good on her joints.

Feeling a hundred years old, she sat on the edge of the bed and scrubbed her hands over her face before silencing the alarm. She was tired enough to wish she could just sleep through the alarm, but she knew better. The watch had been a gift, but it had come with conditions—a promise. It was a simple watch, nothing fancy, but it had been given to her by a friend, one who rarely asked anything of her. And when Nikki gave her word, she tried to keep it.

With that mind, she shoved up off the couch and made her way down to the kitchen. She walked into the wall and scowled when she banged her elbow. The impact sent nasty little jolts down her arm.

"You've got to take better care of yourself," she muttered, echoing the voice of her friend, Kirsten, the woman who'd given her that watch just a little over a year ago.

I will, Kris. Promise.

But Nikki wasn't so certain she was keeping that promise.

Her refrigerator was practically bare, just some chicken, a few eggs and a hunk of cheese. The orange juice had expired a few days ago, but there was her ever-present supply of Diet Coke. She might run out of food, milk, juice and almost everything else, but she'd never, ever let herself run out of Diet Coke or coffee.

In the corner was something on a plate that reminded her of her science experiment in ninth grade.

The store was a definite must for the upcoming day off.

She'd have to take that day off too.

Tomorrow. She'd take tomorrow.

She had to go into town and get her prescriptions refilled and she'd promised her dad she'd come by. With her luck, if she didn't her nagging brother would tattle on her.

Wrinkling her nose, she pitched the juice, the science experiment and what was left of the chicken, but guilt wouldn't let her ignore food altogether. She sliced off some cheese and grabbed one of the soft drinks. With the cheese and her Diet Coke, she leaned against the counter and grabbed the amber bottle of prescription pills.

She studied the bottle with a grim sigh and wondered, for the millionth time, how she'd found herself here.

This wasn't the way things were supposed to turn out.

Not at all.

Opening the bottle, she muttered, "Suck it up, princess."

She tossed back one of the small yellow pills and ate the cheese, drank her soft drink. It filled the empty hole in her stomach. Plus she knew if she got a call from a certain somebody tomorrow, when she was asked a certain question, she could honestly say, "Yes, I'm eating."

Her body felt weighted down as she dragged herself upstairs. Too many nights of catnaps and the migraine from hell, and she was ready to crash. But she wanted a shower—needed it.

She stripped as she made her way into the large, dark blue shower just off her bedroom, leaving a trail of clothing behind her as she went. Shower. Then bed. Shower. Then bed.

She deliberately kept her mind blank, although she was so tired it would be a miracle if she could manage any sort of coherent thought even if she tried.

While she rinsed off though, her blissfully blank mind turned traitor. She wasn't as tired as she thought, because the memories rose up, rushing at her like a freight train, unstoppable, unasked for. Unwelcome.

Time wasn't healing her wounds. Wasn't it supposed to?

God, she pleaded silently. *Will it ever get any easier?*

The pain was just as shattering now as it had been then. It clawed at her, filling her chest, then belly with hot, lancing little darts of pain. Her throat constricted until crying was punishment, but she had no control over the tears that swam in her eyes, the sobs that filled her throat.

With the water pounding down around her, she slid down the shower wall to huddle in the corner, wrapping her arms around her shivering naked body. She thought wildly, *It has to get better. It has to. Sometime.*

"You're almost there, sis. It's just up there..." Rain pounding against the windows, the roof. So much rain.

"Almost there, fella."

"Eat! Momma, eat!"

"Just a few minutes, Jas—"

The impact...the crash. Pain exploding in her head and dimly she could hear her brother swearing in the seat next to her.

Jason crying...

"Jason!"

The drop-off—have to keep away from the drop-off.

Another jolt. More pain...

The world spun around her, horrendous crashing and above it, she heard a baby's terrified cry.

But then, even as the crashing continued, that crying...it went silent.

Forever silent.

"Jason..."

It was the sound of her own voice that brought her back to herself. Huddled on the floor of the shower, freezing. The water battering her body was icy and it stole the breath from her lungs. Shaking, she turned the water off and climbed out of the shower.

She didn't want to look at the mirror, didn't want to see her ravaged face, didn't want to see the body she had let get too thin.

Grabbing her robe and a towel, she stumbled out of the bathroom to her bed. She rubbed her hair until it was mostly dry and then stared off into the distance.

They said time healed all wounds, but three years after

she'd had her heart shredded, she was still bleeding out.

Her little boy...

Closing her eyes, she said softly, "Jason..."

She'd survived, barely, losing his dad.

It had damn near killed her, but she'd survived. Because of Jason.

Falling back on the bed, wrapped in her damp robe, she thought of his little face, those dark eyes, so like his father.

His father.

Wade Lightfoot. At one time, that man had meant the entire world to her.

He had *been* everything to her. He had meant more than her books, her writing, her dreams to leave her rather sad, miserable childhood behind her.

He had been her entire life.

And then he had gotten another woman pregnant.

She'd survived that, and she'd even managed to be happy eventually...because of Jason.

Losing that little boy, that... Well, she wasn't technically dead. Her heart still beat. She breathed.

But she hadn't felt truly alive for three years.

New Albany, Indiana

The hot summer sun shone brightly down on the little house. A For Sale sign was in the yard, topped by a bright red sign announcing to the world that this house was sold. Toys dotted the lawn, and a crop of wildflowers bloomed under each window. Freshly painted shutters gleamed under the noonday sun.

He'd lived in the house for a little over six years, but it

hadn't ever been the home he'd hoped it would be.

Too many ghosts.

He was finally putting those ghosts to rest.

Shoving the door open with a booted foot, Wade Lightfoot walked out of the house, three boxes precariously stacked in his arms.

A gleefully laughing child darted in front of him, a yapping puppy at her heels. Wade stumbled and the box on top, one covered with dust, fell to the ground, falling open as it hit the concrete.

A familiar picture fell out—one he hadn't seen in years. But he hadn't ever forgotten it either.

Automatically he diverted his eyes and started to reach for it without looking, intending to pack it away with the rest of his memories. But then his hand slowed, stopped, and he turned his eyes back to the smiling faces looking up at him.

Damn, we looked so innocent...

It was Nikki and him at her senior prom. He had worn a monkey suit, had even gotten his hair cut. Her shy grin and tousled hair at odds with the flirty black dress she had worn. He smiled, remembering how she had dieted for two months, exercising like some aerobics instructor from hell, losing twenty pounds, to fit into that dress.

He looked up to check on Abby as she shrieked. Her uncle Joe had caught her up in a bear hug. Slowly, knowing he shouldn't, he righted the box. Photographs, notes, souvenirs from some local amusement parks jumbled inside as he reached in and pulled out a picture at random.

Their first real date. Lori's Christmas party.

The day he realized just how *right* it felt to be with Nikki. It was more than friendship, and that was a little scary. This girl was from the wrong side of town, but worse, she was only seventeen and had more problems than he had ever imagined

18

anybody having.

She was three years younger than him, but in her mind she was already far older than him. She'd seen things, dealt with things, he hoped he'd never have to see.

He'd seen some ugly things in his work, but only in his work.

He was an EMT and he often saw the ugly side of life. It touched him, but it hadn't shaped him.

It had shaped her all right. She'd lost two friends to drive-by shootings, her mother to suicide and for as long as he'd known her she'd done her damnedest to keep her younger brothers from falling into the dangerous lifestyles too often prevalent where she'd lived.

It had shaped her all right. Giving her a spine of steel and the resolve to get the hell out.

There was something else inside that box.

A book. The first one he'd seen, a year and a half after she'd run out of his life.

She'd gone and done it—exactly as she'd always said she would.

Sighing, he went to put the book back in the box and tried to tell himself to do the same with the picture, but he couldn't. He found himself staring at it, at the younger versions of them.

At Nikki in her black dress, her eyes laughing as she stared at the camera. If he closed his eyes he could still remember the smell of her flesh, how she felt in his arms...

"Daddy?"

He started, looking up into dark eyes so like his own. Abby. "Yeah, darling?" he asked, amazed his voice could sound so calm after spending heaven only knew how much time lost in memories.

"I'm hungry." She flashed him an engaging grin and held up her stuffed cocker spaniel puppy and added, "Skip's hungry too."

"So is Joe," his older brother said, mounting the steps.

He nodded, ran his hand over the picture, feeling a familiar ache in his chest. He tucked the picture back inside the book then slid the book back into the box.

Out of sight, but never out of mind.

She was no longer a part of his life...no longer his.

That was that.

Chapter Three

Morning found Nikki at a tiny hillside cemetery, the old-fashioned kind that had a little white chapel in front of it. A white picket fence surrounded the cemetery and a tiny stream ran through it.

It was one of the loveliest sites she had ever seen. Peaceful and quiet. That was why she had chosen it.

Her entire world lay six feet below in a tiny coffin, clad in his Easter Sunday suit, his precious Mouse tucked under his arm.

JASON CHRISTIAN KLINE
BORN MAY 11, 2006 DIED SEPTEMBER 2, 2007
Beloved Son
I Am With You Always, Until the End of Time.

She closed her eyes as her mind drifted back to that time of brief consciousness in the ER when she had awakened after the accident.

"Jase…"

She didn't know where that weak whisper had come from. Licking her lips, she tried to call out louder so he would hear her better. When he was playing it damn near took an earthquake to get his attention. "Jason..." The second pathetic whisper was only minutely louder than the first.

She tried to open her eyes but couldn't. Reaching up, she encountered gauze. Searching fingers roamed her face. The gauze bandages covered the top half of her head. What in the hell...

"Ms. Kline? Are you awake?"

She turned her head in the direction of the voice. "Where am I? What's happened?"

"I'm Dr. Lawrence, Ms. Kline. You're in Wayne County Hospital. Do you know where that is?"

"Yes. It's in Monticello. What am I doing here, Doctor?" she asked, telling herself not to worry. Jason was fine. He had to be. She reached up to shove the bandages off her head and another voice intruded.

"You need to leave those bandages be, now," the soft, cool female voice said. "You had some trauma to your face and we have to be careful."

"Who are you?"

"Leanne Winslow. I'm one of your nurses. How are you feeling?"

"I hurt. Will you please tell me what happened?" she asked, reaching out, encountering a soft gentle hand. Another hand rested comfortingly on her shoulder.

Above her head she didn't see the glances exchanged between nurse and doctor or how the doctor compressed his lips and nodded.

"Honey, you were in a car accident. Remember?" Leanne said. The bed dipped beneath added weight and the soft voice was closer.

"The storm..."

"A tornado passed through two neighboring counties. It was a pretty bad storm. You were in a car accident. You were run off the road. Remember?"

The prodding made her try to remember. The sluggish black curtain that obscured her mind wouldn't let her think too clearly. "Not much. My son?"

The hand on hers tightened. "I am so sorry," the nurse said, her voice sounding odd. "Ms. Kline, your son is gone."

She heard those last words and the black curtain suddenly cleared. She remembered. Jason's tiny little body gone cold, his eyes sightless. Pain roared up through her, biting, slashing and clawing until she wanted to scream with it.

She couldn't though. Her throat was tight. Whimpering noises came to her from far off as she drew her knees into her chest, shrugging off restraining hands.

He couldn't be gone. He was all she had left…

Again, darkness…

In a cool hospital room that hummed with machinery, the young woman lay on a hospital bed. She had been comatose for five days, ever since awakening in the ER to hear her son was dead.

During that time she hadn't so much as flickered an eyelid. The doctors were unsure whether or not she would snap out of it. They had found no physical reason for the coma and were certain it had been caused by the trauma of losing her son.

They couldn't say whether she would wake. It could happen any minute. It could happen never.

The room was dark and quiet, save for the steady beep of machinery in the corner.

Nikki gained awareness slowly. First of the sheets beneath and above her, then of the faint itchy feel of her skin. She shifted her hips and noticed another oddity, a tube strapped to her thigh. A catheter.

She swallowed, her mouth dry, her throat tight. Her nose, the area behind it felt strange. Slowly she lifted a hand and probed her nose with tentative fingers. Another tube. They had put a feeding tube down her nose, inserted through her left nostril.

When her eyes opened, she squinted automatically, prepared to not be able to see clearly. Instead she saw a gauzy white light. Bandages. Her searching fingers found the end of the bandage, peeled back the tape and unwound it.

Clarity. She could see everything clearly, from the clock on the wall, to the drab painting, to the room number on her open door.

She hadn't been able to see a damn thing more than two feet away without her glasses in years. Too many years.

Outside her door one nurse was bent diligently over paperwork while two others stood at a tall desk, speaking quietly.

Nikki plucked the little rubber probes from her body, dropping each one over the rail before seeking out another. As the machine attached to those little probes began to beep steadily, she plucked the third one from her breast.

The nurses were rushing in as she reached up for the tape that secured the feeding tube. Before they could reach her, she had already pulled it out and dropped it on the sheet next to her. She barely blinked at the sharp pain it caused.

A familiar voice stayed her hand as she was reaching beneath the sheets. "Easy, Ms. Kline. That won't be quite so easy to remove," one of the nurses said. This one was clad in baggy blue scrubs. A nametag at her breast read "Leanne Winslow".

Nikki recognized that name.

Her hand fell from her thigh, catheter forgotten as she leaned back. She reached out her hand and it was caught in a strong grip. She squeezed it, closed her eyes and whispered, "My son's dead, isn't he?"

"I'm afraid so, Ms. Kline." Her soft pretty blue eyes were filled with distress and she sat on the bed next to Nikki for the second time.

Biting her lip, she turned her head away. "What about Shawn? My brother?" Her voice was calm, abnormally so.

"He's fine. Just a concussion and some bruises. He went home the next day," another nurse said softly, sounding glad she hadn't been the one to break the news.

"But Jason didn't make it," Nikki whispered quietly. "He's gone."

This time Nikki turned her face into the offered shoulder and started to cry silently.

Now

She came back to awareness at the sound of gravel crunching several hundred feet away.

Just like that, he had been gone. One minute he had been playing happily with his plastic keys and Mouse, and now he was buried under six feet of cold earth, all alone.

Nikki had spent nearly a week in a coma. The day after she woke, she had walked out of the hospital against medical advice. Well, more like shuffled, almost crawled, right up until her dad realized if he didn't help her, she *would* crawl. Hell, if she could have done it the day she woke, she would have.

But she'd left, alive, and ironically enough, with an unexpected cosmetic repair. Her eyesight was suddenly perfectly normal, the intense pressure that had caused her nearsightedness relieved when glass had cut her retinas.

She had left the hospital in better shape than she had entered it.

Jason had left it in a body bag.

Thankfully Nikki didn't remember him being taken away. The time after the wreck was a blissful blank.

Now she sat quietly in the cemetery by her son's grave, reflecting on the things they would never do. Not exactly therapeutic thoughts, but Nikki wasn't in the mood for therapy today.

Her depression weighed down on her shoulders, and she knew realistically that this wasn't normal, that she needed to be talking to somebody about this.

But even after three years, she wasn't ready to let go of her grief. It seemed it was all she had left of him, and once she stopped grieving he'd truly be gone.

A gentle breeze drifted past, ruffling her hair and bringing with it the scent of wildflowers. The scent of honeysuckle teased her senses and she remembered taking Jason for a walk on the hillside very close to where he rested.

It had been only two months before the accident. They had had a picnic and he'd toddled after butterflies and come back with a fistful of honeysuckle, which he had shared with her before trying to eat it.

They had waded in the stream, the very same stream that ran through the cemetery. Jason had laughed in delight as tiny fish no bigger than her little finger had darted around their feet.

"You're going to be old before your time if you keep this up, sis," a voice said softly, jerking her out of her reverie.

She turned her head and squinted up at Shawn. "Hey," was all she said, not responding to his words. "What are you doing here?"

"I saw your truck on my way to work," he said, kneeling beside her. His left eyebrow was neatly bisected by a thin scar.

That, and the scars he bore inside, were his only physical reminders of the accident.

There were scars inside. She sensed it, wished she could help him...but she couldn't even help herself.

Jason had been like a little brother to Shawn. He'd adored the baby from the first and talked about how he'd teach him to wrestle, to go fish...all the cool boy stuff. Stuff Shawn hadn't ever had much chance to do himself.

"You ever wonder what would have happened if we'd just stayed at the store that day?" she asked softly. It was a question she'd asked herself a hundred times. A thousand.

"Only a few dozen times a week," he said.

As she looked over and met his gaze, he shook his head. "And you know as well as I do, those kinds of questions will drive us crazy. Some stupid drunk hit us, Nik. You weren't speeding. You weren't doing much of anything except driving in the rain. Bastard hit us, ran us off the road. You can't blame yourself."

She just shrugged.

She could blame herself. And she did.

"Y'know, you're going to be late for work," she told him, turning back to study the headstone.

Shawn shrugged. "I doubt they'll mind." And even if they did, he didn't care. How could work be that important when he looked at her and all but saw the dark cloud she had wrapped around herself? He settled on the grass next to her, uncertain of what to say. When he had been little, he had always run to her when he had been hurt. Nikki had always made the pain go away. And even when he had been nothing more than a street punk, causing trouble and raising hell, when he was in trouble, it had been her he had gone to. She had always fixed it in some way.

It didn't seem fair that after so many years of patching him

27

up and kissing away his tears that he wasn't able to take away any of her pain.

"Jason is probably the sweetest angel in heaven, sis," he said, looking at his feet as he spoke. He could feel himself turning red to the roots of his hair and he had no idea where those words had come from.

"I bet he is," came her soft whisper.

And looking over, he saw the beginning of a smile on her face.

The words, wherever they had come from, had been the right ones.

Before Nikki got out of her truck she donned a dark pair of sunglasses and forced her unruly hair into a stubby ponytail. She hadn't really thought she would be recognized when she had decided to use her own name on her books. She really hadn't thought that far ahead. She had only wanted them to sell.

They had sold though, and she hadn't exactly been in the best frame of mind when she was dealing with the contract negotiations. If she had thought things through, if she had listened to the agent she'd signed with, she would have gone with a pen name. She would have done something to have some modicum of privacy.

Now it was a little too late.

Besides, in a town the size of Monticello, everybody knew everybody else's business. The hat and the sunglasses wouldn't fool many people, but if it helped a little she was all for it. If she lived in a larger town she'd have more anonymity than she had in Monticello. In the past few years it had come to where she couldn't go much anywhere without somebody hailing her down to talk about books.

My little girl wrote this. Isn't that something...

I got a book. Can you help me...

And lately, total strangers who were just in town to fish were recognizing her. Nikki wasn't ever going to let another picture be taken of her, and her webmaster had taken down the one they'd conned her into putting up. Now if she could just get it off the back of the books...

For a while she hadn't minded the attention too much, but as time passed she started to crave solitude. People and questions were coming to grate on her nerves something bad. It was just a sign of her worsening depression, she suspected, and if she were smart, she'd just make the drive to Somerset where she was less likely to be noticed, but she didn't have the energy.

She made it all the way through the store without any problems and was finishing up in the dairy section. She just might make it out of the store, she realized. It even had her mood climbing up a few notches—instead of toxic, it was just slightly hazardous.

She added a carton of yogurt and some cream cheese. As she went to turn the cart around she promptly ran into somebody else's.

"Damn it," she muttered, but her voice was lost under the sound of baskets crashing together and groceries tumbling to the floor.

A sheepish smile crossed her face and she said, "Sorry about that." She would hit somebody whose cart was beyond full. Kneeling, she picked up a carton of cookies and Donald Duck orange juice. She placed them in the basket before stepping away.

The guy had knelt in front of a dark child of four or five, his face hidden as he scooped up items from the floor.

"No problem," he said, although his voice belied his words. He sounded a tad—okay, he sounded a *lot* irritated.

Nikki was about to make a quick getaway, but then he stood. And revealed his face.

A very familiar face, one that haunted her dreams on a regular basis. His hair was shorter, cut at his nape, and his face had thinned out just a bit, the dimples at the corners of his mouth now slashes in his lean cheeks. But the eyes were the same, deep bottomless pools of brown velvet.

"Wade," she whispered. Her eyes, stricken, then landed on the child's face. A little girl, a little mirror of her father.

And of Nikki's son. She wore a red T-shirt decorated on the front with a sketch of a bright-eyed puppy. A baseball cap in that same candy-apple red sat on top of thick black hair that fell razor-straight to her tiny shoulders. She held a stuffed cocker spaniel, a mirror image of the way Jason had carried his precious Mouse.

A knife slowly embedded itself in Nikki's heart, started to twist.

For a moment his face was blank, and then his eyes narrowed. She was unable to move as he slowly reached up and tugged her sunglasses off.

"Nikki," he breathed, his eyes lighting as though from within.

He took a step closer and brushed her cheek with the back of his hand.

That gentle touch shattered her like glass. Flinching, she grabbed her purse and took off running down the aisle. She had her keys before she was even out the door. Swallowing a sob, she dodged an elderly couple glaring at her with censure in their eyes.

As she dove into the dubious safety of her SUV, Wade came striding out the main doors of the grocery store. "Nikki!" he shouted, his little girl perched on his hip.

She spared him only one glance as she started the engine

and threw it into drive. The little girl was staring up at her father in confusion, her dark hair streaming around her face.

The sight of it sent tiny daggers plunging into Nikki's heart.

Dear God, she thought.

And unable to go home where she'd just sit and brood and cry, she ended up making the forty-minute drive to Somerset, tears streaming down her face the entire time.

What in the hell...

Wade stood there, dumbstruck, as Nikki peeled out of the parking lot in a Ford Explorer, leaving a bit of rubber on the pavement as she went.

His mind was a total blank. He didn't know what to think.

Nikki was *here*.

And she'd just run away from him...

"Daddy, who was that?"

Blankly he turned his head to look at his daughter. Abby was staring up at him, her small, sweet face puckered with confusion. His silence wasn't helping.

"Daddy, was she a friend of yours? Do you know her?"

"Yeah, sweetie. I know her," he finally said, talking not exactly easy considering how his vocal cords seemed to have frozen.

"Why did she run away?"

"I guess maybe she had somewhere to go," was all he said, casting one last glance out at the highway, eyes following the path the black SUV had taken.

What in the hell...

Chapter Four

Later that night Nikki stared dully into the freezer, eyes unseeing as she put away half-melted ice cream and nearly warm chicken breasts. She continued to stand there, staring woodenly, until the cold air on her already chilled flesh snapped her out of her daze.

Finally she realized she had been putting canned goods and dishwasher detergent in the freezer as well.

After removing what didn't belong, she shut the freezer and dropped to the floor, exhausted.

"What's he doing here anyway? Whatever happened to Texas?" she asked the empty kitchen. "He was supposed to move to Texas."

Folding her arms at her middle to ward off a very real pain brought on by her misery, she leaned forward as a sob built in her throat.

Why now? I'm just starting to stand on my own two feet again.

Liar.

She wasn't standing on her own two feet—she was just sort of wobbling. She was barely existing. But, hell, she *was* existing. She didn't need to have somebody holding her hand to get her through the day and she got *through* the days, damn it.

The little girl... The sight of her had been like a dagger into her already bashed, bleeding heart. A healthy, beautiful, alive little girl. The pain was more than she could bear.

Then

"Nikki?"

She looked up from her keyboard, eyes bloodshot and weary. Typing on the slow, old word processor she'd bought at a yard sale a few years ago didn't do jack for her headaches, but it was a damn sight better than trying to use a typewriter.

What she wouldn't give for a computer...

Shawn was slumped against the doorframe, hands shoved deep in his pockets. "Your boyfriend's at the door. Want me to tell him you ain't here?"

Wryly she thought, *I must look worse than I thought.*

Shawn was almost acting protective. The sixteen-year-old barely had two words to say to her anymore—especially after she'd physically thrown his girlfriend out on her ass when Nikki had found the girl snorting coke in their cramped kitchen.

She must really look like shit if Shawn was feeling bad for her.

"Nah, he can come on up, Shawn. But thanks."

He only shrugged and walked away. She swiveled in her chair to face her mirror. Yep. She looked like hell. Bloodshot eyes, face pale and strained, hair messily shoved into a ponytail. Her ripped, sleeveless sweatshirt had certainly seen better days, and her cut-off shorts weren't much better.

Not only that, they bagged slightly at the waist, evidence of her lack of appetite in the past week.

She turned back to her keyboard as footsteps echoed on the steps, tapping away at the keys, putting half-formed ideas into words. She worked a few minutes more, even after Wade slowly entered the room.

Still too angry to make the first move, she continued to work.

Finally finished, Nikki skimmed the rough draft and then she saved the file on the slow word processor. She really, really wanted a computer. But college was proving damned expensive, even with her scholarships, so she'd just have to make do for a while longer. Besides, for the most part, when she really needed something faster, she could use the computer at Wade's.

Well, *usually.*

Spinning around, she found Wade staring out the window, his posture slumped, head bent. Finally, his voice sounding rusty, he asked, "Did you make it home okay?"

He was, of course, referring to the night a week earlier when he'd driven away from the store in a fury unlike anything she had ever seen in him.

Cocking her head, she coolly said, "It looks that way. I don't appear to be the worse for wear." Well, not really. Nothing some sleep, a shower and a meal or two wouldn't fix. *And you...*

He sighed, looking even more miserable, if possible, and flung himself on her unmade bed. He had his arm over his eyes, and his hand was clenched so tightly his knuckles were bloodless.

He looked utterly dejected, Nikki thought with mild amusement.

If she didn't know better, she would think he was feeling guilty for picking a fight over nothing. And he damn well ought to. However, Wade never felt guilty about anything. Feeling guilty meant you had done something wrong, made some sort of mistake. Things like that were below him.

She couldn't gloat for too long though. He looked too awful. "I caught a ride home with Connie," she said.

Wade's lower lip was still puffy.

Nikki still couldn't believe she had hit him. But, damn it,

the way he had acted...

Wade's hoarse voice broke the silence when he said quietly, "I'm sorry. I had no right to do that, no right to jump all over you. I don't know what in the hell came over me."

"Don't you?" she asked, her voice remote.

With a sigh, he lowered his arm and sat up in bed, swinging around to sit on the edge of it. Looking her right in the eye for the first time since entering the room, he grimaced. His skin was unnaturally pale, dark blue circles under his eyes.

"I was jealous," he said simply. "Maybe I worry about you thinking about... Shit, I dunno. Dating. You never really did that. We've been together the past two years, and up until you started hanging out with me you never messed with dating. You didn't have a chance to play the field the way your friends did. You would have every right to wonder."

"I never have wondered," Nikki said quietly. "The girls my age think I'm damn lucky to have found myself somebody. The guys my age aren't worth the trouble. But that's beside the point. You came in with guns blazing and attacked me simply for talking to a guy I work with."

"He'd like to do more. I know what a guy looks like when he's interested. And he's definitely interested."

Sighing, he scrubbed his eyes with the heels of his hands. "But that's not the point either. You weren't encouraging him and that's all the matters. I should have had more faith in you." He stood abruptly.

Startled, Nikki was slack when he pulled her out of the chair and into his arms. Wade yanked the rubber band from her hair and buried his face in it, breathing deeply. Silently she locked her arms around his waist and stood there, feeling vaguely as though something was wrong. Something else was going on, but what it was, Nikki didn't know. Her internal radar was sending out signals.

He began rocking back and forth, and instinctively she tightened her arms. Turning her head, she pressed a kiss to the side of his neck, cuddling against him, trying to ease some of the tension that was rolling of him in waves.

She gasped out a breath as Wade swept her up in his arms and went to the bed, cradling her in his lap.

That internal radar was screaming now. They'd fought before and he hadn't acted like he was afraid she would slip away.

"Wade, what's going on?" she asked, cupping his face in her hand and forcing him to look at her. Nikki searched his eyes for some clue but all she saw was torment and guilt. She was almost afraid to ask, but knew she had to. "Is there something I need to know about?"

He closed his eyes and Nikki felt her stomach drop. She waited for him to tell her, but all he did was bring her hand to his lips and kiss it. "I just don't want to lose you," he said, raising his head and staring at her intently.

"I'm not the one who left," she reminded him softly. Then she shrugged. "It was a fight. It's not the first and it won't be the last. I...I shouldn't have hit you."

"You've got a mean right hook, Nikki," he said, a ghost of a smile on his face. "But I deserved it. I'm sorry. The entire thing happened because I'm an ass."

With a forced smile, she replied, "You are an ass." Then she shoved aside her misgivings. Everything was okay. "It's all right, Wade. It's over."

"It's not all right," he insisted, cupping her face in callused, gentle hands. "It's not, baby. I'm sorry for everything I've done that hurt you. I'm sorry for things I said and did and thought that weren't fair to you."

She only tucked her face against his shoulder, looking away from those intent eyes. Meeting them only made her vague feelings of wrongness return.

Nikki had to bite her lip to keep from asking, "What things?"

A month had passed since that day. Buried in her writing, working part-time and dealing with a few extra summer courses, she had her hands full.

There was also the minor detail of a wedding.

They were getting married.

A quiet, simple wedding, but they were getting married. Shortly after their honeymoon was over, she'd start back at U of L for her third year of nursing school.

Yeah, she had her hands full, all right.

Hunched over Wade's computer, she focused on her book. Two hours—she was giving herself two hours. Then she'd get her stupid, endless homework done. She'd get the damn homework done and then she might even have time to work on the book some more.

Wade slept like the dead on the couch.

The broken-down, secondhand couch was comfortable but not that comfortable. He wasn't interested in sleeping in the bedroom though. When she'd mentioned the bedroom a weird look had crossed over his face and he'd shut down, shut her out. Distracted, she hadn't thought much of it, but as she forced herself to turn off the computer, she looked over at him. Nikki had thought he liked the little ranch house they'd picked out. But maybe she was wrong. He ended up at her dad's apartment every morning after work, and slept there on her narrow twin bed until she got home from work.

To top it off, his sleep was fitful. Often he'd wake the minute she got home and tumble her down onto the bed with him, holding her tightly against his side as he drifted back into uneasy slumber. Wade insisted nothing was wrong, just that he was working too hard, busting his ass to save more money for the honeymoon.

Her mind drifted around in circles, trying to pinpoint if she had done something or said something to make him act this way. There had been the fight but it wasn't the worst they had ever had.

Since then they hadn't fought about anything. Wade, in fact, went out of his way to keep things quiet between them.

She didn't even realize he had woken until she heard him whisper, "C'mere, Nikki."

She smiled and rose from her chair. Stiffened muscles protested as Nikki stretched and forced them into action. She bent over at the waist to touch her toes briefly before she went to couch, perching on the edge.

Watching her with burning eyes, Wade waited for her with an outstretched hand. As she settled against him, his arms closed around her and he pulled her down next to him. With a turn of his body, Wade neatly tucked her under him. "I love you," he rasped, his voice intense. "I always will. If I ever lost you, I don't know what I'd do."

She opened her mouth, determined to find out what was going on with him, but then he settled his mouth over hers, and the question, like all thought, flew out of her head.

Things were good...for a while.

Three more weeks to be exact.

Her wedding dress, something that seemed too beautiful to be real, hung in her closet, minute adjustments made in the waistline. Satin ballet slippers dyed to match resided in a box close by.

Everything was already set. Decorations were at the church. She had already mailed the thank-you cards for shower gifts and there wasn't anything left to be done except the wedding itself.

The wedding was to be small and simple, since they had to pay for everything themselves. Even the honeymoon was simple, a four-day weekend to Gatlinburg. A real honeymoon would have to wait.

It was Tuesday, hot, humid. The air was so thick and muggy even breathing seemed like work. The rain started sometime after noon, a steady downpour that didn't seem in any hurry to end.

But she didn't care about the rain, because she had just gotten the call.

Nineteen years old, and she had just gotten *The Call*.

She still couldn't believe it. She'd written everything down just to make it feel real. But it didn't feel real. Couldn't feel real.

Wade... She needed to tell Wade. Determined to do just that, she borrowed her dad's truck, something she rarely did because she hated driving a stick shift, but she hardly noticed it as she drove over to Wade's in a daze of excitement.

Hands shaky, a smile a mile on wide on her face, she pulled into the driveway and danced up the porch.

The deafening silence when she threw open the door should have warned her.

How could silence sound so ominous?

That silence... Yes, it should have warned her.

Her excitement was gone. Forgotten as misery, shock and anger roiled inside her. She'd completely forgotten about the notes she had in her pocket. About the call. About everything.

Nikki now stood on one side of the kitchen, staring out at the thunderstorm that had rolled in only minutes earlier.

If asked why she had driven over, Nikki would have admitted she didn't have a clue.

Wade was across the room, on the floor, face buried in his hands, shoulders and hair wet with rain.

When she'd first arrived a few minutes earlier, Nikki had found him sitting outside on the deck in back, oblivious to the rain that was pounding down.

She'd thought something was wrong. Had thought it was one of his parents. But it wasn't.

He'd been holding a pregnancy test in his hand.

A positive one.

And Nikki hadn't taken any pregnancy test.

That damning bit of evidence now sat on the kitchen table, and she found herself staring at it again, acid burning in her throat.

"I can't believe this is happening." She wanted to scream it, but she couldn't. She barely had the breath to even speak.

"Baby, I'm so sorry," he whispered. "Damn it, I'm sorry."

Sorry? Yes. She imagined he was.

She bit back the hot, burning words that sprang to her lips, because once she gave into the anger, she wouldn't think to ask the questions, and damn it, she wanted the answers before she exploded. Before she lost it.

She deserved answers, damn it.

"Who is she?" Nikki asked numbly, her face gone stiff. She wasn't hurting yet. It hadn't really hit her, but she knew the pain was lying in wait. It was like a man who had suddenly had his leg cut off and could feel nothing for the shock of it.

When he didn't answer, she whirled and snapped, "Who in the hell is she?"

Raising his head, Wade stared at her from brown eyes. Those eyes, always so warm and full of life, looked cold and lifeless. Before he even said it, she knew.

"Jamie Sayer," he said, his voice almost soundless.

That was when the pain came, ripping through her like a forest fire, consuming everything in its path.

Jamie... Of course, it was Jamie. The beautiful, sleek brunette had been chasing after Wade for as long as Nikki had known him, longer. Wade hadn't ever been interested in her. Nikki hadn't ever really worried about her, and man, what a fucking mistake *that* had been on her part.

Looks like the perfect little prom queen had finally gotten him.

"Jamie," Nikki whispered, her tongue feeling thick, her throat raw.

As the pain tore into her heart and the pressure built in her throat, she stared at him. Her knees gave out then and she slid to the floor, a mirror of Wade's dejected slump. She drew her knees up and held them clutched to her chest as she started to shake.

"Jamie," she said again, this time biting the woman's name off. "So...when did this happen? How long has it been going on?"

How long have you been making a fool of me?

"Nikki, don't..."

"Don't what?" she demanded. "Don't ask for details? Considering you just destroyed me with this little bit of information, I think I have right to know some details." Her voice rose with each word until she was shouting.

Wade flinched as she became more graphic, looking disgusted with himself for doing to this to her.

"Nikki," he said, his voice pleading. "I was drunk, so damn drunk I don't even remember it. I didn't know what in the hell I was doing. Hell, I was probably too drunk to remember my own name."

"You'd obviously forgotten mine," she snarled. Her gaze dropped briefly to the region of his fly and she bitterly added,

41

"And you obviously weren't too drunk to get it up, were you?"

Blinded by tears, she stumbled into the living room. She scrubbed them away. *Hold it together. Hold it together.* She had to. For a little while, at least. She took a deep breath, trying to force some air into her tight lungs, but the knot in her throat made it almost impossible.

She had to know. She hated herself for it, but she absolutely had to know. Turning to face him, she asked quietly, "Tell me something. Is she the first? Or just the most recent?"

"It only happened that one time, Nik. Just the one time. That one time. I swear to God. I wouldn't have hurt you like that," Wade insisted, moving cautiously to stand closer to her.

Looking into his bleak eyes, Nikki cursed herself for being a fool. If she had learned anything from her father, it was that things like this seldom happened *just once.* But she believed him.

It didn't make the pain any easier to bear.

She bit back against the wave of agony that rolled through her like a bout of nausea as she grabbed her purse from the table and headed out the door.

Wade moved like a bolt of lightning, blocking her. "Nikki, you can't just walk out," he pleaded, reaching for her.

Her shoulders rose and fell in a helpless shrug "What else can I do, Wade? What am I supposed to do? Damn it, I don't even know how to feel."

"Damn it, Nikki," he rasped, pulling her against him, his forehead dropping to rest against hers. "Damn it all to hell."

Pulling away from him, Nikki looked at Wade and flatly said, "I am in hell."

With a vicious jerk, she tore away from him, moving backward until there were several feet between them. "And I can't even figure out what I did to bring this on," she told him.

"Nikki..." Wade reached for her once more, his hand stretching out.

Nikki stared at his hand, entranced, for a long moment. And then she looked up, met his eyes, mutely shook her head. She turned on her heel, ran for the back door and headed out into the rain. She didn't know where she was going, but she couldn't let him touch her. Couldn't let him get too close. She'd fall apart for certain then...

She dodged a mud puddle and headed for the trees, wishing for the first time that this place weren't so isolated. A nosy neighbor right now would help. Wade caught up with her, snagged her elbow, and she slid, causing them both to end up on the wet grass. As rain fell around them, he stared down at her with anguished eyes. Removing her glasses, Wade covered her face with kisses, hot little nipping ones at her mouth, gentle soothing ones against her streaming eyes.

Don't let him do this to you. It's over. Just get out of here. The tiny voice whispered over and over in her mind while her heart pleaded with her to stay. *It's over. This will be the last time, the very last... Don't you deserve one more time?*

After an internal war, Nikki reached up and locked her arms around his neck. One more time. She had to have just one more time. Hot hands slid under her shirt, stroking rain-cooled skin. She gasped, arching up. A jerk of one of the hard hands popped the buttons on her worn cotton shirt, baring her breasts to him. Through the damn lace of her bra, he nuzzled her nipple before taking it into his mouth, nipping and licking until she whimpered beneath him, clutching his head close to her.

Nikki's hands raced down his shirt, freeing buttons and streaking over smooth, hard, muscled planes as Wade fought to free her from the wet denim of her shorts, shoving his own jeans down just far enough.

Positioning himself between her legs, Wade whispered, "I'm sorry, but I can't wait. God, I need you so bad." Then he arched her hips up and drove into her, burying himself to the hilt.

She cried out as he filled her, stretching her. Above her, Wade moaned deep in his chest, his body shuddering. One of his hands knotted in her hair. The other caught her knee, pulling it up, opening her body. He slid deeper and she whimpered as he shifted angles, the head of his cock rubbing against her in the sweetest way.

She clenched around him, her nails biting into his arms.

"Damnation," he whispered. He stiffened above her, then pulled out and drove inside her, again and again, harder and harder, until he was lifting her with each deep thrust.

Overhead, the storm continued, rain pounding down, thunder crashing through the sky. Nearby, lightning flashed. The smell of ozone mingled with the scent of sex and sweat.

Pleasure slammed through her like a runaway train, sending her flying before knocking her flat. Her breath caught and held in her throat and she squirmed against him, seeking more.

Wade bit at the side of her neck, and she cried out, light exploding behind her eyes before everything dimmed. And he kept on moving. Drained and panting for breath, she lay passively in his grip until he reared up and grabbed her behind her left knee, hooking his arms under her legs and opening her body wide, leaving her unable to move. She whimpered slightly in protest, then gasped in dazed pleasure as he fell forward again, driving deeper.

"Look at me," he whispered. "Damn it, you look at me."

She turned bleary eyes to his as he slowed his pace until he was barely rocking against her, each tiny movement rushing through her like fire. Her eyes focused on his and he rewarded her with a twist of his hips that had her gasping for breath, then whimpering with gratitude.

Then Wade resumed his pace, holding himself back until

she arched up weakly, groaning out his name as one final orgasm rolled through her.

He stiffened above her, pinned her hips with his and held her in place as the fire spread from her body into his, joining them.

Seconds later he slowly collapsed against her.

It was over in moments, but left Nikki weak and shaking, feeling as though the lightning had struck her instead of just flashing in the sky overhead. Shuddering, she didn't protest when he turned onto his side, tucking her body snugly against his while they waited for their hearts to slow and their breath to return. The rain slowed to a gentle mist, cooling overheated bodies until goose bumps covered their flesh.

Sometime later Wade roused enough to right his jeans. He gathered her clothes and tucked them into her arms before taking her in his and rising, carrying her out of the rain and into the house. He laid her on the bed, heedless of their filthy bodies, spooning up behind her, tucking her against him. His arms locked around her middle as though he never intended to let go.

It was after midnight when she finally freed herself. She hadn't slept. Her mind had chased itself in circles, but there weren't a lot of choices left to her.

Turning, Nikki paused to look at him, light from the hallway casting half his face into shadow. He looked exhausted. She had noticed the lines of strain forming around his mouth and eyes, but she had attributed them to work. She knew otherwise now.

It had been guilt. And it had probably been guilt that had dulled his appetite to the point of not eating. Weight he hadn't needed to lose had melted off, leaving him leaner than normal. There was nothing on him but muscle and sinew.

Gently, she brushed back a silky black lock of hair that

had fallen into his eyes. Then, as a sob threatened to burst free, she turned away.

Silently, Nikki gathered her filthy clothes, just as she silently laid her diamond engagement ring on the dresser next to his keys and a mess of coins. Then she slid out of the bedroom. She dressed quickly, donning ruined shorts, tying her ruined shirt in a knot at her rib cage to keep it closed. She grabbed her purse and keys and was out the door without looking back.

If she looked back, she'd never be able to leave.

Now

Nikki came back to herself slowly, sitting in front of the refrigerator, cold and aching inside as though the years hadn't passed.

As though it had just happened.

She wiped away her tears and shakily pushed herself to her feet. Nikki rested briefly against the counter before moving woodenly into the living room. She had left that night, thinking it was all over.

But it hadn't been.

For on that final night something had gone incredibly wrong. Or incredibly right. That turbulent night, their bodies soaked with rain and sweat, Wade had planted a child in her. And by doing so, he had saved her life.

Painful as it was, even Nikki couldn't deny the irony of it all. She was the one who ended up like the interloper, for by the time she knew about the baby, Wade and Jamie were married. She had known it would happen once she walked away, although that wasn't entirely *why* she had walked.

Nikki had seen the damage that had happened when two people didn't trust each other and she wasn't about to start her life with a man she could no longer put her faith in.

But she had known he'd ask Jamie to marry him—out of duty. And Nikki had known Jamie would say yes.

Wade was miserably old-fashioned sometimes. She knew he'd make himself do it, even if it made him miserable, even if it made her miserable.

So while they had gotten married and lived in the house Nikki and Wade had picked out, Nikki had hidden away like the interloper.

But only for a few more months.

By the time Halloween rolled around, she and her family had settled in Monticello in a rented house while they waited for their own house to be built.

Their own house.

Nikki had hit the publishing jackpot—selling one proposed and two completed books, selling the books for more money than she'd ever thought to see in her lifetime.

It meant less than nothing to her. All that had mattered was Jason.

And now even he was gone.

Chapter Five

Wade stood outside the bookstore, staring inside at the display.

It was a salute to local writers, featuring none other than Nicole Kline.

Local.

He owned the first book in the insanely popular young adult series she'd written, although he hadn't read it. He hadn't followed her career, and he hadn't ever attempted to look her up. He'd been tempted more than once, and more than once he'd found himself on Google, typing in her name just to see what he could find out about her, only to make himself stop before he could do it.

Whatever she had done with her life, it no longer included him, and he had no right to know a damn thing about her, no right to contact her. He knew it.

But it was more than that... He needed to focus on the life he had with his daughter, and he didn't know how well he'd be able to do that if he let himself get focused on the girl he'd lost.

But ever since he'd seen her in the grocery store in Monticello there was the tearing, burning need to know. Need to know *more*.

He tucked his hands into his back pockets and rocked back on his heels as he counted the books featured. Three of them. There was a TV series supposedly being based on the series.

Idly, he wondered if she was rich as Midas now.

He went into the bookstore to the display stand. He took down one book, the one that had drawn his attention. It was the first in the series, the one he already owned, but it had a new cover.

The rendering on the front was what had caught as his eye as he wandered through the mall waiting on his mother and Abby to finish up their girl's things.

The guy looked just like him—or at least it looked like he had had five or ten years ago, and if he'd been the leather-wearing type.

Opening it to the first few pages, he scanned them over.

As he scanned the acknowledgements page, a knot settled in his throat. She'd always written. Even before they'd started dating. He knew she couldn't remember a time when she *hadn't* written.

But as much time as they'd spent together, he hadn't ever read her work.

It was something he often kicked himself over because he knew how much it had meant to her and he should have supported it more. Should have treated her so much better than he had.

Even though he hadn't ever read her work, he recognized some of the names on the acknowledgements page, recognized turns of phrases she'd used.

The next page was blank save for these words:

This is for all the people who said I could do it. And all of those who said I couldn't.

He turned to the copyright page, staring once more at the date there. Staring at it still gave him a shock, though not as bad as had the first time he'd seen it.

That first time it had been one brutal, vicious punch.

It had been almost eighteen months to the day since she'd walked out. Abby had been nine months old and a sheer terror. At his wit's end, he'd pushed her into the bookstore, hoping he could find something bright and noisy that would keep her occupied so he could finish his Christmas shopping.

He'd seen her book sitting right by the cash register.

Once he'd gotten past the shock, he'd realized he had the answer to a question that had plagued him for a while. She had shown up at his house that last day, her eyes bright and shining with a secret.

Rain had soaked her clear through, plastering her white cotton Oxford to her torso, her wet hair clinging to the shape of her skull. She had practically danced onto the deck, face glowing, shouting that she had unbelievable news.

This is for all the people who said I could do it. And all of those who said I couldn't.

Wade hadn't been one of the ones who said she couldn't do it, but he didn't know that he'd really expected her to do it.

How many writers tried to make it happen? And how many never did?

But she had done it...and in a big way, it seemed.

What had she been doing in Monticello? Did she live around there?

Hell, why would she be living in the middle of nowhere? He'd moved to the small Kentucky town because he needed to get away from the violence in Louisville—he was approaching burn-out, hard and fast. He needed the quiet, the slow pace.

But why would a successful writer want to live there?

Maybe she didn't. Maybe it was like a vacation home or something. Yeah, that might explain it. After all, the lake was popular. That was how he knew about Monticello. He'd spent more than a few weekends himself fishing down on Lake Cumberland as a teenager with his dad and brother.

Maybe she had a cabin there. Maybe...maybe she had a husband.

Shit.

Shit.

Shit.

If she *was* married, would he be seeing her and her husband? Hell, what if they *did* live there? Could he handle that?

Dropping down on the bench, Wade stared morosely into the fountain. All around him he heard the babble of too many people talking at once. Crowded malls on Saturday afternoon weren't exactly his favorite way to spend his time. But he had promised his mother he would bring Abby back one weekend a month when he had broke the news they were moving.

Abby wasn't happy in Monticello, away from all her old friends, her grandparents and Uncle Joe. He had begun to question the wisdom of this move.

But if he hadn't moved, he wouldn't have seen Nikki again.

At this particular moment, he couldn't decide whether that was good or bad.

It was late Sunday when they returned home. Wade knew he'd be lucky to catch five hours' sleep before he had to be up for his six a.m. shift. As a paramedic he worked twelve-hour shifts for three days a week. It gave him the rest of the week off to spend with Abby and he loved that.

But it could be exhausting, and on so little sleep it would be worse.

Fortunately, nothing much seemed to happen around here.

During his first week on the job, the runs had mainly consisted of chauffeuring little old ladies to the doctor's from the area's lone nursing home. There were some drug or alcohol related issues, but they were the minority here, not the norm. Broken bones, accidental injuries, those were the normal. Once, a little boy had eaten one of his grandmother's suppositories and his mother had screamed over and over that the old woman had poisoned him.

It was a relief in itself to be away from gunshots and stab wounds. He was off the night shift and far away from the violence of Louisville. Wade prayed never to see it again.

One memory in particular haunted him, and probably would for years, maybe the rest of his life. A four-year-old boy shot by his older brother because the little boy had threatened to tell his parents the older brother was smoking cigarettes.

That four-year-old child had died beneath Wade's blood-stained hands and Wade had known he had to get out or he was going to break.

It had happened right before his upcoming vacation and when he had come back from vacation, it had been to turn in his notice.

They were getting out.

Shoving those memories firmly to the back of his mind, Wade dressed a sleepy Abby in her PJs. With a soft sigh, she turned on her side, pulled her blanket up to her neck and slipped right back into sleep.

Wearily, Wade dragged himself to his room, checked the alarm and fell down face first on the mattress without bothering to undress.

Dreams awaited him.

They weren't bloody, but they weren't pleasant either.

"Aw, shit," Wade groaned, then instantly wished he hadn't.

His head was ringing from too much booze the previous night. A thousand tiny soldiers were playing reveille with glee in his skull. Bright early-morning sunlight streamed through shades he had forgotten to pull and the light was killing him. Or at least he wished it would. The inside of his mouth tasted horrible, of stale whiskey and beer, and felt as dry as cotton.

But all of it had been for nothing because he vividly remembered what had driven him to Zack's—that fight with Nikki. Shit. He'd been a jackass.

Why in the hell had he gone and picked the damn fight to begin with?

His lower lip throbbed like a son of a bitch from where Nikki had decked him. He reached up and gingerly probed the area, figured he ought to be glad she hadn't just broken his nose.

Wade forced himself to roll over, knowing he had to get out of bed. He needed to go find Nikki and apologize, although damn if he had any idea how he was going to make the drive with the marching band he had playing inside his skull.

Eyes wide open, he stared at the ceiling above, wishing he could undo the past twenty-four hours.

Forcing himself to sit up, Wade cradled his aching head in his hands. He waited for the world, and his stomach, to stop spinning before he even tried to stand.

"G'mornin," a husky, female, unfamiliar voice drawled from behind him.

Wade froze.

His head came up, and he briefly wondered if he was dying and this was an auditory hallucination.

Slowly, dread curdling low in his belly, he turned.

And stared.

Damnation, what had he gone and done last night?

Jamie Sayer, her midnight hair tumbled and attractively disheveled, peered up at him with sleepy, sated cornflower-blue eyes. And she was as naked as he was. Shaking, he rose, trying to get his frozen vocal cords to work.

"What are you doing here?" he finally croaked, headache forgotten as shame and revulsion ate its way up his throat.

She frowned and sat up slowly, tucking the sheet around her as she did. "Don't you remember?" she asked softly, her eyes darkening.

"Remember what?" he growled. "I might have been drunk, but it would take more than that to invite you here."

"I drove you home," she reminded him. "You were too drunk to do it, so I volunteered. Zack was pretty wasted too."

"That doesn't explain what you are doing in my bed," Wade said through clenched teeth. "Or what you were doing at Zack's. I don't remember you showing up there, and I doubt he invited you." He spied his jeans laying in a tangle on the floor, next to something silky peach. As he jerked his jeans up, it fluttered down to the floor.

Staring at that soft bra, Wade swallowed against the bile rising in his throat.

Damn it, what had he done?

Jamie seemed not to notice his discomfort as she stood and pressed her body against his, arms wrapped securely around his neck. "It was everything I had always dreamed it would be, Wade," she whispered in his ear. "It was perfect. I always knew you loved me."

For a moment he was frozen, arms held rigidly at his sides as he tried to make his brain function once more. What in the hell had happened?

Carefully, not trusting his temper or his state of mind, Wade freed himself from her arms and moved away. "I don't love you," he said calmly, turning to face her once there was distance between them. "And I sure as hell can't believe I would invite you into my bed. I don't remember a damn thing, and I sure don't remember you showing up at Zack's."

She smiled softly, shrugged. "You were upset," she said gently. "You finally broke things off with that...girl. I know you had feelings for her, but she's not right for you...not good enough for you."

"Not good enough for me?" he snapped. Shit, *he* was the one not good enough for *her*. "I had a fight with her—that's not the same thing as breaking things off with her. Although after this she's going to want to boot me out on my sorry ass. Damn it, how could I do this?"

She paled in anger. "You don't have to sound so disgusted. You can't talk to me like that. I'm not your little slut from the projects."

"Sluts aren't confined to projects, angel," he drawled. "I may not remember last night, but I do remember other times when I clearly told you I wasn't interested. In fact, I think I even told you to just stay the hell away from me."

"You don't mean that," she whispered, her eyes filling with tears. "I know it was wrong for me to push it like I did last night, but I just love you so much."

"I want to know what happened last night," he said softly, not moved at all by those crocodile tears. Wade had known Jamie all his life, and he knew one thing very well...she was a born manipulator. "I want to know it now and I want the truth."

"Well, you were just so upset, and crying over the terrible fight you two had..." Jamie said forlornly, sitting on the edge of the bed. "She had been so mean to you and made you feel guilty over absolutely nothing. You were just so upset. I...I felt so bad for you. I was trying to comfort you and it just happened."

"Like hell," he snarled, grabbing her arm and jerking her to her feet. He put his face close to hers and said, "I know a lie when I hear it, Jamie. The truth."

"That's the truth," she whimpered.

"Bullshit," he said succinctly. "Part of the reason I wanted to get so drunk was so I'd forget I made an ass of myself, picking a fight over nothing. I do remember being drunk on my ass and blubbering to Zack about what I could do to make it right.

"Besides, one small problem with your story? There's no way I'd go to you for comfort."

Tears spilled out of her blue eyes and vaguely Wade felt some guilt. Damn it, this was just as much his fault as hers. But what was he going to tell Nikki?

He hadn't realized he had spoken that final thought aloud.

"What do you mean, what are you going to tell Nikki?" Jamie shouted. "It's none of her damn business. You're mine now!"

"No." Wade shook his head. "No, I'm not. No matter what happens with Nikki, I won't be yours, Jamie. I'm sorry, but I don't love you. I'm never going to."

Damn, what had he done?

What had he done?

Wade jerked awake just as the alarm went off.

Years later, that dream, the memory of the shame and dread, could still turn him into a mess. Dragging himself out of bed, Wade shed the wrinkled clothes on the way to the bathroom. His stiff back screamed at him and his eyes were gritty from lack of sleep. A tension headache was already throbbing behind his eyes.

Hot water was the only cure for this. Lots of it.

Turning his face into the hot spray, he let the water wash away the cobwebs and the oily feel that remembered guilt left on his skin. His stomach churned and burned, letting him know it would be another Rolaids breakfast. Hands braced against the tiled wall, he prayed the day would be better than it had started.

It got worse.

He came face-to-face with a young hazel-eyed man with brutally short ash-blond hair. A man who looked ready to kill him. He topped Wade by a good four inches and was lean muscle from the neck down. Those shrewd, cold hazel eyes studied him, hate burning in them.

Wade had been gassing up the ambulance when the Harley pulled into the gas station. Wade admired its clean lines, his gaze wistful and a bit envious. He'd always wanted a bike like that, but a bike like that took more money and more time than he had.

He had lifted his eyes to comment on it only to find the rider shucking a helmet and moving to stand toe-to-toe with him, his dislike palpable.

It was difficult to place him at first. But something about the way he moved registered as familiar. As did the way his chin lifted insolently. But it was those shrewd hazel eyes that finally clued him in. Even back when he had been nothing more than a mouthy hoodlum, this one had been a force to be reckoned with. Of course, back then Wade had worried one day Dylan Kline would end up in prison before he turned twenty.

Obviously not.

One thing hadn't changed though. Those eyes could cut a man off at the knees from ten feet away.

There was nothing left of the sullen boy he had known. Aside from the color of his eyes, he didn't resemble Nikki much, save for the spiky long lashes and sulky mouth. He had always been long and lean, but in the past few years he had filled out.

"Dylan," he greeted, removing the nozzle and replacing it before screwing on the tank lid. "You're looking well." *And strong enough and ready enough to rip my guts out.*

"What are you doing here?" he snapped, his words clear and precise, none of the gangsta drawl left.

"I live here," he said calmly.

"Since when?" Dylan demanded, those hazel eyes narrow.

"Since four weeks ago. I suppose your family is here now?" Two Klines in Monticello pretty much killed his hopes that Nikki was staying here in some vacation home. Damn it.

Dylan just continued to stare at him.

Probably trying to figure out how he'd like to start tearing Wade apart—start at the feet? Or at the head?

"Lived here long?" Hopefully, Dylan would see the sense in not mauling him in broad daylight. He was, relatively speaking, the calmer of the Kline brothers.

If Shawn were here blood would already be flowing.

Wade was honest enough to admit it—very little blood would have been Kline blood.

"Stay away from Nikki, buddy. She's had enough grief in her life. She doesn't need you to adding to it. Again," Dylan warned, his eyes glinting with a promise. *Just give me one reason*, he was saying. *One good reason.* And then, he turned and stalked away.

Close call. It wasn't all that long ago that Dylan would have pounded into somebody he had taken such a dislike to, without even waiting for a reason.

Wade did wonder a bit at the reversal in loyalties. There had been a time when Dylan Kline hadn't even spared his older sister a second glance. His only loyalty had been to himself.

But then again, what did he know anymore? He hadn't seen either of them in five years.

Still, it was weird.

Wade had never seen Dylan stand up for anybody but himself, much less bother getting into a fight over anyone. Shawn might have done it, but only because he was a natural-born brawler. He would have done it for the fun of it, not out of any loyalty or love for his sister.

Time apparently did change things.

Chapter Six

Wade spent the next few days convincing himself he shouldn't hunt her down. There was no point in it.

No point in rehashing old times. No point at all. So much time had passed and they hadn't parted fondly.

Better to just leave things as they are, he told himself as he went to bed Tuesday night.

Wednesday morning he woke with the sole intention of tracking her down. He had to at least talk to her, if only this one time.

It wasn't hard to find out where she lived either. The beauty of being a celebrity in a small town, he supposed. Although he doubted Nikki cared for it much.

After dropping Abby off at her preschool, he headed out of town. The thirty-minute drive gave him more than enough time to question his motives. He insisted all he wanted to do was clear the air. They had been friends once upon a time, and it was only right that he try to get things on a friendly note between them.

Wade didn't believe a word he told himself. The winding road led up a steep hill completely covered in trees. Gravel crunched beneath his tires and he began to wonder if he had misread the directions. Surely she wouldn't be living this far from...

The trees suddenly opened up to reveal a large cabin-style house constructed of wooden beams and glass.

He didn't have to wonder whether he had the right place because he recognized the gleaming black Ford Explorer parked in the semicircle drive.

The front of the house seemed to consist of little more than windows. And damn, what a view. It was practically perched on the face of the hillside, overlooking a deep valley that was bisected by a wide, lazy creek. Rolling waves of impossibly green grass surrounded him, marked here and there with the chaotic colors of wildflowers.

The glass shimmered under the sun, sparkling bright. The porch spanned the entire width of the house, a comfy swing at one end. The treated wood gleamed a soft, mellow golden brown. Birds sang and called from tall, graceful oaks. Toward the back, he caught a glimpse of sun reflecting off water. A pond.

This was very different from the cramped, dirty three-bedroom apartment she had grown up in. It was actually about as far away from it as she could get...and he figured that right there would explain why in the world she'd chosen to move here of all places.

She'd wanted to get away from that place, that trapped, confined little hellhole where rarely a night passed without hearing sirens wailing, where the walls were stained with water, mold and smoke, and where the only scenic view she'd ever been able to find had come from within the pages of the books she read, or the stories she'd created for herself.

"Looks like you managed to do just that, Nik," he said softly, pride moving through him. Pride...and regret. He wished he could have been there with her as she made this walk.

Gravel crunched under his shoes as he headed for the front door. He mounted the steps slowly, studying the fine construction. This place must have cost a fortune. Intricately carved oak and beveled panes of glass made up the front door. That alone probably cost more than he made in a month.

Who would want to live alone in a house like this? Surely it was too big for just one person. If ever there had been a place built for raising a family, this was it. Married. She had to be married.

Five years had passed, certainly long enough for her to have found somebody and fallen in love.

No, Wade thought, his gut wrenching. Damn it, he didn't know if he could stomach the idea of her belonging to somebody else, even though rightfully he had no hold over her. He'd lost that right years ago, shattered it straight to hell.

But what if some guy answered the door? Or worse, a child?

Gritting his teeth, he raised a clenched fist to pound on the door. Tucking his hands in his pockets, he half-turned away to wait. And pray it would be Nicole answering the door.

"Damn it, I'm not yelling!" Nikki yelled at the phone. "And don't tell me to calm down."

Fortunately, it was on speaker and she was standing by the window.

So her editor and one of her best friends wouldn't likely be nursing a busted ear drum.

Kris sighed and said, "Nikki, sweetheart, I know this pisses you off. Trust me, it makes me mad too. But we can't do anything more than what we're doing."

"Don't give me that. It's not fricking enough. Why in the hell do people have this sense that they are entitled to just *take* whatever they want? Shit, you got any idea how hard I had to work just to be able to buy a couple of books a month when I was in high school? And most of those were *used*. But damn it,

I *paid* for them. I didn't *steal* them." She drove a hand through her hair, glaring at the computer. She should be working—she *needed* to be working, but she couldn't damn well concentrate after seeing that website come up *again*. "They aren't entitled to just take whatever the hell they want, Kris. It's not right. It's so far from right, it's sickening."

It made her sick, twisted her gut in a way that was almost physically painful, and for the next little while, at least until her rage passed, she wouldn't be able to write.

"They *aren't* entitled," Kris said. "I know that. You know that. But we can't convince them."

The ache in her chest wasn't letting up, but she hadn't expected it to do. "There are times, Kris, I swear, there are times when I wish I didn't do this."

"Honey, please, please don't tell me that."

"Sorry. I'm not going to lie about it. Putting all that time and work into those books and having people just take it makes me feel like shit—and they expect me to be *grateful* too. That's like rubbing salt in the wound."

"I know."

"Hours, Kris. I spent sometimes twelve, fourteen hours a day writing. I bust my ass on those books. I do contests. I write myself into surgery. Half the time my back forgets its natural shape because of all the time I spend sitting at my damn computer. I spend thousands every fricking year on research, on contests, on promotional crap, on the damn website..." Her voice trailed off and she sighed, resting her forehead against the window.

The most frustrating part of all was that it was a violation, not just a legal one, although that pissed her off too. But this went deeper than that.

These books, she worked so damned hard on them. So hard.

"If I'd known this fight was waiting for me, I don't know if I would have signed up for this," Nikki said quietly.

"So you're going to let the ones who don't respect you ruin it for you? Ruin it for those millions who *do* respect you?" Kris said, her voice flat.

"Shit," Nikki went to shove her hands into her pockets, only to realize the low-slung yoga pants didn't *have* pockets. "No. *Those* readers deserve better. They are the reason I keep going, and you know it."

"Yes. They're worth it, baby."

"Yeah." Nikki smiled tiredly. "I know." Then she sighed and shifted around, resting her hips against the windowsill.

"So I just keep sending take-down requests and searching the stupid internet for this crap. I'm a writer, damn it. I'm supposed to be writing, not messing with this."

"Then don't," Kris said. "You can either forward the information to me and we'll handle it or you could get an assistant to handle it."

Nikki cringed at idea of an assistant. Somebody in her house. No. No, thanks.

It was a discussion they'd had a hundred times before and would have a hundred times again. Blowing out a breath, she said, "You know I can't just ignore it." She rested her head against the window again, staring outside. "My work, Kris. If I can't be bothered to protect my work I've got no right expecting somebody else to do it. It doesn't matter if it takes time away from writing or not. I'll handle it."

"Honey, plenty of writers in your shoes do let other people take care of this for them. That doesn't *mean* they don't care. It bothers them as much as it bothers you. But you let this get to you, and it gets you depressed and it pisses you off and that interferes with your writing and if you'd just—"

"It's my work, Kris," Nikki interrupted, her voice soft but

firm. "How other writers choose to handle it when somebody steals from them is their business, but when somebody takes a book I spend months of my life on and just passes it out like it's nothing, it makes me feel like...like it's nothing. Like *I'm* nothing. Like all the writers are nothing...just automatons out there to create something for people's amusement. We do our damnedest to bring them a few hours of pleasure, some entertainment and these people treat us like we're nothing, like we don't matter. It's not right. I work damn hard on those books, Kris. All of us do. It should mean something."

"You're right, and you know I feel the same way. But can't you find another way to handle this?"

"By *not* handling it?" Nikki snorted. "Nope. Not in my make-up."

Nikki looked at her computer.

Right now, save for her brothers and a slowly healing relationship with her dad, the books saved on the computer were pretty much all she had in the world.

Although, logically, even if that weren't the case, she'd still be the same way.

The job she did was a hard one, one that seemed to get less and less respect with each passing year. Writers were expected to do more, produce more, for less and less. If she was going to keep writing, then she was going to keep protecting the work she'd devoted much of her life to.

"I can't pass it off, Kris. So you'll just have to keep listening to me rant," she said, knowing her editor wasn't going to be surprised.

After all, she'd been having this discussion with her for the past two, two and half years. Granted, the discussions had been getting more heated lately.

Kris chuckled. "Well, that doesn't really surprise me. Besides, this gave me a reason to get out of a meeting I didn't want to go to. Taking a call from you, even when you're on a rant, is a lot more fun."

"Well, if the meeting is still going on, I could rant more. Want me to go on a tirade about the people who feel information should be freely shared? We can see if they'll be the ones to pony up the dough to start a fund to provide for the housing, insurance and daily living expenses of all writers, as those writers are expected to work for nothing..." Nikki smirked as she said it. "Maybe they'll be willing to pay for the hand surgery I'm probably going to have to have next year."

Kris groaned. "Nikki, enough. Look, let's talk about the book. It's due in three months. How is it going?"

"Almost done." She doubted she'd need the three months, but that wasn't a bad thing. She was going to need a little more time before she started work on the next book in her contract. She flexed her left hand and rubbed her wrist but it didn't do anything to ease the vague ache there.

"Almost done. Awesome. Tell me about it."

"Well..." Nikki paused for about five seconds and then said, "It's a book."

"You are a pain in the ass."

"Yeah. It's sticking pretty close to the synopsis I sent in," she hedged.

"That oh-so-descriptive one-page narrative? Fine, fine. Keep it close to your chest. Just hurry up and get it to me. And what's this about surgery?"

"I will. Probably in the next few weeks...because I've got a feeling I'm going to need some time before I start on the next one," Nikki said. "My left hand's starting to act up. Pretty bad."

Kris didn't need any more details. Eighteen months earlier Nikki had gone through surgery on her right hand and the doctors had advised she'd likely be facing surgery on the other one at some point. Apparently some point had arrived.

"What about that voice software?"

Nikki grimaced. "Sometimes I can go into the groove with it, and other times? Not so much. Helps a lot when I'm editing, actually."

"But not with the writing."

"Well, considering how miserable I am while I'm editing, I'm willing to take all the help I can get," Nikki said. "And it will get better, I think. I just need to work with it more."

She glanced at the clock. "Speaking of work, I need to do just that. My slave-driving editor will kill me if she hears I'm talking on the phone all day."

Nikki heard the motor long before she saw the vehicle. She'd finally gotten into a rhythm with the story and she'd actually used the voice software too.

Damn it.

It would figure.

She stifled a groan as she saved her work.

Who in the hell could that be? Whoever it was, they weren't welcome. Her dad and brothers all worked, so it wasn't likely to be any of them. Besides, they would have called.

From the large floor-to-ceiling window in the living room, she watched. From time to time, she caught a glimpse of shiny black paint and silver chrome. It rounded the bend as Nikki tried to remember if she knew anybody who drove a truck like that.

Glancing down at herself, she sighed. The white tank top and black yoga pants weren't really company clothes, but as she hadn't really invited anybody to come for a visit, did it matter?

She did pause by the bathroom to splash some water on

her face and pull her hair up into a ponytail, but that was all the effort she wanted to expend.

By the time she was done a knock sounded on the door. Through the beveled cut of the glass, Nikki could make out a dark shadow. The polite smile she had fixed on her face wobbled, then collapsed, when she opened the door.

Wade.

He was staring out over the verandah, hands tucked into his back pockets. He turned as she went still, his eyes sweeping over her from head to toe, much as she was gazing at him. Finally, their eyes met, but she still didn't have a single word to say. Her heart was pounding fast and hard.

You still look the same, she thought helplessly as her eyes searched for changes. His face looked a little more solemn and he looked like he had filled out a little more in his chest, but other than that and the shorter hair, he hadn't changed much at all.

Maybe if I close my eyes and wish hard enough, the past few years will just fade away, she thought, leaning against the doorjamb, swallowing. *Just a bad dream...*

And then she kicked herself. No. She wouldn't undo them, even if she could. Not for anything would she give up the brief time she'd had with Jason.

Wade looked so exactly the way he always had.

But she had changed. Nothing in her life was the same now. Nothing at all. And as empty as her life was, she didn't think there was room in it for the likes of Wade Lightfoot.

Thank God, he was alone. She couldn't take it if he had brought his daughter with him.

"Nikki."

"Wade."

He looked away, a sigh escaping his lips. He

looked...flustered. Under her steady gaze his hands left his pockets, thumbs hooking in his belt loops as he rocked back on his heels. She could still remember the pleasure those hands had been able to evoke.

"I was surprised to see you here," he said, his voice sounding tight and rusty.

"Were you?" Nikki asked calmly, trying very hard to pretend she hadn't taken off running from him. She didn't quite succeed. That dark red flush, the very bane of a redhead's existence, spread up from her neck, heating her flesh, staining her cheeks, but she determinedly ignored it.

Wade blew a sigh out, his eyes narrowing. With irritation written all over his face, he said, "I was even more surprised when you took off running like a jackrabbit, Nikki. I've never known you to run before."

"I'm hardly the same person you knew, Wade. There's a lot about me you don't know."

"I wouldn't think turning yellow would be something to be proud of."

Nikki narrowed her eyes. "It's not a matter of turning yellow. I didn't want to see you or talk to you. So why hang around?" That was mostly the truth, right?

"Fair enough," he said with a slow nod. "How long have you lived here?"

"A while. We moved here after we left Louisville."

"You and your brothers."

"And my dad." She leaned against the door jamb, crossing her arms over her chest. She supposed she could be nice and invite him inside. But she didn't want him in this house, in her safe haven. It might be empty, but it was some place that was free from memories of him and she'd rather keep it that way.

"Your dad." A faint smile curled his lips. "How's he doing?"

"Good. Actually, he's better than he's been in a long time." The past five years had been sober ones for Jack Kline, something Nikki still couldn't quite believe. But then again, he'd had one hell of a wake-up call. When your twenty-year-old, formerly healthy daughter collapses right in front of you, it tends to scare even the most stalwart of men.

"That's good. I've seen your books. Bought them, as a matter of fact. Congratulations, Nikki. You did exactly what you said you would do," he told her, his eyes gleaming. "I'm proud of you."

She just stared at him, careful not to let him see that those words had any effect on her. They *shouldn't*. Not at all. But they did. In a flat voice that she hoped covered her chaotic emotions, she told him, "I couldn't care less if you're proud of me or not. I didn't do it for you. It wasn't about you or for you. It never was."

With a careless shrug, Nikki added, "You never really cared all that much about it anyway. It has nothing to do with you."

His mouth spasmed slightly and he said wearily, "No. I don't guess it does." He studied her again, his eyes narrowed and intense. "Yeah," he finally said quietly, as though to himself. "I guess you have changed."

"It's to be expected, I'd think. I'm not the person I used to be, any more than you are the person I thought I knew," Nikki said. "I certainly never would have expected what you did to me. Or expect you to hide it the way you did. I wonder, if Jamie hadn't gotten pregnant, would you ever have told me?"

"No," Wade said, clearly and without hesitation. "I wanted to. Hell, it was killing me inside. But I couldn't lose you. It was the wrong decision. I know that now. Hell, I knew then. But if she hadn't been pregnant, you never would have known." His eyes met hers straight on, unblinking and steady.

Looking away, Nikki absently rubbed the back of her neck. Why did it still hurt so much? Hadn't enough time passed for her to be over this by now, over him? "Well, at least you can be honest about it now," she said quietly. "But it's a little late." Closing her eyes, she summoned up her strength. Then she looked back at him coolly. "What are you doing here, Wade?"

"I guess I wanted to apologize," he told her, turning away. He walked to the edge of the verandah and braced his elbows on the railing. A breeze lifted the edges of his hair, tugging at them, while the sun gleamed down on it. Broad shoulders strained at the seams of his shirt. His voice was lower as he spoke again. "I made a lot of mistakes with you, Nikki. I hurt you. And I'm sorrier than you will ever know."

Nikki's eyes closed briefly and she lowered her head. Pressing her fingers to her eyes, she thought, *Sorry...? He is sorry?*

With a sigh she looked back at him, her eyes searching for something she couldn't quite define. She had experienced too much grief in her life over the past few years to wish it on another, even somebody who had hurt her as much as he had.

He meant it. Wade looked...tired. As if the past few years hadn't been easy on him. Despite what had happened, she hadn't wished him ill. She had never wanted him to be unhappy.

He was though. There was unhappiness in those dark eyes, in every line of his body.

Nikki moved out of the doorway, shutting it behind her. In her bare feet, she padded over to the porch swing and sat. Drawing a knee to her chest, she studied him. "Apology accepted, Wade."

"Just like that?" he asked, turning to face her. With disbelief in his eyes, he stared at her, watching her closely. "Aren't you going to rant and rave, or give me the cold shoulder?"

"It's in the past now, Wade. I've never wished you ill. It just wasn't meant to be with us, and I've accepted that," she said, shrugging and looking away from him. "It wouldn't do any good to rant and rave now."

Damn, I'm good. Nikki could almost believe it herself, almost convince herself her heart wasn't bleeding inside. But the past seemed like it was just yesterday, the pain still every bit as true as it had been then.

But convincing herself wasn't what mattered. All she had to do was convince him. Make sure he didn't know she hadn't accepted or dealt with anything, at least not very well. Make sure he didn't know she woke up crying at night for their son...and yes, very often for him.

Frowning, Wade stared at her. With a heavy sigh, he looked away. "How have you been doing the past few years? Did you finish college?"

"No." How could she tell him that she'd never gone back, that her interest in it had been gone, that she'd been too depressed to care about a nursing career at that time? And later, when she had been interested, the doctor had strictly forbidden it. She hadn't needed that stress then. After that, when she had Jason, she had been too happy, too satisfied to need anything else.

And now...now she just didn't care. About anything.

"Why not?" Wade asked, another frown darkening his face. "I guess with as big as your books got, you didn't need it, but it always seemed to be one of the most important things in your life. That and writing."

"No," she corrected. "*You* were the most important thing. Writing is just a part of me. Nursing fell way below you."

Closing his eyes, Wade swore quietly under his breath. "Damn it, Nikki. You always did know how to twist the knife."

Nikki ignored him as she added, "Besides, nursing didn't seem quite so important once things with the books took off. A writing career turned out to be a lot more demanding than I'd expected anyway. *Writing* turns out only to be half of what I end up doing. I didn't need to juggle both, so I decided not to."

A half-truth. Nursing school fell by the wayside and she never made the attempt to pursue it as writing became her focus. But for a while even writing hadn't mattered all that much.

Writing had still been important, but it hadn't been the all-consuming passion it had once been. It was important because it was a job, how she provided for her son.

It wasn't until Jason was suddenly gone that she started to cling to her writing like it was a lifesaver. During her pregnancy and while Jason had been alive, she had written only because she had been determined to make certain her son had a good life, better than her own childhood had been.

Later, after she had come home to an empty house and stared at Jason's empty room, the need for her stories had resurfaced. Like a drowning man clings to a life preserver, she wrapped herself in her make-believe worlds and tried to forget. And while she wrote, for a little while, she'd been able to.

Without the stories she would have lost her mind. It was all she had left now…

A feeling of despair was rising in her, her throat tightening, her eyes stinging. An empty house, a handful of books and an empty nursery.

Damn it, if you get right down to it, I don't really have much at all, she thought bleakly.

Determined to keep thoughts like that away, she said the one thing guaranteed to help her get back on track, to get refocused and to get him the hell off her mountain.

"Your daughter looks just like you, Wade. I imagine you and Jamie are very proud of her."

"Jamie's dead."

Just as she congratulated herself on the return of her

composure, she felt her foundation crumple under her. Shaken to the core, she closed her eyes as his words echoed over in her mind.

Jamie's dead. So calmly, so flatly stated. *Jamie's dead.*

"What?" she whispered.

"Jamie's dead. She died three years ago, Nikki."

It was then that she finally noticed he wore no wedding ring.

Jamie's dead.

Nikki felt as though the ground had opened up under her, leaving her standing on thin air. Scrabbling for purchase.

The woman she had spent years hating was suddenly no longer alive to hate. One hand went to rub at her stomach, which was churning with all the stress she was keeping bottled up.

Shakily, she said, "I'm sorry." Her gaze flew up to meet his, certain she would see total desolation there, but all she saw was a distant sort of regret before he turned away, staring out into the trees that lined the northwestern side of her property.

Wade was silent for so long she wondered if he was going to speak at all. When he finally did, his voice was so quiet she could hardly hear him.

"Don't be. She was miserable with me, Nicole. I did the best I could, but I couldn't give her what she wanted. She never could understand that I didn't love her, that I was only there because of Abby. She had my name and a ring, but nothing else."

Turning to her, Wade stared at her with intense eyes, mesmerizing eyes. Unable to look away, Nikki sat helplessly as he moved closer to her. He sank down on his knees in front of her, reaching out to trace the line of her jaw with a feathery touch. Softly, he said, "She could never understand that in my heart, I still belonged to you."

"Don't say that, Wade. We ended the night you told me she was pregnant." Jerking her face away from his touch, Nikki gave a harsh laugh. "Hell. We were over the night you spent with her. I just didn't know it."

"None of that changed the fact that I loved you. None of that changed the fact that I still do love you." Still staring at her with those dark eyes that held her pinned to her seat, he lifted her left hand, studying it intently. Gently, he pressed a kiss to the back of it. If he noticed the trembling, he didn't remark on it.

"No wedding ring, Nikki. But is there somebody in your heart now? Am I going to have to fight to get you back?" His voice dropped as he spoke, as he hooked one hand behind her head, drawing her closer.

His softly spoken words, dark hypnotic eyes had soothed her, lulled her into believing, into hoping, dreaming. *If only*, she thought wistfully.

The gentle touch of his lips on hers broke her out of her spell.

"No," Nikki said, her voice faint. "No." Her voice was stronger this time. She shoved him away and shot to her feet, moving to the far railing. "I'm not interested in rekindling an old flame, Wade. I'm certainly not interested in reliving the past or rebuilding something between us."

"Why not?" Wade asked, moving on silent feet until he stood so close she could feel his body heat warming her back.

Turning around, she pressed a hand against his chest, determined to keep him at a distance. It wasn't enough though. And it didn't help. She could feel the heat of him, the warmth. She could feel his heart racing against her hand.

This is too much, she thought desperately. *Too much.*

Harshly, she said, "You turned out to be everything I hate in people. You betrayed me. You lied to me."

Wade flinched at her words like she had slapped him. And then she turned her back on him, staring out in the trees.

Nikki's words lashed at him, pouring salt into the still-open wounds of his heart. His guilt over what had happened had never eased, but he had succeeded in burying it. Now it returned in full force, making his gut clench and his throat constrict. Reaching for her, he started to speak, "Nikki—" But she cringed away from his hands.

Nikki flinched away when he turned her around to face him. "I don't want you touching me, Wade," she said, her voice thick. "I don't want you here. So go away."

Without waiting to see if he listened, she edged around him and headed for the door. Without sparing him one last glance, she disappeared inside the house and locked the door behind her.

Well, that went rather well.

He cursed himself as he drove away, shaken. He hadn't meant for it to go quite like that. He certainly hadn't expected to see a cold, quiet woman in place of the stubborn, hot-tempered girl he had known.

She was just a shadow of herself, her eyes sad and distant. He couldn't see any of the thoughts going on in her mind.

He had always been able to read those eyes, know what was going on in that quirky mind of hers. It was very disturbing to look into those eyes now and see nothing. Absolutely nothing.

Hell, Wade. What did you expect? Did you think she would throw her arms around you and tell you how much she had missed you?

While he hadn't been expecting it, he had been hoping for a warmer reception than he had received. *Damn optimistic fool.*

Chapter Seven

For three days Nikki existed on catnaps. When she finally crashed the nightmares had her waking in the night, screaming, fighting, struggling with a seatbelt that no longer held her pinned in the seat, fighting to get to a child she had buried three years earlier, while the father who had never known his son stood by and watched with emotionless eyes.

The nightmare had been so awful, now she feared closing her eyes again. Working was impossible.

Eating was impossible.

Thinking was impossible, and she knew she needed to snap herself out of it.

She couldn't let seeing Wade do this to her—she couldn't. Not if she wanted to stay anything even resembling sane.

Sometimes it seemed her grasp on sanity was already pretty tenuous, and she knew if she didn't get a grip that grasp would go from tenuous to non-existent.

The best thing, the logical thing to do was push him out of her mind. *Stop thinking about Wade. Stop thinking about the little girl. Stop wondering... Stop thinking about Jamie, what had happened.*

It didn't concern her, after all.

None of it did.

But she couldn't help it.

Staring out the window, her computer sitting untouched behind her, she rested a hand on her flat belly and wondered, unable to stop herself, if Jamie had felt that amazement, that joy, that *fear* when her tiny little baby had moved inside her for the first time. Had she cried when the ultrasound showed a healthy baby? Had she cried when she had learned she was pregnant, carrying the baby of the man she loved more than life itself?

Nikki hadn't cried. She had been too stunned, too shocked.

Then

"Nikki, I don't think you understand the gravity of the situation here," Dr. Moriarty said, his eyes kind. "You almost waited too long to come in here. You're in bad shape. We can help you, but the baby…"

Logically, Nikki knew he was only telling her what was best for her. And it wasn't like she had exactly *come* in either.

That was the worst of it.

She'd collapsed, passed out right in the middle of the living room. Her dad had called *911* and she had ended up in the emergency room, where she was informed about something she had never, never had expected to hear.

She was pregnant.

And she was in almost the worst physical shape imaginable on top of it.

"No," she repeated for the third time, her voice shaky, practically soundless. She sat motionless on the exam table, wearing a shirt that had fit her months before, but weeks of depression had sapped her appetite and she had lost far, far too much weight.

"Nikki, listen to me. You have developed an irregular heartbeat, something that's due to your malnourished state. Collapsing the way you did was nothing short of miracle,

78

because it forced you to get medical care. We can help you—you're young, and up until recently, you were very healthy. Despite your current condition, you're strong. But that baby...according to the information you've given me, you are well over three months pregnant. You are severely underweight, badly malnourished. I imagine the blood work will show that you have all sorts of electrolyte imbalances, vitamin and mineral deficiencies.

"If this was just you we were talking about the problem would be fixed easily enough. We can get you healthy again, but it's too late for that little baby. The first three months are critical. I seriously doubt you could even carry it to full term. If you did, the child could have numerous problems, mental and physical handicaps. The first trimester is the most important time for a fetus development-wise. That is when the groundwork for a healthy baby takes place. Your baby's groundwork is...precarious. It probably wouldn't live very long."

Her father stood staring out the window, hands buried deep in his pockets while they listened to the doctor. As he reached up, patting his pocket, she knew he was craving a cigarette, that he could practically feel the smoke burning its way down his throat, soothing his shaking hands.

And a drink, he probably wanted a drink. She wanted to feel angry about that, but she couldn't. She just couldn't. She was having a hard time feeling much of anything. It had been that way for the past three months. She felt nothing, not even the anger, not even the self-disgust part of her *wanted* to feel for letting herself sink this low.

She felt nothing... No. That wasn't entirely true. She did feel something now. She wasn't entirely sure what it was, but whenever she rested her hand on her belly and thought about the little life there, she felt a strange mix of fear and delight. And hope...

There was a baby in there...her baby. Wade's baby. A child

they had created together, a child struggling to live, despite her not taking better care.

She couldn't get rid of it. Everything inside her screamed out even at the thought of it.

"Nicole, are you listening to me?" the doctor asked, his voice gentle.

She nodded. "Yes."

"Do you realize what I'm telling you? This pregnancy could put a strain on your body. One that could kill you. You are not healthy. Your body has probably forgotten what it's supposed to do." The doctor paused, his expression grim, as though he wasn't sure he'd explained himself well. As though he was convinced Nikki didn't understand what he was telling her.

She did though. She understood exactly what he was telling her.

"I understand, Dr. Moriarty," she said, meeting his gaze although it was hard. It had been weeks, longer, since she had made herself talk to anybody, even her brothers, even her dad.

"Do you? Do you really?"

"Yes." She licked her lips and nodded. She lowered her gaze, studied her hands, a bit stunned by how thin they were, how frail. She'd done this herself. She'd done this...let herself just fade away.

Like your mother, she told herself.

Now the self-disgust made an appearance. Setting her jaw, she looked back at the doctor. "Up until this fall I was a student at the University of Louisville's School of Nursing. I'd planned on specializing in neonatal nursing or pediatrics. I do understand, and while I realize I don't look like somebody capable of taking care of herself, I know how serious this is, and I know in all likelihood that I probably won't be able...able to carry this baby to term. But I can't have an abortion. I can't."

The doctor sighed, smoothing a hand down his tie. Then he

slanted his eyes toward the quiet man waiting by the window. "Mr. Kline," he said, trying a different tactic.

Jack Kline looked as though he'd aged ten years since he'd stepped inside the office, but the look in those eyes was resolute, every bit as unyielding as the look in his daughter's gaze.

"She's made her choice, Dr. Moriarty. I'll support her, regardless of the outcome," he said quietly, his voice gravelly and rough from the years of abuse he had heaped on it.

Sighing, the doctor rubbed the back of his neck. "Very well. It's your choice. I'm going to refer you to Dr. Gray. He's new in Somerset, practiced in Louisville for quite some time..."

"I completely agree with Dr. Moriarty," Dr. Gray said as he pored over the blood work and ultrasounds he had been sent. Wire-rimmed glasses perched on a thin blade of a nose, while wide, intelligent blue eyes studied the records and lab results.

"This is going to be extremely risky. Nikki, he wasn't lying when he said this pregnancy could kill you. You're malnourished. You have an arrhythmia. According to your physical from your previous physician in Louisville, you didn't previously have one, so we're going to have to assume this is a new development.

"Do you understand what that means?" he asked, studying her with intense eyes.

Nikki sat on the table and struggled not to give in to the urge to lie down, to rest. She was tired, so tired. But being tired, hiding away and sleeping were the reasons she was here. Ever since she had walked away from Wade three months ago, she had been hiding. Hiding, sleeping, pretending the outside world didn't exist, and look where it had landed her. Look what it had done to her. Look what it might do to her baby.

She was done with it.

She hadn't ever been weak before and she was completely disgusted with herself for what she saw in the mirror now. So instead of lying down on the table, she sat up and held the doctor's gaze.

"I have to try," Nikki said softly. "I know there are options...for others. But there aren't options for me. I have to try."

Sitting on the wheeled stool in front of the exam table, Dr. Gray took her hand. "You understand, I can't guarantee anything. I can't even guarantee your own safety should you continue with this pregnancy."

"I know," she said, forcing herself to smile.

"It's going to be an uphill battle no matter what."

An uphill battle didn't quite describe it.

She went nearly a month overdue, delivering at forty-three and half weeks. Jason was small, but he was perfect. Alive, healthy and hers.

Hers...and Wade's. Conceived in a fit of fury and desperation that last time in the woods. Conceived while pleasure racked her body and agony tore its way through her broken heart.

If she were stronger, if she were any less selfish, maybe she would have told him.

But she couldn't. The wounds were too raw.

He was married now—married to Jamie and they had a little girl. One of Shawn's friends from Louisville had heard the news. Nikki had overheard him tell Dylan and Dad.

No. Jason was hers and only hers.

Now

Nikki came back to herself slowly. Her eyes were dry and burning, the pain she felt too deep for tears. Crying brought her no release. Beneath her questing hand her belly was smooth, flat and hollow. She felt horribly empty.

The room down the hall stood with the door closed tight, the toys untouched, the crib unslept in and the laughter forever silenced.

Chapter Eight

Avoiding Wade became habit.

She saw him in a store—she left. She saw him walking down the street—she turned around and went the other direction. Sometimes he let her get away with it. Other times she had to ignore him until he gave up.

It was easiest when he had his daughter with him.

He didn't seem to want the kid to realize there was a problem.

So it was easier...in some ways.

In other ways it was harder.

So much harder. The girl's dark eyes, her dark hair, even her smile, everything about her reminded Nikki of Jason. Everything. Part of her wanted to cradle the child close. Another part of her wanted to get as far away as possible.

If she had thought about it for even five seconds, she would've realized the Fourth of July parade in the small town was exactly where she was likely to run into the little girl, and she never would've left home.

By the time she figured it out, it was too late. She was too late and cornered by a pint-sized kid on a mission.

"Why don't you like my daddy?"

Cornered. On Main Street with Abby Lightfoot and no sign of her father in sight.

Why me?

"Well?" the little girl demanded impatiently, her hands going to her hips in a gesture that mimicked her father's.

"Uh," Nikki said, uncertain what to say. "Uh, who said I didn't like him?"

"Anytime he tries to talk to you, you take off. That's not very nice," Abby informed her, her face prim. Polite.

Despite herself, despite the turmoil in her heart, amusement curled inside her. Reaching up to scratch her nose, Nikki hid her grin. She could see the hand of Wade's mother in this child. A very precocious child too. Geez, what sort of four-year-old was this?

"Just where is your dad? I don't see him and I don't think he wants you running around by yourself," Nikki said, kneeling and looking the little girl in the face. The girl smelled of baby lotion, candy and innocence.

Dear God. She looked so much like Jason. Nikki could feel the razors slicing into her heart and she wondered how it was possible none of it showed.

"This is important," Abby said, sounding very adult. "Dad will understand. Now, why don't you like him?"

"Are you sure you're only four years old?" Nikki asked, buying time while she struggled to come up with an answer that wouldn't be a lie, but wouldn't make this precocious little girl upset.

"I'll be five in April."

"Ah. That explains it," Nikki said sagely, nodding her head. Never mind that April was months away.

Unable to resist the urge to touch, she reached out and stroked her hand down Abby's raven black hair, soft and thick. "Honey, it's not that I don't like your dad. But we've had some problems in the past and it kind of hurts for me to be around him."

Would she understand that? Nikki wondered.

Solemnly, the little girl nodded. "That's what he said. But you know, when somebody hurts you it helps if you let them say they are sorry. Did he hurt you?"

"A little," Nikki said, her smile weak and shaky. *That's the understatement of the century.*

With a bright, happy grin, Abby said, "Then just let him say he's sorry and things will be better. I know he's sorry, otherwise he wouldn't look so sad when he sees you."

Nikki wasn't able to answer for just then, Wade swooped down out of the crowd, snagging his daughter and catching her in a tight hug. "Abby Lightfoot, what were you thinking running off like that?" he demanded, his eyes closed tight.

"I'm sorry, Daddy," Abby said, twisting away until her father released his death grip and saw Nikki standing there.

"Thanks for watching her, Nikki," he said gruffly, transferring her to his left arm.

Nikki shrugged. "She sort of found me, Wade." As quickly as she could, she averted her eyes, ready to escape into the crowd.

"Don't you ever take off like that, little girl. That's just asking for all sorts of bad things," Wade said, looking from Nikki to his daughter.

"I'm sorry, Daddy. Please don't be mad. It was real important," Abby said softly, her eyes sober, her mouth pursed in a pout.

Nikki watched as Wade fought not to melt under those sweetly spoken words and Abby's face properly solemn and chastised, utterly repentant.

Nikki knew without a doubt that should something else important come up, the little girl would do just as she had. Would Jason have been like this? Sweet and stubborn, determined to get his way?

Turning away, Nikki started to find someplace else to watch the parade, only to have Wade snag her arm. She looked up and met his eyes without speaking.

"Why don't you watch the parade with us?" he asked, his dark eyes caressing her face. His hand was warm on her arm, and despite the heat of the day she felt goose bumps rising, felt her pulse kicking up a notch or two.

"I don't—"

"Dad, I think you need to say you're sorry first," Abby interrupted before Nikki was able to make good her escape. "After you say you're sorry, you can be friends again. Then she can watch the parade with us."

"Is that right?" Wade asked, studying his daughter's face. "Are you sure that's how it works?" All the while, as he talked with his daughter, he drew Nikki closer, his hand cupped around her elbow.

"Of course it is. Now say you're sorry. That's all she's waiting for," Abby stated, a very adult look on her little face. For all the world, she looked like a kindergarten teacher correcting two unruly students.

Wade turned his eyes back to Nikki, smiling slightly. "I am sorry, Nikki. I thought you already knew that," he said quietly.

"See, now wasn't that easy?" Abby asked, squirming until her father set her down. Then she grabbed Wade's hand in one hand, Nikki's in the other, and pulled them closer to the front of the crowd. "I knew that would help."

Nikki stood next to the little girl, a frozen smile on her face.

Just walk away, she told herself. *Just take your hand back and walk away.*

But she couldn't find it in her heart to wipe that happy smile off Abby's face.

The hot summer sun beat down on her bare shoulders and arms but did nothing to warm her. Her scoop-neck tank top

87

and cut-off denims had been comfortable earlier, but now she wished for sackcloth, a sweater, turtleneck and jeans, anything to warm her chilled flesh.

What was she doing here? She was watching a Fourth of July parade with the man who'd cheated on her.

She was insane, absolutely insane, just begging for punishment.

With one eye on the clock, the other on the parade, she prayed for it to end quickly.

Wade wasn't certain what had prompted Abby to go seek out Nikki, but he was damn glad of it. She was standing less than two feet away, and though Nikki had yet to say a damn thing without being prompted, she hadn't taken off in the other direction. Yet.

Something told him she was just biding time. His instincts proved right when he caught her eyes dart to the clock in the square for the second time in only minutes.

He shifted until he was standing more behind Abby and Nikki than beside them. One hand rested on his daughter's shoulder as she leaned against Nikki's side, laughing at the clowns and squealing at the floats that went past. He kept his other hand fisted in his pocket to keep from wrapping it around Nikki's waist.

A gentle breeze fluttered her hair around her face. She'd cut her hair, those gleaming chestnut strands were cropped to chin length and even curlier than before. Again, her glasses were missing. She wore no jewelry, no make-up, and her nails were ruthlessly short. Her soft mouth was set in a firm line, her solemn eyes were fastened on the parade and she looked neither up nor down the street.

She could have been standing before a firing squad with all the pleasure she showed.

Nikki didn't want to be here. Wade knew that as well as he knew his own name. She was here though. That was something, right? Closing his eyes, he inhaled, dragging the scent of her skin into his lungs, heating up blood that already pumped hot. His eyes fastened on the soft skin of her neck and shoulders, bared by the tank top she wore. If he put his mouth on her there, where her neck and shoulders joined, would it still make her gasp?

If he rubbed gently, would it still make her sigh with pleasure?

"—fireworks with us?"

Wade snapped his head around, looking down at his daughter. Abby was tugging on his pants with one hand, the other holding tightly onto Nikki's, as though she too feared Nikki would disappear into the crowd the moment she had the chance.

"Sorry, baby. I didn't hear you."

"I want to know if Nikki can watch the fireworks with us," she repeated patiently.

He looked up to find Nikki staring straight ahead, her eyes blank. "She's welcome to if she wants," he said quietly, already knowing what her answer would be.

"I can't. I promised my family I would come by after the parade," Nikki said, giving Abby a half-hearted smile. "Let's just finish watching the parade together, okay?"

Wade sighed as Abby looked away, her face fallen. He picked her up and settled her on his hip. "Maybe next time, brat," he whispered in her ear and nuzzled her neck. "Okay?"

Nikki said nothing. Hell, the way she stared at the spectacle on the street you'd think she was utterly fascinated by the damn parade. Wade knew damn well though that she wanted nothing more than to get the hell away from him.

For the next thirty minutes she ignored him. Except for her

brief answers to Abby, Nikki might as well have not even stood there. She kept her eyes straight ahead, not once looking over at him. Wade knew, for he didn't take his eyes off her.

Frustrated, he wondered how much longer she would persist in ignoring him or running away. How could she ignore him when the very thought of her was enough to set his blood afire? When just being near her managed to make him feel both achingly empty and oddly complete at the same time?

Damnation, he had missed her.

He wanted her back.

Wade hadn't expected her to continue to ignore him for as long as she had. She wasn't even willing for them to just be on friendly terms. She had made that abundantly clear.

How long would she keep this up?

Nikki jumped involuntarily when a hand settled on the curve of her hip. Stiffening, she tried to move away, but the crowd had gotten a little too close.

She aimed a quelling glare up at Wade, only to find him talking to Abby. All around the crowd talked, music played, children laughed. The noise buzzed in her ears, but she heard none of it.

A tiny shudder raced up her spine as his thumb moved up and down. On bare skin. The bottom of her top barely touched the waistband of her shorts and now his hand was kneading her naked flesh. Long, clever fingers played over her waist while she tried hard to ignore it.

She wasn't succeeding. Her stomach felt warm and jittery. Her heart pounded harder. Her skin felt far too tight, hot and prickly.

Damn it, how much longer until this thing's over? she thought wildly as her insides continued to do a slow meltdown.

Her shoulders ached with the effort to keep tension in her body, to keep from relaxing against him. It would be so easy just to let her head fall back against his shoulder, let him wrap her in his arms.

Why was he doing his? Hadn't she made it clear she wanted nothing to do with him? Why was she still standing here? Abby no longer held her hand in a death grip, wasn't looking at her every few seconds as if to say, *Isn't this fun?* Nikki could have left several minutes ago, so why she was torturing herself?

She stood frozen as Wade shifted until he was standing just behind her and slightly to her right. That hand slid around her middle and exerted enough pressure to pull her flush against him. The heat of him was enough to brand her flesh.

Her eyes closed as Wade leaned down and whispered in her ear, "You don't want to stay away from me any more than I want you to. Don't keep running away, baby."

"Stop it," she bit off, her own whisper harsh.

"Stop what? Stop dreaming about you? Loving you? Can you stop thinking about me? Is it really that easy for you?" he asked in a low voice, nuzzling her ear gently.

Her eyes flew open as Wade's hand slid under her shirt again, now caressing her midriff with agile, knowing fingers. She grabbed his hand, stilled it with her own and slipped away from him.

"The parade's over," she said, her voice hoarse, heart pounding. Her palms were damp and her hands were shaking. And he had hardly touched her.

She shot a strained smile to Abby. "I've got to run, sweetheart," she said, then, unable to resist, she tousled the girl's silky black hair. Without another look at Wade she lost herself in the crowd.

Nikki sat silently on the deck while her father cooked steaks on the grill. A lukewarm can of soda sat untouched next to her while she tried to figure out exactly what she was going to do about Wade.

He wasn't taking the hint very well, but that was simply because he didn't want to.

He had decided he was going to get back in her life and that was exactly what he intended to do.

I could go to New York, she thought, chewing her lip. Kirsten had been nagging her to come up for a visit. But she hated New York. Hell, she could hardly stand to go to Louisville anymore.

Besides, the thought of running away galled her.

So what did she do?

What she had to do was make him understand she wanted nothing to do with him. But how was she going to do that?

He knew, in that way of his, that she wasn't dating. He figured that left the field wide open for him. He was going to keep coming around until he wore her down.

So how do I keep him from coming around?

Make him mad. Narrow that field a little bit.

His temper didn't appear to flare as easy as it used to, but Nikki figured if she got him mad enough, kept him at a distance, she could handle him. She couldn't handle him coming around coaxing and wooing.

So she just had to figure out a way to piss him off.

An angry Wade was a lot easier for her to handle than one who teased and flirted.

Wade froze in action, his hand hanging limp at his side

instead of reaching for his wallet. The teller at the window repeated, "That will be twelve dollars, sir."

Automatically, he paid her, accepted the tickets and moved away. Abby chattered away about the upcoming movie, but for the life of him he couldn't process anything she said.

Nikki was here with a tall, lanky man he recognized dimly. It was the guy who owned one of the two repair shops in town. That bastard had one tanned, muscular arm wrapped securely around Nikki's waist as he led her into the theater, head bent low, murmuring into her ear.

Son of a bitch, he fumed silently as he let Abby tug him through the double glass doors and into the line at the snack bar. What in the hell is she doing with that guy?

Searching the lobby, Wade's eyes narrowed as he spotted them in the line next to theirs. He saw red as the guy stroked his hand down Nikki's cheek...and she *smiled* at the guy, a real smile, one Wade hadn't seen in years. A smile that had that lone dimple flashing and her eyes crinkling up at the corners.

Was this why she wouldn't give Wade the time of day?

How in the hell could she do this? Why in the hell would she do this?

Shit, she was dressed up in a killer little dress that left much arm and leg bare, and left very little to the imagination. It was a deep apricot color and it displayed a lithe, toned body and made her skin glow. Her full mouth was painted the same shade and her eyes were made up to look huge and slumberous. She'd pulled some of her hair up into a loose knot and long sparkling earrings danced and gleamed as she cocked her head to look up at him.

Impotent fury swelled in him as he watched them leave the lobby, but it paled next to the rage he felt as they walked side by side into a theater that was showing a sexy new thriller. He had asked her to go see it with him just three days ago, and she had said she wasn't interested.

"Movies don't do much for me anymore, Wade," she'd said, voice cool and disinterested.

Through ninety minutes of cartoon antics, Wade sat rigidly, his hands clenching and unclenching as he thought of the two in the theater next door. How long had she been seeing him? Why hadn't she said anything? Why hadn't he seen them together before now? Why was he sitting here when he could be one theater over, murdering the bastard with his bare hands?

Something on the screen had all the kids shrieking with glee while Wade sat thinking about making the man next door into a eunuch.

He managed to calm himself on the drive home. This was the first time he'd seen them together. In fact, Nikki was always alone. So maybe this was just a one-time thing. After all, she wasn't completely indifferent to him, and as honest as she was, if she was serious about this guy she would have told him.

Hell, Nikki would rejoice in telling him she was unavailable. Not that it would have stopped him. She would have rubbed it in his face time and time again, just like a sadistic slave master would rub salt in the wounds of slaves he beat.

No... There was nothing going on. Right?

He'd calmly go talk to her the next day while Abby went to the big community picnic with the twins next door. And if he didn't like the answers he heard, he would...he would... Hell, he'd figured that out then.

But Nikki wasn't home the next day, and it wasn't until he got back into town that he figured out why.

She was also at the community picnic.

With the same damn guy.

Chapter Nine

A man could only be so patient.

Wade sat in the shadows of the porch, staring into the darkness. She wasn't home and it was nearly midnight. She hadn't been home all night. He knew because he had been sitting here waiting for her.

Nikki was out with him again. No big surprise. She had been out with Dale Stoner nearly every weekend for the past month.

He would give it an hour more, then he would go looking for her. And God help them both if they were at the mechanic's house.

A tiny little voice in his head berated him while he sat brooding.

You're being an idiot. She doesn't want you. Haven't you figured that by now? You need to get over it, go home, because when she sees you playing stalker on her porch she's going to kick your ass.

Shut up, he thought, grinding the heels of his hands into his eye sockets. *Just shut up.*

"He can't have her," Wade said aloud.

But she wants him. Not you.

"Too damn bad," he snarled, rising to his feet and pacing. He'd wear a damn hole in this wood if she wasn't home soon.

Wade was right here waiting for her to settle down and let the past go, and she was running around with Gomer Pyle.

And God help Gomer if he tried to go inside with her.

God help them both if—

Down the hill gravel crunched. And he could see headlights. He retreated back to his shadowed corner, waiting.

Nikki sat quietly in the seat. Dale was acting...odd. Even for him. In fact, he had been acting different the past few nights they'd been out. And she couldn't figure out what could be wrong. He didn't seem mad, but he wasn't exactly happy either.

Out of the silence he said, "I want to come inside. I need to talk to you."

She turned her head but could hardly see anything in the darkness of the car. "Okay," she said, her voice cautious. "Is something wrong, Dale? The book giving you trouble?"

Dale was a writer too. It was how they had met. He had actually just sold his first book—a fairytale, modern-day version of *The Princess and the Frog*. Not only had he written the story, but he had also illustrated it.

"No," he said, his voice rough. "Not a damn thing wrong with the book. Unless you consider a hillbilly mechanic who fancied himself a storyteller a little strange."

"You're not a hillbilly, and there's nothing wrong with being a mechanic. Hell, I was a high school kid who fancied herself a storyteller," she said, her brows lowering over her eyes at the cynicism she heard in his voice.

"You're different," he murmured, a soft sigh escaping him.

"No, I'm not. I want to tell stories. You want to tell stories. We both do it... That's what we are. No difference at all."

The silence stretched out until Nikki just couldn't take it

any more. "Dale, something's up," she said flatly as he pulled into her drive. "Stop brooding and just spill it."

Dale laughed, the sound totally without humor. "Yeah, there's something up. But I really doubt you want me to spill it."

As she waited for him to come around the car, she ran her tongue over her lips. Her gut was feeling tight and raw and it didn't help any as she saw the look in his eyes as he helped from the car. Ever the gentleman, Dale was. But this time, after helping her alight from the car, he didn't release her hand. In fact, he tugged her closer, grasped her chin and lifted her face. "Yeah, there's something wrong," he repeated. "This."

And then he fit his mouth over hers while Nikki stood there motionless. Shocked. Stunned.

Oh, hell.

Gentle, strong hands cupped her chin and Dale rained loving kisses over her face while she stood passively, unsure of what to do. "I can't keep doing this, Nicole." He groaned, burying his face in her neck, his strong arms locked around her back. "I can't. You're all I've thought about for years and it's killing me to be this close to you, knowing you don't want me for anything more than a friend."

Hard, hot hands trailed over her shoulders and arms, caressed her back as he whispered, "From the moment I saw you, I wanted you. Every moment since."

Nikki had to strain to hear him as he whispered into her hair. As he sought her mouth again, hot little darts of pleasure raced through her. He was so warm, felt so good against her. And he was safe. Dale wouldn't ever hurt her. She had felt enough love in her life to know what it was like to receive it and there was love and heat twined together in his embrace.

"Just give me half a chance, Nikki. I swear I'll make you happy," he promised.

It was tempting.

So tempting.

She was so lonely...

She couldn't. Tempting or not, lonely or not, she couldn't do it.

It wouldn't be fair to him.

He deserved so much better than a woman with only half a heart.

"Dale, I can't," she whispered. "I just can't. I'm sorry, but—"

"Nikki, please—"

Reaching between them, she rested her fingers against his mouth, shaking her head. "Dale, I can't. I'm sorry. This wasn't fair to you," she said quietly, putting distance between them as they spoke. "And as much as I would like to, as flattering as it is, it's no good. I'm not whole—I don't think I ever will be."

If I had a choice in this, I would pick you. Staring at his almost poetically beautiful face, she shook her head and repeated once more, "I can't. I can't give you what you want, and if I can't do that it's not right to pretend otherwise. It's not fair to you."

"Maybe you should let me decide that. I want you," Dale said, his voice whisper rough, his hands gentle and caring as he eased her back against him. "I'll take whatever you can give me. I just want you."

With a sad, faraway look in her eyes, Nikki smiled at him. "If I've learned one thing in my life, it's that we can't always have what we want. I'm sorry, Dale." She reached up, cupped his cheek in her hand. "If I could have chosen, Dale, I would have chosen you. You mean so much to me. You got me through some very rough times, and I'll never forget that. But I can't be what you want. Or what you think you want."

"I know how I feel. I know what I want and don't want."

"Yes, I guess you do." Rising on her toes, she pressed her lips to his jaw. Man, she felt like an utter bitch doing this to him. Why hadn't she known? How could she have not seen this?

Because you never looked. You never thought to look. He's always just been Dale.

"I'm sorry."

Dale stroked her cheek, his own eyes sad and wistful. "So am I. Does he have any idea how big a fool he was to let you go?" he murmured, shaking his head.

Wade stood in the shadows, unable to breathe, unable to see, his anger was so great, so deep. He was touching her, kissing her, and she was letting him. His gut roiled and churned and blood pounded thickly in his head. Hands clenched and unclenched spasmodically.

Yeah, maybe he didn't have any right, but logic didn't exactly exist for him when Nikki was in the picture.

He had one hand on the railing, ready to leap, when Nikki pulled back, shaking her head.

What were they saying? They spoke too quietly for him to hear. Heads bent close together, the mechanic's large hands holding her as if she were made of the finest porcelain. They spoke in low whispers, their voices too quiet to carry.

Nikki touched her hand to Stoner's face and shook her head. She was telling him no, Wade realized as the other man pulled away, his hand lingering on her cheek for a moment before he got in his car and drove away.

Wade moved quietly until he was standing at the head of the steps, and waited for her to turn around. He didn't know what he was going to say now, but only one thing mattered.

She had sent him away.

Moments passed, and still she stood there hugging herself tightly, shoulders slumped, head hanging low. A picture of total desolation.

"Have a good time?" he finally asked, keeping his voice flat, when Nikki continued to stare in the darkness. Only he could tell he was quivering inside with both rage and relief.

Nikki jumped, startled. Her hair swung around her face as she spun to face him, her eyes wide. Hands went up, clenched and ready, until she recognized the voice, the vague shadow standing there.

"Wade," she gasped, her voice unsteady.

He continued to stare at her, at her slightly swollen soft mouth, at her sleepy eyes. Another man had touched her, had made her look lazy and satisfied. How many times had Gomer put that look on her face? How many nights had she spent in his arms while Wade suffered and sweated them out alone, aching and miserable?

"What are you doing here?" she asked, her arms falling to her sides, hands curled into loose fists. She might not look so ready to defend herself against an intruder, but she definitely looked ready for a fight.

Then again, he might have been deluding himself. When it came to him, she was more in the mood to either ignore him or just walk away.

Her eyes narrowed. "Are you going to answer me?"

He shrugged and said, "Waiting for you to come home." He moved down the stairs and closer until he stood only two feet away. "Out awful late, aren't you, Nik?"

"You know, I must have lost the memo about when my life suddenly became your business," she said, her voice cool. "Now why don't you get the hell off my property?"

"Why? Is lover boy heading back up here?"

"If he is, it's no business of yours." She shrugged.

"I see him here again, I'm gonna tear him apart," Wade drawled, his voice friendly, his smile bright and vicious. "And then I'll lock you up and throw away the key."

Locating the keys, she snorted and moved around him. "Get over it, buddy. I'm not yours. That's over with. In the past."

"It's our past, present and future, doll," Wade promised, following her up the stairs. He trapped her by the door as she fumbled with the lock. "And I've learned from past mistakes so the future is bound to be better."

"Wade, I don't see how my future could possibly be worse than my past," she said calmly, finally unlocking the double locks on her door. "However, I also don't see how my future has anything to do with you."

Temper suddenly gone, Wade lowered his head to nuzzle at her neck as she spoke. Gently, he nipped at her earlobe and smiled to himself when she shuddered.

"Everything you ever do in life is going to have something to do with me," he said quietly, catching hold of the doorknob and holding it firmly shut. He lowered his head enough to speak quietly against her ear, not touching her, but standing close enough that the scent of her swam in his head.

"Just as everything I do will somehow include you. We're part of each other, Nik. The same way my heart is a part of me, the way your brain is part of you. It's been that way for years, even when we were miles apart and I was married to someone else."

Nikki said nothing. She just stood there, her back to him, her head lowered. Gently, Wade made her turn, lifted her chin in his hand and stared into carefully blank eyes.

"I love you," he whispered. "I never expected to see you again. But I've always known I'd go to my grave loving you. Can you tell me you don't feel the same?"

To the grave... His words echoed over in her head. Hell yes, she'd die loving him. She had already been to the edge once though, because of his love. She wouldn't ever let herself get that way again.

Nikki's eyes slid shut and she turned her head, the smooth sweep of hair hiding her face from him. "What I feel for you is not what I felt eight years ago. Or even five years ago," she murmured, her throat burning. Gathering her courage, she met his eyes and said, "Things change, Wade. Feelings can change. Especially when somebody rips your heart out of your chest and smashes it. It makes it much easier for feelings to change. Or disappear altogether."

Damn you, Wade, she thought half-hysterically. *Just leave. Now. Before I fall apart.* Nikki knew damn well there was no way she was going to be able to keep her distance if he kept this up.

Cupping her cheek in his hand, he asked softly, "Do you really expect me to believe you feel nothing for me?"

"It really doesn't matter what you believe, Wade. It only matters what I believe," Nikki stated simply. She forced a sympathetic smile when sympathy for him was the last thing she felt.

"Poor Wade," she clucked, shaking her head. "You lose a silly little girl who adored you and gained a wife who only wanted to own you. Once she had you, she probably didn't even know what to do with you."

Ducking out of his arms, she moved a few feet away, sliding him a sly glance from under her lashes. "How was your vapid little bride, Wade? Did she keep you happy?"

The porch light illuminated his face enough for Nikki to watch his jaw clench and his eyes narrow. But he continued to stand there like he had no intention of ever leaving. "Now the wife's gone and you think you can get that silly girl back." Nikki moved closer to him and gently patted his cheek like he was a five-year-old child.

"It's a pity you just can't accept the fact that silly girl doesn't exist any more. Even more pitiful is the fact that I would have been anything you wanted me to be, given up anything, become anything," she whispered passionately. "Life's not very fair, is it?"

"Nice try, Nikki," he said, his voice hollow. "I'm very impressed. You can be quite the bitch when you want."

"I've developed a number of talents over the years," she said calmly, even though her heart was pounding away.

"Obviously. You never used to lie so well." He caught her chin in his hand and arched her face up to his, lowering his mouth until not even air separated her lips from his. And he hung there, waiting, for a long moment.

"Fortunately," Wade whispered, his breath fanning across her face. "I don't give up that easily. I'll be around, Nikki."

And then he was gone.

Long legs trailing out from under her SUV, Dylan cursed loud and long as he attempted to finish doing something or other with her oil. Nikki sprawled on the grass nearby, listening with amusement. For a guy who pretended not to understand simple English, he was very...fluent in certain aspects of the language.

After one particularly inventive phrase, Dylan muttered, "Eureka," and emerged from beneath her car, liberally covered with grease and grime and God only knew what else. She would never understand the love-hate relationship both of her younger brothers—and so many other men—had with motor vehicles.

"I suppose you're going to want to come in and clean up," she said, arching a brow at him.

"Considering I saved you a trip into town and some money changing the oil and all the other crap you forget about, it's the least you can do. And I wouldn't mind supper."

"Don't you have a date or something going on? I thought you and um, Cyra, Catie... Which is it? Didn't you have plans?" she said, shoving herself to her feet and stretching.

"Cairey. And we broke up."

Cairey...right. Cairey. Studying him, she echoed, "Broke up?"

"Yeah."

Waiting silently, Nikki stood there watching him.

With his back to her, Dylan finished gathering up his tools, his shoulders lifting and falling as he sighed. Finally, he looked over his shoulder at her and shrugged. "It wasn't working out, Nik. That's all."

Nikki continued to stare at him, her head cocked. A lazy summer breeze drifted by, tugging at her hair as she rocked back on her heels, tucking her hands into her pockets. "It took you eight months to figure that out? You used to be a lot quicker than that."

He sighed, wiping his forehead with his arm before aiming an aggravated glance in her direction. "She was messing around with some guy she met in Somerset. I didn't know."

"I'm sorry."

Turning his head, Dylan gave her a small smile. "Why? You never liked her. Too shallow, I think you said. Among other things."

"You did like her, or you wouldn't have spent all that time with her," Nikki said, shrugging her shoulders.

"I don't know if I liked her or not. She was really just a way to pass the time. Just interested in having some fun. That was all I wanted. But I'd just as soon not have fun with her on Friday," he finished cynically, his eyes cold, "and on Saturday, she has fun with some college kid in Somerset. Besides, it's not like I'm going to be around much longer. She was pissed off I wasn't changing my mind about the army. This was probably her attempt at payback."

Nikki followed him into the house, wondering if she sounded as bitter and world-weary as he did. Probably worse.

Nearly an hour later, Dylan mentioned Wade's name.

Nikki froze momentarily, then she went about adding milk to potatoes as she listened to him. She watched her hands, making sure they stayed steady. Dylan didn't miss much these days.

"I saw him and his little girl in the store. Looks like he's settled in, sis," Dylan said, leaning back so that his chair was propped on the two rear legs.

"It would appear that way, especially since they've been here all summer," Nikki said dryly. "Feeling guilty you didn't throw him a housewarming?"

"Naw. But I thought you might be," Dylan said, shrugging his shoulders. "Seeing as how you two were so close. Pretty little girl."

"Yes. I know." Without even closing her eyes Nikki could picture that little girl. So much like Jason. Her eyes started to sting with tears she quickly blinked away.

"Are you going to tell him?" Dylan asked, his voice close.

Nikki went still as he rested a hand on her shoulder. Her head fell forward and she sighed. "No. It doesn't concern him."

"He was Jason's father. How can it not concern him?"

"Because he wasn't there. He had his own little girl to raise. Jason was mine," she whispered savagely. "*Mine.* He wasn't there, Dylan. I had to do it alone. I am not going to share it with him now so he can try to put together the pieces when there's really nothing left," Nikki said, her voice harsh. She shrugged away his hand, moving aside.

"He ought to know."

"No. I'm not going to dredge it back up merely to satisfy a father's rights. It would hurt me too much and I'm just now healing," Nikki snapped, her eyes flashing at her younger brother.

"You're not healing." Point blank, simply stated. That was Dylan. That was so very Dylan.

She stared into his eyes, same shade, the same shape as her own. "I'm fine."

"You're not fine." He jerked a shoulder in a shrug. "And if it was me, I don't think I'd be fine either. I miss him, too, Nik. I don't know how you handle it. But don't look at me and tell me that you're healing, that you're just now starting to do it, and that's the sole reason why you don't tell that man he had a little boy. If you have other reasons, fine. But don't lie to me."

"Shit." Averting her eyes, she wondered why she bothered. It wasn't like it did any good. Lying to Dylan was like lying to herself. She could fool her father to some extent, and sometimes she could fool Shawn but she couldn't fool this one. Taking a deep breath, she made herself meet Dylan's gaze once more.

"If Jason had lived, maybe it would be different. I could handle it if Wade found out and wanted to be involved in his life. But Jason is gone. My memories—they are all I have of him. And I shouldn't have to share those with somebody who didn't even know he existed." Then she squared her shoulders and added, "And it doesn't concern you, so I suggest you stay out of it."

Dylan held his hands up and backed away, silently saying it was her call but he didn't agree with her.

He didn't have to agree. He just had to keep his mouth shut.

Sweat poured down the back of her neck, over her shoulders, to pool into her bra as she pedaled the bike up and over the crest of the hill. As the road leveled out, Nikki wiped a gloved hand over her forehead and tried to steady her breathing. Sports bra, tank top and bike shorts were all soaked with sweat. The muscles in her legs were quivering so badly she could barely keep her feet on the pedals.

Three hours on twisting hilly roads did more to improve her state of mind than anything else could. It had the added benefit of making her so damn tired she'd probably collapse on her bed and sleep like the dead. After two sleepless nights and restless days, she would give almost anything for one peaceful night of rest.

She rounded the final curve and stifled a groan as the trees gave way to reveal her home and the shiny black Ford Ranger. So much for falling into bed right after a quick shower and meal.

Nikki gritted her teeth as she swung off the bike by the porch. She paused only long enough to make sure her shaky legs would hold her before she pushed the bike onto the wooden deck.

Wade and little Abby were perched on the porch swing, moving idly back and forth. She was suddenly the focus of two pairs of dark eyes, one shy, hesitant smile from the little girl and a bright, easy smile from Wade.

"I don't recall inviting you up here, Wade," she said coolly as she opened the front door. Cool air rushed out to meet her and she sighed in relief as she moved inside.

She didn't see the look they exchanged behind her back.

"I didn't know you still rode," he said after catching up with her in the kitchen.

She'd taken a few seconds to tuck away the bottle of Lanoxin. It wasn't likely he'd look at the bottle, but if he did he would know what it was for and that wasn't a talk she wanted to have with him.

Ever.

After draining a glass of water, she turned her head and leveled out the hostility in her eyes before saying, "I was riding before I ever met you. I like it. I didn't do it simply because you did."

Then she forced a deep, calming breath into her lungs before giving Abby a tired smile. "How are you doing, Miss Abby?"

"Okay," Abby whispered, looking all around. "You have a pretty house."

"Thank you," Nikki responded, her smile a bit more relaxed. It hurt so bad just to look at the child, but at the same time it somehow soothed her battered heart. "I like it myself. There's a TV through there if you'd like to watch some cartoons. I know there's SpongeBob somewhere. My brothers love SpongeBob." She pointed in the direction of the living room, wishing she were callous enough to dislike the child simply because of who her mother was.

She knew it was terrible, but part of her wished she could dislike the girl. It would be one patently simple way of alienating Wade.

But Nikki couldn't do that. Children were too precious—it was a lesson she knew all too well.

Moments later, the child safely stowed away in the living room, watching talking mice, Nikki returned to the kitchen.

She splashed cool water on her overheated face and dried it before turning her eyes to the man sitting negligently at her table. His legs sprawled out before him and he had a can of soda in one hand.

"Why don't you make yourself at home?" she drawled, her voice sugar sweet. She soaked a rag with cool water and lifted it to her nape, swiping her neck and chest and arms with it, taking perverse pleasure as his eyes heated.

"Don't mind if I do," he returned, sipping at the drink and winking at her over the rim. His eyes, however, lacked the lightheartedness that was in his words.

As she pressed the cloth to back of her neck, Nikki closed her eyes, trying hard to ignore him, but it was damn near impossible. She could feel his eyes on her as she swiped the cool rag over her hot flesh.

The pounding of her heart had nothing to do with him, she insisted. It was from the exercise, only the exercise.

"Need some help?" Wade offered, his voice going low and rough as her eyes opened and she studied him, her face flushed and damp, body gleaming slightly from her exertions.

Recognizing the look in his eyes, Nikki stopped playing with fire and threw the cloth into the sink. "What are you doing here, Wade?" she asked flatly, crossing her arms over her chest and leaning against the counter.

"I came to see you, of course."

"Why?" she asked, her eyes narrowed. Hostility all but radiated from her.

"Must be the charming company. You being such a gracious hostess and all." Her anger rolled off his back. He had been in high spirits for several weeks now. Nikki hadn't been seen around town with Gomer Pyle since that last weekend.

Little rumors were floating around that Stoner was packing up and leaving town. A For Sale sign posted at the garage confirmed said rumors and Wade had grinned for an hour after he had seen it.

"You really can't take a hint, can you?"

"You shouldn't be surprised to see me here, Nikki. I told you I wasn't giving up," he reminded her.

"I didn't say I was surprised. Disappointed is more like it." Running a fingertip over the rim of her discarded glass, she studied him quietly from under the shield of her lashes. "Don't you think you've done enough?"

His cheeks flushed a dull red and he looked away, sighing. "I guess I deserve that."

"And worse," Nikki added quietly.

"You're making this as hard as you can, aren't you?" Wade demanded, resisting the urge to slam his own glass down on the table. Carefully, he sat it down and stood, his hands going into his back pockets. "Nik, I'm not going away. You might as well get used to that."

"Oh, you'll go away. Sooner or later you'll figure out I'm not who I used to be and I'm not somebody you want to be around." Somber hazel eyes drifted to the sound of childish laughter coming from the living room and she said, "Certainly not somebody you want your daughter around."

"You've always loved kids. And I've never seen a kid you couldn't enchant. Why wouldn't I want you around her?" he asked, watching her.

Nikki turned away, gazing out the window. Finally, she turned her head to him and her eyes were sad. "I'm not who I used to be. I keep telling you that, and you just won't listen."

Moving up beside her, he cornered her between his body and the counter. He saw the alarm in her eyes and braced himself. She always struck out when she was feeling threatened.

Never one to disappoint, she tossed her head back. In a voice as cold as winter, she said, "I can't look at you or your child without seeing her and remembering what you did."

Cupping her cheek in his hand, Wade sighed. "I'm not here to remind you of what I did. I just want to be with you."

I just want to be with you.

Those words tore at her heart. He made it sound so easy...

"Being with you does remind me," she snarled, slapping a hand against his chest as he leaned closer. The heat of his body rushed out and filled hers, making her feel more overheated than three hours of trail riding ever could. His eyes, so full of love and promises, seemed to mock her.

Wade was so full of life.

And she was so empty.

"You are making my life a living hell. Don't you think I've had enough of that?" she demanded, her voice shaking with the rage and pain she lived with.

His eyes glittered, the only proof that her words had any effect. Slowly, Wade leaned down and brushed a light kiss across her flushed cheek. "I don't want to hurt you. I never wanted to. I'll never do it again."

"Then stay the hell away from me!" Nikki cried, jerking her head back away from his. Shoving both hands against his chest, she tried to move him away, but he wouldn't budge.

"You hurt me just by being around me. Stop coming around. Why in the hell are you still coming around?"

"I keep coming around because I love you. And you love me," he whispered, covering her hands with his and leaning down to kiss her averted mouth. One hand caught and held her chin as he rained kisses over her cheeks and closed eyes. "I messed it up the first time, doll. But can't I have a second chance? I'll never hurt you again."

As he covered her damp mouth with his, Nikki quaked. And prayed. First for him to stop. Then she prayed for him not to.

Wade wrapped his arms around her waist and dragged her closer, dark delight spiraling through him as her arms clamped around his neck and shoulders. He tasted salty sweat and soft skin on his tongue as he trailed a line kisses down her neck. Helplessly, Nikki rocked against him, and he shuddered before taking her waist and boosting her onto the counter top.

Moving between her legs, Wade rocked against the V of her thighs as he covered her mouth for another kiss.

He nipped at her lower lip with his teeth and then darted his tongue into her mouth while one hand pulled her hips to the edge of the counter until only cloth separated him from her. Nikki stiffened slightly as he moved against her, but he paid it no heed. She wanted him. There was no denying that...and he wanted her. She could taste it in his kiss, feel it in the hungry moan that vibrated up from his chest.

Her belly jumped as he ran his hands down her thighs. Unwittingly, she wrapped her legs tightly around his hips, never wanting to let go. For a little while...she could forget.

Cupping her breasts in his hands, Wade dragged his thumbs over the nipples, and she mewled as they tightened, throbbed under the sturdy cotton of her sports bra. Her hands went back to balance her weight as he grasped the bottom of the shirt in his hands and pulled.

Blood pounded in his temples as she arched against him, a weak moan falling from her lips. *Mine*, was all he could think. After all the time that had passed, she was still his in every way that counted. Her words might be saying no, but her body, her clinging hands were saying something totally different.

One lean hand cupped her, feeling the damp heat through the thin material of spandex. Nikki vibrated under his hand and whimpered as he massaged the heel of his hand against her damp cleft. He lifted his head and watched as her eyes darkened and her breath caught.

Triumphantly, Wade smiled as she started to convulse

under the pressure of his palm. Quickly, he seized her mouth with his just as a rush of liquid warmth soaked both the spandex and his hand.

Mine. And all that mattered was marking her, making certain she knew just how strong his hold on her was.

Intent on peeling that spandex from her, Wade delved his hands inside her clinging shorts, wanting her naked and open. Distantly the sound of laughter and kid's music penetrated the fog in his brain.

Abby.

"Damn it," he muttered, his head dropping forward to rest on her shoulder. Nikki was shuddering against him, her hands clenching at his shoulders and back. Sweet heaven, Abby. He had totally forgotten his daughter was in the other room, just twenty feet away.

He raised his head to look at Nikki. Her face was flushed, her lips swollen and red from his. Her large hazel eyes were soft and unfocused, full of need. Damn it, what timing.

Nikki dropped her head, taking several shaky deep breaths before she released his shoulders and pushed at him. "Let me down," she whispered, her voice faint.

Wade did so, knowing if he didn't move, he would take the chance, regardless of where Abby was. Clumsy, she clambered down and stumbled away from the counter. Quickly, she jerked her tank top back on before moving around until the table separated them. Then she turned those hazel eyes on him, her lips parting as she drew in deep draughts of air.

"Damn you, Wade," Nikki whispered, her voice rough and unsteady.

Grimacing, Wade agreed silently as he leaned back, adjusting his jeans. He sure as hell wouldn't be doing much sleeping tonight. "Nothing like a little trip down memory lane," he drawled, crossing his arms over his chest and waiting.

113

"That isn't going to happen again."

"Ever?"

"Absolutely never," she swore, her eyes slowly clearing of the fog.

Nikki kept her hands pressed flat to the table, hoping to hide their trembling. Her knees were weak, watery, and she was having trouble staying upright. Hot, molten need still flowed through her veins and deep inside, she ached.

Idiot. Fool. Why did you let that happen? She asked herself, staring at him from the relative safety of ten feet away, across the solid oak of the dining table. "Never," she repeated, her voice certain.

Too damn bad she didn't feel as certain as she sounded. Her knees still felt like water and her brains like mush. Even the thought of what just happened was enough to make her want to whimper with need. All he had done was touch her and she had exploded.

"That's an awfully long time," Wade mused, drawing one knee up and hooking his thumbs through the loops of his belt. His erection strained against the worn denim that cupped him. His stance was cocky and arrogant, his smile full of promise, eyes glinting with need and humor.

Just looking at him made her mouth go dry.

And he wasn't helping as he cocked his head and studied her with hot eyes. Eyes that studied her flushed face and trailed down her neck to focus on her shirtfront, where her nipples thrust against the sturdy cotton. The corner of his mouth quirked up in a slight smile as he added, "Especially considering your body would like nothing more than for me to come over there and finish what we started."

"What you started."

"I wasn't alone in that, Nikki. I wasn't kissing myself," he drawled, scratching his chin. "One of us just climaxed and it certainly wasn't me."

"It won't happen again," she said, clenching her jaw.

"Why not?"

"Because I won't let it," she answered, her chin rising.

"Why won't you let it?"

"Because it isn't going to change anything. I'm happy with my life the way it is, and I don't want you in it."

"You know something, Nik? I look at you and get the feeling you've forgotten what it's like to be happy. We were happy together once, Nikki," Wade reminded. His heavy-lidded eyes and long smoldering look reminded her of things long past but hardly forgotten. "Do you remember that? There was a time when all we needed was each other to be perfectly satisfied with life."

"That was before I figured out what real life is, Wade," she said coldly, dredging the memory of long nights spent alone. Of a stormy day when she had lost everything. Of rainy days in which she prayed to forget. And of a tiny little grave twenty miles away.

The backlash of pain that filled her nearly knocked her to her knees. She had lost everything that had mattered. She couldn't let anything matter again. She'd never survive if she lost it all again.

Speaking of it, thinking of it was like opening a floodgate. Nikki had refused to let herself think of it, bottling it all up inside, and now it was ready to be set free. If she couldn't control the pain, then she would use it.

Harshly, Nikki said, "You don't know what you did to me. You destroyed me. You tore out my heart and soul and I still haven't recovered from it." The pain spread throughout her entire body, leaving her weak and trembling, throat tight, hands shaking from the raging emotions.

"Nikki—"

"Don't say anything, not a single thing to me, Wade. There is nothing you can say that could make up for what I lost. You can't even begin to comprehend what I lost. But even if you could," she whispered, dashing away tears that leaked over. "It would change nothing. Nothing would ever make up for it."

"I want the chance to try."

She started. She hadn't even realized he had come closer until she felt his hand resting on her shoulder.

"Talk to me," he whispered, cajoled. "Tell me."

Tell him?

Tell him?

She shouldn't have to tell him. He should already know because he should have been there with her when it happened. *I shouldn't have had to go through that alone.* But she couldn't tell him that. He would have no clue as to what she was talking about.

Closing her eyes, Nikki shook her head. "There's nothing to tell, Wade. You told me all in glorious detail five years ago. If you can't figure out what's wrong, then you have something seriously wrong with you."

"Don't give me that," he rasped, shaking her gently. "I know you. I know you inside and out, remember?" His voice dropped, intensified. "I know you love me. I know you want me."

"Wrong. I don't want this! My body might, but I don't. I will never want it." Shrugging his hands away, wrapping her arms around herself, Nikki turned and stared out over her land. Then she closed her eyes. "I don't ever want to care about anybody like I cared for you. I don't ever want to love again. Those kinds of emotions give others power over you. The power to destroy. Like you destroyed me."

Wade's hands froze in the act of reaching for her to draw her back against him. The honesty and the pain in her words pierced his heart and left him bleeding inside. His hands clenched impotently into fists as they fell to his sides, empty still.

Looking at him over her shoulder, her eyes so empty and so lifeless, Nikki swallowed and spoke around the knot in her throat. "Go out of my house, Wade. Off my property and don't come back."

She heard him sigh. Heard him leave the room. As the door shut gently, Nikki closed her eyes against a fresh onslaught of tears.

It took every last bit of strength she had left in her not to reach out to him.

Chapter Ten

"Dunno—two weeks, maybe three." Nikki frowned at the screen.

Need to rewrite the line there.

"Okay. If you can, try to make it two—I'm leaving in three weeks for vacation and I want to see it—you're being more secretive than normal," Kris said. "Unless of course, you want to share details now."

"Nope. I'll jinx myself."

Turning away from her computer, she stared out the window. Her gut clenched and she saw the darkening sky. Thunderheads were piling the horizon. A storm was coming.

"Yeah, yeah." There was a brief pause. "So, what's this I hear about Wade Lightfoot? Ex-boyfriend coming back around?"

Shawn, I'm going to stomp your ass into the ground. It had to be Shawn. Dylan wouldn't willingly discuss anything with Kris, and somehow she couldn't see her dad doing it either.

"Wade is not a boy, nor is he a friend," Nikki corrected, pinching the bridge of her nose with her fingers.

"No. He was more than that, wasn't he?" Kris asked softly, "Want to tell me about it?"

"Nothing to tell. He's determined to pick things up and I want to let them lie. I have to go," Nikki said, her eyes burning. She ached to talk about it. To cry about it. But she was afraid if she started she wouldn't stop.

She settled back in her own chair as a heavy torrent of rain started to fall. No, she couldn't change the past. But she sure as hell could keep from repeating it.

Later that day Nikki stood in front of the floor-to-ceiling windows in her living room watching the wind whip through the trees. The rain had stopped and hadn't started back up, but it would soon. The watery, eerie green-gray light coming through the windows disturbed her. Tornado light.

The knock at the door startled her and she silently prayed, *Don't be Wade.*

Nikki nearly threw her arms around Dylan's neck when she opened the door to reveal her younger brothers standing there, arms laden with Chinese takeout and movies.

"Is this the best you two can do on a Saturday night?" she asked, trying to keep from laughing with relief. "Come and see your sister?"

Without responding, Dylan pushed past her to set the food down while Shawn displayed his movies. "We have *Tango and Cash*, both of the *Transformers* and *Judge Dredd*." He tossed them on top of the TV before dropping on the sofa and propping booted feet on the coffee table.

Dylan was emptying the bag as he announced, "I've got sweet and sour chicken, chicken curry and chicken broccoli. Plus a whole mess of fortune cookies."

The brainless entertainment they had brought was welcome, the company even more so. If she was lucky, the storm might pass before she had chance to think about it. But at least she wouldn't have to wait it out alone.

It was half past three in the morning and the credits rolled after Stallone had roared off into the sunset on his futuristic motorcycle. Nikki thumbed the remote and rubbed at tired eyes. She climbed off the couch, leaving Dylan to sprawl over the length of it.

On the landing, Nikki paused, unable to see three feet outside the window. The first storm had passed after eight, but before ten a second had moved in, followed by a third. Each had been more intense than the last. It was supposed to calm by dawn. Because she was so tired, her mind numb, she was able to leave the window without tears welling up in her eyes.

In concession to her brothers, she donned a pair of boxer-shorts-styled pajamas before crawling into the king-size bed. The sandwashed silk felt cool against her already chilled flesh and she quickly burrowed beneath covers. The big bed felt so empty. Hugging a pillow to her chest, she turned her back on the light show going on outside her window. Rain beat against the windows and roof as she huddled in the middle of the big bed, shaking. Whether it was from cold or loneliness, she didn't know.

Closing her eyes, Nikki gave into the weakness inside her and wished for Wade. She wanted him there so badly, had he appeared she would have forgiven him anything. She just wanted him there, holding her, keeping the painful memories at bay.

A cynical voice reminded her that if it hadn't been for Wade, the memories probably wouldn't be so painful.

Her aching heart told her she really didn't give a damn.

Thirty miles away, Wade was suffering as well. Rain brought back memories of their last time in the woods, something he hadn't been able to put out of his mind. Was it because it was the last time? Was that what made it so damn unforgettable, what etched it into his mind?

In the past few months he had tried every viable way to get her to open up, to let him in. Everything from pleading to demanding.

Nikki remained firm. Polite, distant and if he could believe her, uninterested. But he didn't believe it. It was just the façade she put in place. It slipped from time to time, letting him see the raw hunger in her eyes, the need. Nikki still loved him, still wanted him, but she held back, unwilling to trust him.

But Wade was patient.

Hell, I'm being a damn saint, he thought derisively.

Vivid pictures of laying her down on his huge oak bed had driven him to the couch for the night. But sleep was no where to be found. Rain beat against the house as he lay there, unable to sleep, his body tormented by the images his mind wouldn't let go.

What is she doing? Is she awake like I am? Hungry? Too damn hungry to sleep? He wondered what she slept in. Once he had known the answer to that. Nothing. Nothing at all. The few nights they had spent together, she had slept in his arms, her warm body pressed to his without a single barrier between them.

Groaning, Wade flipped to his back and kicked the sheet off the couch. He was hot, his body aching. Every muscle in his body was rigid with tension, and his throbbing cock pressed painfully against the fly of the old cutoffs he wore. Damn it, his cock was so damned hard he hurt with it. And nothing would relieve it except sinking his length into the hot, wet warmth he knew he'd find between Nikki's thighs.

He had half a mind to leave the house, drive the half hour to Nikki's and wake her up. Abby was spending the weekend with her grandparents and he wouldn't have to worry about her. He could simply get in his truck and drive, be there before dawn.

"Stop it," he snarled, pressing the heels of his hand to his eyes.

But the image continued to flicker through his mind, taunting, teasing.

Would she welcome him? Half asleep, Nikki would be less likely to remember she wanted to hate him. He could simply cover her mouth with his and then her body, pulling her beneath him and burying himself inside her before she even had a chance to catch her breath. Before she could wake up enough to remember she wanted to hate him.

And then he would keep on loving her, keeping her from thinking. Could he do it long enough for her to forget she wanted him out of her life?

Maybe. For a little while. Would it be long enough to bind her to him and keep her from slipping away like she wanted?

"Son of a bitch son of a bitch son of a bitch," he whispered through clenched teeth. Why did he torture himself like this?

Why keep remembering how sweet she smelled, how soft she was? How perfect she fit against him? If he just thought of it, he could feel her smooth skin under his mouth, and he could remember how she felt under him, over him...the snug glove of her sex gripping his cock as he sank deep inside her.

Damnation, why did he do this?

Because he couldn't stop himself. Everything reminded him of her. The rain reminded him of that last time. Rising with the sun made him remember all the sunsets and sunrises they had watched together. Tucking his little girl in at night made him wish his woman was there with him.

My woman... Nikki was his. She had been from the beginning and nothing had changed that.

Fuck. I need her...

And if he was in this shape, maybe Nikki wasn't much better off.

It was that thought that had Wade rising with the sun, driving into the horizon.

Nicole stood on the porch, leaning against the column, her silk-clad arms wrapped around herself to ward off the slight chill of the early morning. Her eyes stared sightlessly into the sunrise, her mind troubled.

The stormy weather had passed, leaving a breathtakingly beautiful morning, one that made her feel even emptier inside. A cold chill had settled over her body, one that ran gut deep.

Wade...

He haunted her thoughts. Her dreams, her every waking moment seemed to revolve around him. She was going out of her mind.

And she was tired of fighting him, fighting herself. Maybe...

"Have you slept?"

She looked over her shoulder to see Shawn padding onto the porch, running a hand though tangled hair. His slid an arm around her shoulder, offering body heat and silent comfort. Too cold and lonely to deny either, she only smiled. "A little. Not much."

"Bad dreams?" he asked.

Ducking her chin, she mumbled an answer that was half-fiction, half-reality.

Teasingly, Shawn asked, "Or were they a different kind of bad dream?"

Scowling, a blush rising up her cheeks, she punched him in the gut and moved away. Quietly, she said, "It stormed nearly all night."

"Sis, it's been three years," he whispered, tucking her again against his side, resting his chin on her crown. "You can't spend the rest of your life hiding in your room with the curtains pulled every time it rains. You need to let go."

He was right. She knew that. A grown woman just couldn't run to her room and hide every time it stormed. And she had spent most of her night tossing and turning and thinking about Wade, not Jason. But she hated the rain.

"Letting go isn't the same as forgetting, Shawn. And it's not that easy to do either." She would have said more, but the sound of a motor silenced her. Her shoulders tensed and her gut clenched violently. She knew exactly who it was driving up her mountain when the sun was still hugging the eastern horizon.

Damn it. Not now. "I can't deal with him right now," she whispered harshly.

If Wade was startled by the shiny black classic Mustang in the drive, he was absolutely shell shocked at the sight of Nikki standing half naked in the arms of a blond man who held her all too closely, his shirt hanging open. Both were mussed and sleepy eyed. What in the hell was she doing in the arms of another man when it wasn't even seven in the morning?

Bad enough she spent months with that jerk-off Stoner. But now she was with somebody else?

This is the fucking last straw, baby. Get ready for a showdown, he thought furiously as he climbed out of his truck, murder on his mind. If she thought she could go running to another man she had another thought coming. *Gonna kill that bastard. Who in the hell does he think he is, touching her like that, holding her like he as a right to?* he thought viciously as he took the steps in a single bound.

Nikki stood there sleepy eyed, hair tumbled, face slightly flushed, as if she had just climbed out of bed after a night of loving. Ready to tumble right back into bed for some more.

Over my dead body.

First Dale Stoner and now this. If she didn't still love him, it would be different. But she did.

Cuddling up to the chest of another blond bastard, and it didn't look like she was in a hurry for him to leave either.

He closed the distance between himself and the bastard he intended to kill with his bare hands.

The soon-to-be corpse ran a hand down a silk-covered back and ducked his head to whisper in Nikki's ear. Probably suggesting they go back inside once their visitor was gone. His body practically vibrating with rage, Wade stood motionless as Nikki stepped forward, leaving the blond's arms and staring at Wade with blank eyes.

She stood quietly, her eyes calm.

Damn you, he thought, clenching his jaw. *Don't you know you belong with me? In my arms.*

She should have spent the night with Wade, and he damned well oughta be the one holding her as the sun rose into the clear blue sky. Instead, she had another man who even now was laughing at him.

Then Wade's black eyes met the greenish-hazel eyes of the stranger and the rage drained out of him. Hazel eyes, exactly like Nikki's. And a squared, tougher version of Nicole's soft rounded features. A face so similar to Nikki's they could have identical, except where she had curves, he had only angles.

The youngest Kline. The only one he hadn't come across in the months he had been in Monticello.

"Shawn," he said, his voice slightly hoarse from the residual emotion that had almost eaten him alive. The young punk had grown into a man Wade barely recognized. Formerly long hair was cropped close to his nape, and long sinewy, almost bony arms had thickened with muscle.

Okay, so maybe this isn't the smartest thing I've ever done. He should have stayed home where it was nice and safe. And lonely.

Shawn looked absolutely delighted to Wade, a wicked gleam lighting his eyes, an unholy smile curving his mouth. Gently, Shawn moved his sister to the side and stepped closer, until he was toe-to-toe with Wade, all but snarling at the shorter man.

Pride kept him from moving back, even though he knew in a fistfight with Shawn, he was sure to lose. Wade may be able to hold his own in a fight—but Shawn had damn near written a handbook on streetfighting. Wade had seen the results of his handiwork, and they hadn't been pretty.

The only one who had ever held his own against Shawn was his older brother, Dylan.

Before Shawn could even open his mouth, Nikki planted herself between them, shoving them apart with strong, slender hands.

"Don't even think about it, kid," she snapped, apparently oblivious to the fact that he outweighed and outreached her.

"Easy, Nik. All I want to do is make good on a promise I made myself." And he sidestepped to face Wade once more.

"No."

Flashing a cocky grin, Shawn promised, "I won't kill him, sis. Just maim him a little. Make him remember not to mess with a Kline again."

Without blinking, she stepped hard on Shawn's instep and punched him in the gut.

"You mean little bitch," Shawn wheezed out, glaring at her.

"You watch your mouth," Wade snarled, brushing past Nikki in an attempt to bust the arrogant brat in the mouth. He had almost succeeded when Nikki moved again, this time planting all her five foot four inches in front of him, and snapped, "Keep out of it. What in the hell are you doing here?"

Gingerly setting his foot on the ground, well aware that it would be bruised within a few hours, Shawn bit off, "He's here so I can kick his ass, of course."

"Watch your mouth," Wade repeated. "You still haven't learned how to show your sister any respect."

"And you did?" Hazel eyes flashing, Shawn asked, "Who are you to lecture me on how to treat anybody?"

Nikki didn't even hear Wade's snarled reply. She turned to go inside. Let them beat the hell out of each other. She didn't want to hear about it or think about it.

But apparently other things were planned. Dylan had come outside without being noticed. With an ease that came from years of roughhousing with Shawn, he deflected the first punch and, before anybody could blink, he had Shawn trapped in headlock he had little hope of breaking unless he wanted his neck broken as well.

"What's up?" he asked calmly, as though every morning he stepped into the middle of a soon-to-be blood bath.

"Lemme go, you son of a bitch," Shawn panted. His face was red with anger and effort as he twisted uselessly to try and free himself. "All I'm gonna do is rearrange his pretty face a little."

"Did she ask you to?"

"No, but so what?" Shawn grunted, swiveling his hips, trying to jerk free. "You can't...tell me...you never wanted to...do it yourself."

Casting a wistful glance at Wade, Dylan said, "If she wanted it done, she'd do it herself. She doesn't need us to do it." His wishful eyes clearly made Wade aware that all Nikki needed to do was say the word.

Nikki stood silently, her eyes empty and flat. Her silence told Dylan all too much. It had been months since the grim-

127

eyed man from Nikki's past had shown up, and he was still hanging around Nikki.

That only told Dylan Nikki really didn't want the bastard gone. But God help him if he hurt her again.

"Damn it, lemme go," Shawn demanded.

"Sure," Dylan drawled, letting go suddenly and with a shove that had Shawn sprawling in the grass in front of the porch.

Young pride bruised, he leaped to his feet, ready to battle with both of them, only to come up against the heel of Dylan's hand, and go sliding on his butt again.

"Damn it, why in the hell are you knocking me around for?" Body smeared with mud, eyes flashing. "I ain't the bastard who went and knocked—"

"Shawn." Nikki said, her voice low, hard and angry.

That one word stopped Shawn in his tracks and he dropped his head. "Aw, hell," he muttered, climbing to his feet. "Can't even beat the shit out of a guy anymore. Nobody used to look twice when I got into a fight." Gingerly, he moved up the steps, tossing Wade a look that said "just wait". And then he was gone.

Dylan lingered a moment longer, asking silently if he should stay or go. Wade began to wonder if he wasn't going to have to do battle with one of them after all. But finally, after long moments of silent communication, Nikki just shook her head. "Make sure he cleans up the mud he tracks in. I'll be in soon."

Dylan shrugged and turned on his bare foot to go inside, casting one long, unreadable glance in Wade's direction before shutting the door quietly behind him.

Chapter Eleven

As he watched her, Nikki wrapped her arms around her middle, a tiny shiver racking her body. She met his eyes and just gave him a flat, blank stare. "What are you doing here, Wade? It's barely seven."

"I've been up for hours... Can't sleep."

"So you decided to come up here at the crack of dawn? Strange solution to insomnia."

He shrugged and tucked his hands in his back pockets. "You know, if looks could kill, you two would have been dead the minute I rounded the bend. I didn't recognize Shawn. He's grown up."

"He looks pretty much the same way he did five years ago."

"Not really. He looks like a whole other person. I hear he's training with a contractor, going into construction."

"That's right. Dylan leaves in a few months to join the army. Might even have a shot at military intelligence. Neither one of them have been in trouble with the law in years. Shawn just broke up with the girl he swore he was going to marry, but he's not too upset about it. Dylan just broke up with a girl too, but he says now isn't the time to be starting relationships. Did you come up here to discuss my brothers' plans for the future?" she asked, arching an eyebrow at him.

He ran his eyes over her sweetly curved body, appreciating

every exposed inch. The green silk she wore left a lot of inches exposed. A lot exposed and little to the imagination. His mouth went dry as he found himself staring at her breasts, at the way her nipples pressed against the fragile cloth.

Hell, discussing anything was the last thing on his mind.

"No." He moved closer, backing her up against the wall.

"Back off, Wade," Nikki snapped, her brows drawing together. Her soft, full mouth firmed into a flat line as she leaned back into the wood, trying to stay as far from him as she could. Her eyes were dark, turbulent with emotions Wade couldn't even begin to understand.

"I can't deal with this right now."

"Deal with what?" he asked absently as he lowered his head, eyes focused on her mouth. Her answer went unheard as he groaned and locked his mouth on hers, intent on making every vivid dream, every little fantasy of the past night a reality here and now.

Wade closed his eyes, nearly dying from the pleasure of feeling her moving against him. She felt like an angel, tasted like heaven. Sanity fell to pieces around him as his hands traveled under the silky top to find her bare beneath it. Nothing but soft, smooth skin that trembled under his hands. Wedging himself between her thighs, he ground his erection against her and shuddered.

He clamped his hands over her silk-covered hips, hiking her up, pressing heat against heat. Tearing his mouth from hers, he dragged air into his starving lungs. Her head fell limply back, coming in contact with the exterior of the house, but she didn't even flinch. Throat exposed, eyes closed, she was the very picture of surrender. Wade lowered his head and feasted on the smooth expanse of bare skin between neck and shoulder.

A soft whimper escaped her lips as his mouth brushed against the sensitive flesh of her neck.

As he began the slow journey up to her mouth, Nikki felt her already weak resolve begin to crumple. This had always felt so right, she thought in despair. How could she fight off something that felt as natural as life itself? It might be easier to will her own heart to stop beating. She shuddered when he plunged his tongue into her mouth, his strong hands molding her against him, cupping the curve of her rump, lifting her up.

Nikki gasped. The heat shimmered through her from head to toe, then centered at her neck and groin. The blood in her head pounded in time to the thick, heavy waves of pleasure that washed over her.

Have I lost my mind? she wondered frantically as those waves washed down to pool between her thighs. Her brothers were waiting inside, probably watching their every move. And here they were, ready to go at it like a couple of teenagers. Audience or no audience. And she really didn't care.

Fisting her hands in his hair, Nikki dragged his head back to hers, met his mouth again. Sharp teeth nipped gently at her lower lip before his tongue sought out the tiny hurt and soothed it. One hand left her hip to race up and close over her bare breast, dragging the pajama top up in the process. His thumb scraped over her nipple, drawing it tighter as he kneaded, massaged, stroked her breast.

Wade tore his mouth from hers and lowered his head to nip at her neck, forcing his hands back. The silk top of her pajamas fell back down, covering her.

Sanity made a brief return as he remembered where they were, and the fact that they didn't exactly have privacy. *Not here. Damn it. What timing.*

"Come home with me," he whispered, frustrated need and lust making his voice harsh.

Her voice practically gone, Nikki shook her head. "No."

"Yes," he demanded, biting her earlobe with none-too-gentle teeth. "You want this as much as I do." Pulling away, he stared down at her face that was flushed with hunger. Desire had darkened her eyes until they were nearly black. That wide mobile mouth was red, lips swollen. "Damn it, I could unbutton my jeans and spread your legs right here and you'd love every second of it. I don't think you could stop me right now. I don't think you'd want to."

She closed her eyes and refused to reply. She wouldn't lie about it, but damn it, she didn't have to admit it either.

"If you won't come home with me, then get dressed and come walking with me," he coaxed, his thumbs caressing her ribcage and the sensitive underside of each breast. "I'll take you into the woods and lay you down on the leaves and make love to you there." His voice was low, smoky, full of promises and need. "And I'll make you forget every second you ever spent without me."

The hot words and hot promises in his eyes wound themselves around her like a silken rope, pulling her flesh tight, making breathing nearly impossible. She was tempted. Sweet heaven, she was tempted.

"Wade, I can't," she whispered, the words coming hoarsely. The lump in her throat was making breathing difficult.

"Sure you can. Just go throw on some jeans and come with me," he said, nudging the wet cleft between her legs with his erection. His blue-jean clad legs rubbed against her inner thighs, the sensation almost painful to her sensitized nerves.

"That's not what I meant, Wade," she whispered brokenly. "This isn't going to solve anything." *Understand. Please. I can't keep fighting you, not now. I'm too weak already.*

She saw it in his eyes, the heated fog of lust clearing as he started to actually hear her. She continued to stare at him, knowing he could see that hunger there, as well as her fear and something that bordered on desperation.

Anger started to flash in his eyes, and she braced herself.

"What's there to solve?" he demanded. "You still love me. I love you. We need each other."

"I can't do this," she said, closing her eyes against the pain.

"You don't have to do anything at all. Just spread your legs for me and I'll do the rest," he snapped. "If you can't give me anything else, I'll settle for your body for now."

"I can't do it like that," she said sadly. "It's all or nothing."

"And if I need an answer now?"

Wade could see it in her eyes, on her face. Her throat worked as she swallowed and her eyes glistened with the wet sheen of tears. But her voice was firm when she answered, "It would have to be nothing."

"It's always been all or nothing with you!" he raged. Damn her, he couldn't wait forever. "If you would just learn to bend a little, maybe we never would have had these problems."

She threw his hands off, her eyes going wide. "Me?" she asked, her voice low and shaking.

"Me?" she repeated, her voice rising with shock and anger. "Learn to bend? This is *my* fault? You son of a bitch. You knocked up some bimbo and I'm supposed to *bend*?"

"You're supposed to let it *go*—hell, even if you can't forgive *me*, at least get over it. It's *over*." Frustrated beyond belief, he shook her slightly. "Damn it, what in the hell happened to you? You've turned into a damned hermit. You're barely a shadow of what you were. You think I can't see the pain in you? It's tearing you apart and I can't help but think it's more than just me. You never would have let me ruin your life, not after what I did. I wasn't worth it!

133

"Let it go," he finished, his voice ragged, his brow pressed to hers. "It can't affect us any more."

"The past made us what we are, Wade. It's not that easy."

Watching her from hooded eyes, Wade came to slow realization. She wasn't going to give in. Not now or ever. "If that's the way it is, then I don't think I like what it's made you into. I don't think you like yourself much either."

His words cut at her as her own frustrated desire turned into misplaced anger and hurt pride as quickly as his had. Her eyes narrowed and she knew the hurt she was feeling showed in her face. "If you don't like what I am, you only have yourself to thank. It was you who did this to me. You and that damned slut—"

Before another word had left her mouth, Wade had her pinned against the wall, his hand clamped over her mouth. "Don't ever speak of my child's mother that way, Nik. Don't ever do it," he repeated, his voice low and hard, his eyes glinting like shards of broken black glass.

With a furious toss of her head, Nikki dislodged his hand, glaring. "Ah, yes. I mustn't say anything against the sainted Jamie. Never mind that she took you from me," she snarled, throwing his hands from her.

"That poor little rich girl, she grew up with anything and everything she ever wanted. She had everything. I had *nothing*. Until you. You were mine. You were the only thing in my life that really mattered and she took you away."

How can you defend her? Her heart breaking inside her, Nikki clenched her fists. She had bitten her tongue, had held back for years. And what had it gotten her? Nothing. Damn it, if she had done something *then*, maybe this mess wouldn't have happened.

But she had ignored Jamie, like she knew Wade wanted,

and not done or said a damn thing to the woman who spent months chasing after an engaged man.

"Well, I'll say whatever I want against the bitch," she coldly said, whipping past him to stand her ground in the middle of the porch. She didn't back away as he advanced, just took out the one weapon she had left. "Like a dog in heat, she went chasing after you, no matter how many times you told her you weren't interested. She did everything to catch your eye except strip naked and plant herself in front of you."

Her lip curled up, her voice full of hate and derision, she said, "And to think that your hands touched her. How can you possibly think I would want you after knowing you were with her? That your hands touched her? I don't want them on me. They're dirty."

Wade stopped in his tracks, anger suddenly replaced by pain, deep biting pain. He had never, in all the time he had known her, heard her speak to anyone in that tone. And the look on her face, as though she had found something distasteful on the soles of her shoes.

Dumbfounded, he stared at her. She couldn't mean that.

But one look at her furious face told him otherwise. She didn't want him here. She had told him time after time, but like a fool he had kept coming back.

He needed her so badly, like a dying man needed water, but she didn't even want him touching her. Had he imagined the way she lit up when he touched her? Had he imagined the need in her eyes simply because he so badly needed to see it there?

"You can't expect me to believe you don't want me," Wade said, his voice sounding tight and rusty. "You can't expect me to believe you feel nothing when I touch you." He only wished he was as certain as he sounded.

He watched as she flipped her hair back and shrugged,

carelessly, casually. "It's been a while for me, Wade." She smoothed her hands down her sides, ran her fingers through her tousled hair. "Been a busy few months. Haven't had time to get out much. After Dale left... Well, I'm picky. And there are not too many guys around here who've caught my eye."

Wade looked into her eyes, looked for some sign she was lying, playing out a role. But he saw nothing that could convince him she spoke anything less than the truth.

I don't want them on me.

The words replayed themselves over and over as he stood there, feeling vaguely lost and very confused. The hurt and anger were waging a war within him, ripping at him until he was so damn torn apart he could barely see. Nausea roiled sickly in his gut as her implication that any man would suffice sank in.

Had it come down this? Would fate be cruel enough to place her back in his life, to tempt with glimpses of what could be paradise, only to have his hopes and dreams smashed because she just didn't want him anymore? Had Nikki been imagining somebody else in his place every time he touched her?

"Are you so damn perfect that you never made a mistake, never hurt anybody?" he rasped, growing aware of a desire to hurt her as badly as she had hurt him. Anything, even pain, would be better than that damned disdain that sat so haughtily on her face, surrounding her like an invisible cloak. "Never done anything that you would give anything to have undone? Never done anything that made you feel like the lowest life form on the planet?"

He couldn't see the guilt and the sorrow that started to form in her eyes and he didn't hear the soft apology in her voice as she quietly said, "I make mistakes. I've felt even lower than that. I've screwed up more times than I can count and you damn well know it."

Her voice sounded oddly distant, flat. But it rolled off his shoulders like water as he tried to reconcile the words, *I don't want them on me.*

"Wade, I need time. I'm only human."

The unspoken apology went unheeded by him as he heard in his head, over and over, *I don't want them on me.* The unspoken words he was hearing were *Almost any man would do. You might be handy, but you're not good enough.*

He kept coming back, time after time, needing her so badly, and she kept kicking him in his face. That mental image of him crawling at her feet only to receive a boot in his face for his efforts had his pride kicking in, temporarily masking the pain he felt. He drew himself up, reined in the anger and pain that must be showing on his face.

"Yeah?" he asked, derisive. "I'm not so sure of that. A human would show some forgiveness, a little compassion. That's what happens when you have a heart. And from what I can see you lost yours some time ago. I'm beginning to wonder if you ever had one."

Damn it all, he was done begging. He was done crawling. No more.

Making his own face as cruel as hers had been, he continued, "Hell, I'm starting to wonder about a lot of things. But one thing is certain—" moving closer until he was nose to nose with her, he whispered harshly, "—you ain't worth it."

"Wade—"

Her face was pale. The pain in her eyes registered dimly in some part of his mind, but he didn't acknowledge it. He had his pride. He wouldn't keep crawling after her. He had been patient, understanding. Hell, he had all but begged her to take him back.

And this was what he got for giving up his pride in the name of love.

Coldly, he offered, "And as for time, well, take all the time you need, Nicole. What you do matters nothing to me." And then, without looking back, he walked away from her.

Nikki walked woodenly into the house. It was over. She had won. She had driven him away and away he would stay.

What had she done?

Over the guilt a soft voice whispered inside her, *Exactly what you had to do. You had to be sure...had to be sure you could trust him. Trust yourself. Otherwise it wouldn't have been fair to either of you. Or to Abby.*

But why had she been so hateful?

Sinking down on the steps, Nikki buried her face in her hands. Anger. Hurt. Self-defense. Any one of those would have been right. Or at least, partly right. But the real reason was fear. She was so damned afraid of being hurt again, of losing it all.

"Nikki?"

She looked up, startled. Dylan stood before her, concern in his eyes. He knelt down in front of her, took her cold hands in his. Her eyes stared back into his, eyes so like her own. "Want to talk about it?" he asked quietly.

"No," she whispered, her voice almost soundless. With a gentle tug, she freed her hands and rose on none-too-steady legs.

"What are you going to do?"

She stared at him, her eyes lost. "I don't know," she said faintly. She badly wanted to run away and hide, lick her wounds.

So why don't you? She blinked as the soft little voice repeated itself. *Why don't I?* she asked herself. Hell, it wasn't like she had any reason to stay here, not after what he had told her.

It wasn't like he'd be waiting now, right? Even if there had been a chance at something between them again, she'd gone and ruined that just now.

He was done waiting.

Just when she had started to think, maybe...just maybe...

Too late now. And the wishes and dreams didn't matter if he didn't want her anymore.

A slight shudder racked her body, like an echo of the pain she was holding trapped inside. Closing her eyes, she focused, grounded herself. Why in the hell shouldn't she take some time?

"I'm going to New York."

Wade drove around aimlessly until early afternoon. He restaged the fight time and time in his mind, and in the way of men and women since the dawn of time, he came up with sharper retorts and an even more crippling parting shot.

His thoughts jumped around, leaving that and returning to the porch where she had told him, *I don't want them on me.*

Didn't want him touching her, didn't want his love...didn't want him.

Nikki's words replayed in his mind like a broken record he couldn't turn off. She had finally said what was on her mind and in her heart. If she had done so from the beginning, maybe he wouldn't have wasted all this time trying to get her back.

Wade conveniently forgot she had been telling him just that time after time. He had just decided not to listen.

"Hell, Wade. It's better this way. You know where you stand with the woman. Now you can get over her," he told himself, drumming his fingers on the steering wheel.

Like hell.

Get over her? Not likely to happen.

His heart felt as though it had been ripped out of his chest and thrown, still beating, on the floor.

Chapter Twelve

Nikki sat in the passenger seat, her eyes dry and itching. She knew without looking that she was pale and wan looking. Shawn kept sending her worried little glances and she knew he didn't want to be driving her to the airport. He wasn't happy about her traipsing off, away from home and alone, in her current mood.

"How long are you planning to stay?" he asked, his eyes flicking from the road to her. Accordingly, the black Bronco drifted right.

"Watch the road, Shawn," she snapped, one hand instinctively bracing against the dash. As he corrected the vehicle, she answered, "I don't know. I guess I'll stay until I feel like coming home."

"What is so important in New York?" he asked, frowning but keeping his eyes on the road.

"A better question would be what isn't there, Shawn. Now just let it go, okay?" she answered wearily, reaching up to rub at her temple. Damn, but her head hurt.

"Ya know running away ain't going to solve anything. It's not going to keep you from still loving him. It's not going to change that you want him." Shawn kept his eyes fixed on the road this time, a certain sign of how uncomfortable he was with discussing emotions. "Being in New York isn't going to change any of that. It's still going to be here when you get home."

Nikki remained silent. How could she explain that she needed someplace safe, someplace where she wouldn't see him, as she licked her wounds and tried to start all over again. She needed time to heal a little, her heart *and* her pride. She knew she wasn't going to get over Wade, not now. Not ever. But she needed some distance from him, time to rebuild her shattered defenses.

Nikki needed the bliss of not thinking about the wreck her life had become. Kirsten lived in a social whirlwind and would pull Nikki inside it.

It wouldn't solve her problems, but maybe if she kept busy enough she could forget for just a little while. Right now she was too raw to think about it, to try to put things into perspective.

In a while, after time had dulled the edges a bit, Nikki would think about it, and how stupid she had been.

I don't want them on me.

"Idiot. Fool," Wade muttered under his breath.

A week later he was still kicking himself over the altercation between him and Nikki. This particular kicking was taking place as he sat in the car waiting for his partner to make a run into the café to get their lunch.

Closing his eyes, he relived that argument with Nikki, tormented by the words that had tormented him into walking away.

They haunted him both day and night.

Now they only served to remind him of what a jackass he was. As rain splattered down on the windshield, he listened with half an ear to the radio as he muttered more accusations at himself.

If only he hadn't been pushing so hard. She would have

come around sooner or later. Nikki had all but admitted that. If Wade was totally honest, he could admit he had been waiting for years, ever since Jamie had died, hoping against hope he would have another chance. What harm would a few more weeks, a few months, have done?

With a ragged sigh, Wade closed his eyes and let his head fall against the back of the seat. His eyes were reddened and bloodshot, dark circles beneath his eyes emphasizing his haggard look. He couldn't keep going on snatches of sleep. His job wouldn't allow for it.

His heart wouldn't let him just let go, even though his pride insisted he not go crawling. And that was probably what it would take. He had been a total ass. About all of it.

His mouth compressed as he remembered Nikki's harsh words against Jamie, the first she had given voice to. It made him angry, hell, yes. That was Abby's mother, his childhood friend.

But how could he not expect Nikki to harbor resentment? The entire time Jamie had pursued Wade, Nikki had kept her cool, kept her mouth closed and her wits about her. God knew, if Nikki had been of a mind to, she could have ripped Jamie into so many pieces there wouldn't be enough left to bury.

The blow up he had expected the night he told her of Jamie hadn't happened.

How long had Wade expected her to keep the lid on her temper? With a grimace, he remembered how blind with fury he had been when Nikki had been dating the blond mechanic, how murderous he had felt before he had recognized Shawn. He was lucky Nikki had kept it to words and had held her tongue this long, and God knows Nikki had a lot more reason to be pissed off than he did.

The door swung open, letting in the rain-drenched air as J.D. swung into the cab of the ambulance, two bagged lunches in hand. "Here you go, one gourmet hamburger, complete with grease, saturated fat and sodium. A walking heart attack. And to top that off, there's fries to go with it."

"Thanks," Wade mumbled, taking the bag with a noted lack of enthusiasm. He wasn't hungry. Everything tasted pretty much the same, like sawdust. He knew things weren't going to get any better until he resolved this with Nikki.

"—so here I was, in bed stark naked with this girl, and the Pope is pounding on the door," J.D. said around a mouthful of food. "I ended up jumping out of the fifth floor window, wearing her pink robe and a pair of bedroom slippers. Elvis caught me when I landed and we took a trip out to Vegas."

Glancing up, Wade frowned. Had J.D. been talking long? He couldn't remember a damn word that had been said. "Pardon?"

"I had a feeling you weren't hearing me," J.D. said, shaking his head. "You wanna tell me about it?"

"Nope," Wade replied, taking a bite of the rapidly cooling burger.

As if Wade hadn't spoken, J.D. said, "You know, I'd guess it was a woman problem, but you haven't ever once mentioned a woman, not in the three months we been together. If it wasn't for the fact that you got a daughter, I'd wonder if you knew what women were. But you had to know what women are because you put one to good use at least once." He wagged bushy black eyebrows before taking a sip of his soft drink.

Wade scowled over at his partner before taking another bite of the burger.

"Course, I seen you with that girl, Nikki Kline, once or twice. She don't talk to many guys, so I guess you must be doing something right. I'm surprised her brothers ain't scared you off. I tried to get her to go out with me a couple of times, but any time I talked to her, those two showed up and they got trouble written all over their faces. I heard they were both gang members up in Louisville a few years back," the other medic said, chewing up his fries as he spoke. He paused only long enough to wash the food down with a soft drink before continuing. "Is she who you're moping about?"

"I am not moping," Wade said slowly, spacing each word out. "Now why don't you mind your own business?

"Because my partner can't hardly keep his head out of his ass and this ain't the kind of job you can do if you aren't focused on it," J.D. snapped, his blue eyes narrowing. "If this was a big town you'd already be waist-deep in hot water. But sooner or later something more serious than a broken bone or an upset stomach is going to pop up and you'd better be able to handle it."

Having made his point, the older man turned his attention to his half-eaten lunch, dismissing Wade and his dilemma with the words, "You'd better get things worked out quick. Otherwise you're going to get your ass thrown into the street."

Hell.

Wade turned his truck up the drive, grimly refusing to think about how much he might have to crawl. Damn it, she'd probably call the cops and have him thrown off her property, and wouldn't that cap things off nicely?

But he had to try. Wade had to try to make her understand how sorry he was. And with a whole lot of wishful thinking on his part, he was hoping she would let the sorry incident at her house go. He had to try to smooth things out, apologize and get her to understand.

His life wasn't worth a whole hell of a lot without her in it.

And the man who had sworn to himself he wasn't going to beg was ironically aware that begging was exactly what he intended to do, in front of God and everybody if that was what it took.

Gravel crunched under his tires as he pulled the truck to a stop. The overcast sky promised more rain before the day was out. As he climbed out of the truck, he caught the cool scent of the coming fall on the air. He helped Abby out of the booster seat in the back of the extended cab before turning to the silent house.

Her jacket buttoned up against the faint chill in the night air, Abby snuggled against his chest as they both looked at the empty house before them. Curtains drawn and secured, windows dark. "Daddy, Nikki's not here, is she?" Abby asked, her face puckering in a slight pout.

"No, baby. It doesn't look like she is," he answered gruffly. And from the looks of things, he had a feeling she wouldn't be back any time soon. The house had the vacant air to it of one that was going to be empty for some time.

"She'll be home soon, right? We could wait," Abby said, her eyes hopeful. "We could sit on the swing again and wait like we did last time."

"Angel, I don't think she's coming home any time soon." He turned away, helped Abby back into the car and strapped her into her child seat. He paused by the driver's door, looking back at the house. Where in the hell had she gone?

As the days turned into weeks, and weeks into a month, the house on the hill outside of town remained empty. The questions he started asking of her family went unanswered. Her dad was cool and polite, Shawn taunting and insulting. Dylan was simply silent, staring at Wade with flat hazel eyes that saw too much.

Wade finally heard a rumor she had moved to New York.

No. He told himself she wouldn't just up and leave. Not for good. But all too soon Halloween was over and the holidays were looming on the horizon and he had yet to hear anything more about her.

As his regret died, it gave way to anger. The apologies he had been rehearsing turned to ashes on his tongue. So he had meant that much. After one fight she had just given up and turned away, walking out of his life, not giving him a chance to try to heal the wounds before they festered.

Wade spent several weeks in that mindset, stewing and steaming over it. The anger certainly felt better than the guilt and he was able to function a little better.

After Thanksgiving dinner with his parents Wade returned to Monticello, wondering if he should move back home.

At least Abby would have her grandparents close by and her old friends. And he wouldn't have to live day by day, wondering when she would come back.

If she would come back.

Abby was lonely. Two of her closest friends had started kindergarten and in the careless manner of children, had decided Abby was too young for them play with anymore. And she was unhappy, probably sensing her father's state of mind. It was wearing on both of them.

At least twice a week, he made the long drive to Nikki's house outside of town, up that winding road to see if she had returned. He would prowl the woods behind her home and slowly go out of his mind while he wondered.

Pacing the floors at night, the four walls of his house threatening to close in on him, Wade worried and wondered. The anger was giving way to desperation and dismay. Something wasn't right. The woman who had fled from him wasn't the girl he had known.

Nikki would have stood her ground, dug in her heels and lifted that arrogant chin. Damn it, she would have laid into him, teeth bared. Where had that girl disappeared to? How had Nikki changed so much?

And why had Wade done that? Acted that way? Handed out ultimatums he had no right to hand out?

Why had she let him? Why hadn't she fought back the way she would have before? She had stood there, letting him pile it on her and rage away. She should have torn into him, but she hadn't. She had just taken it.

It was like there wasn't much fight left in her.

And so December dawned, cold and gray, an echo of the grief he carried inside.

Chapter Thirteen

Wade glanced up as his partner dropped down on the chair across from him. His face was grim, his eyes shadowed and dark. "The boy didn't make it," J.D. rasped, his voice raw and strained.

"Damn," Wade whispered, useless anger curling within him. "Damn it."

"Massive head trauma. If he'd lived he would have been a damned vegetable. The mother is still in surgery, but they think she'll pull through. Hell of a piece of news for her to have to hear while she's fighting for her life." J.D. slouched in his chair and rubbed his eyes.

Their shift had ended well over two hours earlier, but neither had been able to leave until they heard the news. Wade was now wishing he had left. He wanted to rip something apart with his bare hands. Knowing he didn't want to know, but unable to keep from asking, he gave in. "The driver?"

"Mild concussion. Mild lacerations. A few bruised ribs from his impact against the safety harness," J.D. said, his voice flat. "Ain't that justice?"

"You boys need to head home."

Wade looked up as one of the ER nurses came into the lounge. A soft, comforting smile on her familiar face, Leanne Winslow settled into a chair next to Wade and took his hand. "You've had a rough night. You need to get some rest. This isn't even your normal shift."

"Saving money for Christmas," he muttered, folding his cold hand around hers. "Any more news about the mother?"

"Some. And it could be good news. She's about four and half months pregnant and the baby is hanging in there. She hasn't spontaneously aborted yet, so that is definitely a good sign. If all goes well..."

Wade grimaced and shook his head. "Too many things can go wrong, especially that early in the pregnancy."

"If she'd been much further along, much bigger, the baby's chances wouldn't be as good. As it is, the little girl is small enough that her mother's body sustained much of the damage. She pulled through surgery but... Well, the pain meds and antibiotics, those are what's worrying her OB right now. At least she's past the first trimester. We've located her husband."

A soft hand stroked over his brow and he fought off the urge to shrug it away. Wade never should have accepted her offer to dinner few weeks ago. But now any time he decided to call things off, he was struck with a bout of loneliness so strong he lost his resolve.

Leanne was sweet, gentle and unassuming. She looked at Wade as though she thought he was some type of god and made him feel like he wasn't a walking disaster.

And Abby liked her. She hardly even mentioned Nikki anymore. The past three weeks had been easier, but he didn't know if that was because Leanne was there or because he was adjusting to the fact that Nikki was gone.

"Wade, you need to go home," Leanne ordered softly, gazing up at him with concerned blue eyes. "Get some rest before that little girl of yours comes home from daycare. With Christmas coming you're going to need that rest."

Rest. That had become a precious commodity in his world. On the rare nights Wade slept for more than four or five hours, he always dreamed of Nicole.

The tasks of working two extra shifts of a week, trying to get Christmas shopping done and dealing with a rambunctious four-year-old were an exhausting combination enough, but when the father couldn't sleep, it made it even worse.

Rest? he thought cynically. Yeah, right. Not in this century. But Wade gave her a tired smile and nodded. "You'll let me know about the mother?" he asked as he stretched his arms over his head and forced his stiff body out of the chair.

"Yes. But she's going to pull though. She's stable and she's young. I just hope her baby makes it. Losing one child is hard enough," Leanne murmured, rising gracefully to her feet. The baggy blue uniform rustled softly as she leaned close enough to peck him on the cheek. "I'll call tonight once you've had a chance to get some rest. You too, J.D. Get some sleep."

She smiled sweetly at him and left the lounge on silent feet. Her ebony hair, wound in an intricate braid, swayed as she walked away. That girl moved like a dancer. She was beautiful, sweet and intelligent, a perfect dream. She was happiest when she was fussing over people.

And, more often than not, two hours after leaving her, Wade could hardly remember what she looked like. Certainly couldn't pull up her image in his mind, couldn't remember how she felt against him, or smelled, or tasted.

"That is a fine piece of work," J.D. murmured as he rose, sliding his rumpled jacket on as they headed out the lounge. "You two serious?"

Wade shrugged. "We've gone out a few times."

"About time. That girl's been practically begging you ever since you moved here. Nice to know you finally developed a brain."

Wade shot his partner a dour look. "That's not a brain you're thinking of, buddy." His steps slowed as he passed by a man being wheeled outside with an armed escort. He was sobbing theatrically and waving his arms in the air as he begged and pleaded with the officers.

"Damned murdering son of a bitch," J.D. whispered under his breath as the two men slowed to a halt. "Listen to him, saying he wasn't drunk at all. That bastard had empty beer cans all over the back seat."

The bastard in reference had kept trying to grab his treating paramedic the entire time she was with him. He had been singing loudly and begging for "a special performance" while Wade and J.D had been laboring over a tiny three-year-old boy, trying to pump life back into him. Bastard was so damned drunk he hadn't really realized he had been in a wreck.

As he sang merrily, unaware of what was really happening, Wade and J.D. had struggled to make that boy live.

They had succeeded only to have the boy die in the ER.

"What's likely to happen to him? In Louisville, some fancy-ass lawyer would get him off with a suspended sentence and community time."

J.D. grunted and raised his shoulders. "He'll be tried for manslaughter. And unless his family is rich, he won't get a lawyer fancy enough to even try to talk down a thing like this. Even then, folks around here don't take too kindly to bastards like that. This isn't his first offense either. Multiple DUIs. He'll do time. But that won't bring that little boy back," J.D. finished savagely, glaring in the direction of the cruiser.

"But maybe it will save another one," Wade said, holding onto that thought. That helped. Not a whole hell of a lot, but it did help. "You have to remember that. If he got away with a slap on the wrist, this would be a hell of a lot harder to handle." He cast a glance up at the cold winter sky as they resumed walking to the ambulance. "Hell of a Christmas that family is going to have."

Once home, Wade shed his clothes on the way to the bathroom and turned the water to as hot as he could stand it. His uniform was saturated with blood and he felt as though his skin was as well. So much blood for such a small child. Sharp needles of water pounded his face and chest as he scrubbed at his flesh.

How was that poor boy's family going to make it? If he lost Abby...

His little girl was all he had. Losing her would kill him.

No parent should ever have to bury a child.

Exhaustion kept him from dwelling too long on that thought. Stepping out of the shower, water sluicing off his body, Wade forced his mind not to go down that road.

He fell face first on the bed without even drying off. Wrapping up in the comforter, he prayed for oblivion.

Waking shortly before Abby was due home, Wade climbed out of bed, his stiff muscles protesting as he stretched. The dull ache of grief resided in his chest but he pushed it aside. His little girl was on her way. And with Christmas only four days away, she was becoming more and more hyper and required every bit of his energy.

Every other word out of her mouth was "Christmas". "Have I been good?" ran a close second. Even without the extra hours he was putting in she would have worn him down. And in two days his parents were coming in to spend the holidays with him and Abby. Which meant he had to clean the damn house.

To top that all off, he couldn't get Nikki out of his mind.

Is she home yet? He hadn't gone up the mountain in two weeks, and he'd finally stopped hounding her family.

How much longer was she going to stay away?

Not that it mattered. Wade had finally given up waiting. He

153

had accepted that this was her way of making a clean break. It was over for her.

But not for him. And that was the most pathetic part of it. Because he was the reason she had decided to make that break. Him and his damned pride. If he had been a little more patient he would have had her back.

And then he had gone and screwed it up.

Again.

Later that night, Abby sat scrubbed clean and dressed in pink and blue flannel pajamas, her eyes focused on the Christmas special on the television. *The Small One*, Wade thought. It was a sweet cartoon, and Abby was enamored with the donkey.

He reached blindly for the phone when it rang, knowing automatically who it was. Leanne's slow southern drawl sounded in his ear and he tuned out the television as he listened. The mother was fine. The baby was hanging in there. He sent a silent prayer heavenward and thanked Leanne for letting him know.

"Are we still on for Christmas Eve?" she asked softly.

"Yeah. And don't forget you're welcome to come by Christmas night when you get done working your shift."

She chuckled. "I may not be in the mood for celebrating by the time my shift is over. You know how holidays are in the hospital. Even here in the country we get our share of folks drowning their holiday blues with Jack Daniels and sleeping pills."

"Cheerful thought," he muttered. And it wasn't one he really wanted because it reminded him of Jamie. She'd drowned her blues all right. But it hadn't been Jack Daniels. It had been Jose Cuervo and sleeping pills. When he'd found her, she'd been in their bed, wearing blue silk, her face perfectly made up. She hadn't written a suicide note, but then again, he hadn't needed one. He knew why she had killed herself... It was his fault. She blamed him for never loving her.

"You sound tired. Didn't you get any sleep?"

"Yeah, but it doesn't feel like it now," he replied, closing his eyes against the glare of the television. The six hours of unconsciousness might as well not have happened. "The extra work is catching up."

"Do you think maybe you should slow down?" Leanne suggested hesitantly.

Nikki would have told him to stop working himself into the ground, or she'd stop him herself.

Leanne wasn't Nikki. She was the exact opposite, which was why he was dating her. "This was the last one. I was only doing it for Christmas."

"Good. You need to take better care of yourself." The way she said it, her words sounded more like a question than a statement.

Cursing himself, he promised, "I'll try," before hurriedly getting off the phone. He was too damn tired to listen to his evil twin berate Leanne for being everything he had decided he wanted in a woman. Or everything he *should* want in a woman.

But damn it all, he didn't want a southern belle who hung onto his every word and couldn't make a decision on her own unless it had to do with the job. She even asked him what she should cook when he came over for dinner.

What he wanted was an acid-tongued transplanted Yankee who would tell him to go to hell before she'd offer to come and cook breakfast for him on her day off.

"Damned fool," he told himself softly as he settled back against the couch.

Nikki stood in the shadows of the alcove, watching the

festivities with weary eyes. Everybody at Kirsten's party was having a blast, save for Nikki. She could only think of one place she wanted less to be. Home.

Shawn had told her yesterday that he'd seen Wade going out with a woman he vaguely knew from the hospital. A pretty young nurse Nikki remembered all too well.

Leanne Winslow had been the one holding her hand when she woke up briefly in the ER after her accident. When she had asked about Jason.

Coal black hair, porcelain smooth skin, eyes the color of the midnight sky. She had been kind and comforting in the ER, and the few times Nikki had encountered her since then she had always been sweet and concerned, asking how she was. Mother Teresa in the flesh—that was Leanne. There was something almost ethereal about the woman.

She would be a prefect mother to Abby. A perfect wife for Wade.

Now that is a cheerful thought...

The third man of the evening to approach Nikki got within three feet before she noticed. Turning her icy eyes his way, she gave him her most obnoxious glare, hoping he'd get the point. The invisible wall of ice she had around her didn't seem to even faze him.

Nikki accepted the offered champagne flute only to set it down untouched on the elegant Queen Anne table behind her. He hardly noticed.

He was too drunk to notice. He didn't notice the way Nikki was edging away from him, didn't notice the look of utter distaste on her face. All he noticed was a streamlined body in a crushed velvet dress of crimson and the pouting, sulky mouth.

As he backed her farther into the corner, he also failed to notice the flash of temper that sparked in Nikki's eyes.

But he did notice the cold champagne that was flung in his face when he slurred out an invitation to go find an empty room somewhere.

As he sputtered and swore, Nikki dodged him, moving quicker than she had in weeks. She dodged dancing couples and gaily laughing groups of people.

All around people were celebrating. Not celebrating Christmas, the holiday season or even the weekend.

They were celebrating life.

No wonder she didn't want to be here. She didn't have any life left in her.

Shutting herself in the library, Nikki settled in a huge leather chair overlooking the estate and wished she had not wasted the champagne. She could have used a drink.

Her wish was granted when the door opened to reveal Kirsten, clad in a floor-length figure-hugging gown of sparkling emerald green. A slit that went all the way up her thigh was the only thing enabling her to walk. Without that strategically placed slit all she would have been able to manage was a shuffle.

In her elegant, ring-clad hands, she held drinks. A flute of champagne for herself and a Bloody Mary for Nikki.

Nikki accepted the drink with a smile and toasted her hostess. "Hell of a party," she said before taking a drink of the spicy concoction.

"Yes, I noticed your enthusiasm as you threw perfectly good champagne at one of the junior editors. He's being escorted home as we speak. Donald doesn't appear to hold his liquor all that well." She tossed Nikki a catty little smile before adding, "He swears up and down you propositioned him, and then when he accepted, you threw your drink at him. You little tramp." Kirsten settled herself against the desk and took a delicate sip of champagne as she studied her friend.

Nikki's only reply to that was a snort.

The girl looks like hell, Kris decided.

Some might think the weight loss was an improvement. She now had the model-thin look that was so popular, particularly in New York. The hollowed cheeks made her eyes look larger and the rich material of her dress clung lovingly to her torso before ending in a flirty little skirt inches above her knees. The dress, deep red and flattering to Nikki's svelte new figure, actually belonged to Kirsten. It had been altered only the day before.

Kirsten's attempts to take her shopping had failed, even though she knew very few of Nikki's clothes fit her anymore. And she owned nothing that could be worn to Kirsten's annual holiday bash at her parents' house in Long Island.

Not that she really wants to be here, Kirsten thought wryly. Hell of a compliment. She was boring her best friend out of her mind.

Of course, Kris had known this party would hold no interest for her.

No. This wasn't an improvement. Kirsten saw only despair in that face, pain in those sad eyes. That sleek body was a result of her appetite fading into nothingness. Nikki didn't look slim and sexy. She looked ill.

Nikki forced herself to eat regularly, but she couldn't down more than a few bites out of any meal.

"Is your dad upset that you're not going home for Christmas?"

"A little. We'll celebrate when I go home in January." Nikki drank again, emptying the glass and setting it aside as she shifted her body to face Kirsten.

"Have you set a date? Got your ticket?"

"Yes, mother. I'm going home to face the music."

Kirsten shook her head and sighed. "Nik, you're welcome here as long you like, but we both know you're miserable. You're going to be miserable anywhere until you put this behind you. And you can't do that here."

"I'm aware of that," Nikki said, her voice quiet. "I just need a little more time."

"Time isn't going to help this. If you'd put it to rest it would, but not until then. You hardly eat. You hardly sleep. You walk around looking like a damned zombie." Kirsten sat her champagne flute down with a snap and moved closer. "You have got to either let him go or go back and fight for him. But this has got to stop. Or you're going to end up the way you did five years ago."

Nikki lowered her lids slowly over her shadowed eyes, tipping her head back to meet Kirsten's angry glare. "I'm not that bad off."

"Yet." Kirsten started pacing back and forth, her heels sinking into the thick piled carpet.

Where had the anger come from? she wondered. Nikki was hurting. Kirsten knew that. She had reason to. She wasn't sulking over nothing.

But Kris desperately feared this was just the beginning of another downward spiral.

That thought not only angered her, it frightened her as well.

"You're not that bad off yet, but you will be. Before much longer you'll be in the hospital again, hooked up to IVs, tubes running this way and that. Your dad is going to be sitting there, begging you to fight and I don't think you have much fight left in you, Nicole. He's already come home once to find somebody he cared about dead. He wasn't able to save your mother. He doesn't deserve to lose another woman he cares about."

Swallowing the lump in her throat, Kirsten paused long enough to blink away the tears burning her eyes, "Damn it, Nik. He isn't worth this, Nik. I don't think any man is, but if he's worth this much grief, then why aren't you fighting for him?"

"That's easier said than done," Nikki murmured, her voice thick with tears. She failed to notice the angry and frightened tears that glittered in Kris's eyes. "And he doesn't want me. There's no point."

Wrong words.

"No point," Kirsten repeated slowly, her cat green eyes narrowing.

"No point? So you'll just mourn yourself into the grave this time?" Kirsten snapped, whirling to face the younger woman. "That's where you are headed this time, little girl. Your heart can't take the kind of abuse you heaped on it last time and I'm not talking about the emotional heart. Damn it, it's a wonder it didn't give out on you last time. It can't take that strain again and you know it.

"It's been five years since you pulled yourself out of that hole, and you're still popping Lanoxin every day. You will never be able to stop taking those drugs, Nikki. They are your lifeline and one more little injury to your heart could kill you. It will give out if it's put through much more strain, honey. You're going to end up having a heart attack or worse.

"And you don't have Jason to latch on to this time. He's not here this time to keep you going."

"I'm not that far gone. I'm still perfectly healthy—"

"Bullshit," Kirsten said succinctly, her voice hard, sharp as shards of broken glass. "You're a damned mess. Over *him*, a jackass that slept around on you, had two women knocked up at the same time. He got some woman pregnant one night, drunk out of his mind, angry over a fight he started. Doesn't that strike you as kind of stupid, being that upset over it? How many times have you told me about how angry you were with your mother when she put up with this kind of shit from your father? Why is Wade any different?"

Nikki didn't answer, just stared at Kris with haunted eyes.

"I can't believe you waste your time and your love on such a pathetic bastard, Nicole. Not just once, but twice. You're letting him put you through hell all over again. I can't help but wonder how many others he's got on the sly while he's been chasing you. Why do you even bother with him?"

Quietly, Nikki said, "Wade isn't like that."

"Oh, the hell he isn't," Kirsten replied, slashing at the air with a sharp gesture, rings flashing fire. "He's a no good, lying, cheating, hick of a bastard who wouldn't know a good thing if it bit him in the ass."

"I love him, Kris. He's not a bad man," Nikki snapped, her own eyes narrowing this time.

Kris managed to suppress the pleased smile. "Then damn it, go back and fight for him. He spent months chasing after you. Do you think he'll give up that easily?" That spark of anger settled her a little. Nikki hadn't shut down quite as much as she wanted people to think.

"He's seeing somebody else," Nikki reminded her, the hollow ache in her chest spreading. "He's found somebody else."

Kirsten snorted. "So he up and got married already?"

"They're dating."

"Oh, the sacred covenant. Dating." Sarcastically, Kirsten said, "And here I am encouraging you to go break up this happy union. Oh, wait a second, this is the man who got another woman pregnant while he was engaged to you. Oh, yes. He's definitely a man who honors his commitments."

"If he's dating somebody, it's because he's lost interest in me."

"You left," Kirsten said, spacing each word out slowly. "You've been gone for months. He might think you're not coming back, so he's probably trying to get on with his life. Hell, your dad said he's been asking about you all over town. He even had the nerve to approach those lunatic brothers of yours. *That* right there shows how desperate he is. If he could afford it, he'd probably be hunting you down."

"I doubt that. You didn't see him that day, Kris. He's fed up with me."

Kirsten rolled her eyes. "He's a *man*, sweetie. When men don't get what they want when they want it, they pout. That's how men are. But they get over it." Kneeling in her dress wasn't a wise thing to do, but she did it. Emerald green silk stretched but held as Kris caught hold of Nikki's hand and whispered, "You need to go home, baby. He's got to be worth fighting for, or you wouldn't be such a mess."

"And if he really doesn't want me?" Nikki asked, her voice ragged. She clenched Kris's hands tightly as the tears welled up in her eyes and spilled over. "If I go back and he doesn't want me, what do I do then?"

"You'll go on," Kris whispered, freeing her hand and brushing back the younger woman's tousled hair. Her eyes were swirling masses of pain. If this was what love could do to you, Kirsten wanted nothing of it. "Honey, you'll just have to go on. You're strong, stronger than you think. You'll be just fine.

"But," Kris said, smiling softly. "I don't think that's going happen. He loves you, has loved you for years. He isn't going to give up that easily."

A soft, muffled cry came from Nikki and Kris shifted, wrapping her arms around her, whispering, "It's okay... Just let it go." She stayed there as the sobs ripped out of Nikki's throat.

The storm passed quickly and Nikki swiped a hand over her eyes, smearing already ruined make-up. Sheepishly, she hugged Kirsten. Then she sat back and heaved a ragged sigh. "I haven't told him about Jason. If...if he wants to try this one more time, he's going to have to know about his son."

"Damn it, Nik." The words came out on a huff. "Why haven't you told him yet?"

Grimacing, Nikki said, "Stubborn. I kept telling myself I didn't want him back, that my past wasn't any concern of his. I guess I figured if I told him, that I'd forgiven him and was ready to try again. And..." Her voice trailed off as she stared past Kirsten's shoulder, her eyes distant.

"I was scared to," she finally admitted. "I still am. I...I don't think I can take being hurt like that again, Kris. It'll destroy me."

"He hurts you again, I'll destroy him," Kris promised. "But something tells me he'd sooner chop off his arm than hurt you again. If he was the jerk I wanted him to be, he wouldn't have hung around as long as he did when you kept being a cold little bitch to him."

"You don't know the half of it," Nikki murmured, dashing the back of her hand over her eyes. Then she eyed the black smears on her hand. "I'm a mess."

"I've told you that already," Kirsten reminded her. Gingerly, she got to her feet and heaved a sigh of relief when she did so without hearing material ripping. "I don't know why I chose this dress. I can't even sit down in it."

"That's probably why you chose it. You like seeing eyes pop out." Nikki gave a weak, watery smile as she rose to her feet as well. "The person who designed it must have been a man. They don't think of things like that. But you look great in it."

"I've been told several times tonight that I'd look better out of it," Kirsten quipped, flashing a smile at the younger woman. "I know I'd certainly feel better out of it." She slid a sideways look at Nikki and asked, "What about you?"

"I don't think it matters to me one way or the other, but for propriety's sake you ought to leave it on," Nikki replied, her voice droll.

"I meant, do you feel better?"

"No," she replied honestly. "But I will."

Chapter Fourteen

On January 9, Nikki went home to face the music. The flight to Lexington passed uneventfully and much, much too fast. As she disembarked, she set her shoulders, mentally prepped herself, reminded herself of the talks with Kris. Wade had spent months trying to get her to open up to him—if he had been at all serious, one bad fight wasn't going to dissuade him.

And even if it had, that just proved things never would have worked out between them and she'd be better off knowing.

Blah, blah, blah, blah...

Her long leather coat swept her ankles as she entered the terminal, looking for familiar faces. Shawn's face was the first she saw. Or rather, she saw his head as he bent it to whisper in the ear of a girl who would stand a good six inches over Nicole. Behind him stood her Dylan, leaning against a pole and gazing into nothingness. Her dad stood to the side, searching the crowd with impatient eyes.

They hadn't seen her yet.

Nikki resisted the urge to melt into the crowd and take off running. Ireland. Australia. Scotland. Any place. The Arctic Circle would be fine. Afghanistan would be fine. The Bering Sea.

But she didn't. She was getting tired of running.

Tugging off the loose gray beret, Nikki shifted her way through the flow of people until only ten feet or so separated her from her family. She was five feet away before they recognized her.

Jack's eyes glanced over her absently before drifting away. Seconds later they returned to her thin face and he sighed, shaking his head in resignation.

The thin, sad little waif before them bore little resemblance to the healthy woman who had left. Only the sad eyes were the same. Sadness had eaten away at her literally, until she was just a shadow of herself.

Jack doubted she'd weigh a hundred pounds. Violet half moons lay under her eyes and Jack wished that for five minutes he could be alone with the boy who had done this to his little girl. Again. He pulled her into his arms, stifling the second-nature instinct that had him wishing for a drink.

"How are you, baby?"

Nikki forced a smile and promised, "I'll be better now that I am home." She hoped she wasn't lying.

Dylan was scowling at her when she turned to him. "You look like hell. Doesn't that rich girl in New York know how to feed people?" he demanded. His mouth was compressed to a tight thin line, his eyes narrowed. "You were supposed to come back better, not worse."

"She knows how to feed people. I just forgot how to eat," Nikki told him, her mouth quirking in a slight smile before she moved away, letting him shoulder her carry-on.

The animosity between her brother and friend was a long-standing one. Kirsten had taken one look at her brooding baby brother and steered far clear of him. Dylan simply ignored her, never speaking more than five words to her unless he had no other choice.

Nikki suspected Dylan had noticed the elegant lady from the first moment he had seen her. *Really* noticed.

She also suspected she knew exactly why Dylan avoided

Kris so completely. Kris had only been a junior editor when she had met him the first time, but she was far more successful than he would ever be He was a street punk from West Louisville. She was a classy educated business woman.

And if she knew her brother at all, the fact that he had what could be considered a crush on her that wouldn't go away would only add fuel to the fire.

She arched a brow at him, unable to keep from wondering how long those two would avoid each other. The inevitable would happen sooner or later. Under her patient stare, Dylan scowled and repeated himself. "You look like hell."

He hugged her close and Nikki sighed, relaxing for just a minute. But then he straightened up and stared down at her with shrewd, knowing eyes. "You didn't outrun it, did you?" Dylan asked quietly, studying her shadowed eyes. "But I don't guess you expected to."

"No. I guess I didn't," Nikki agreed, turning away from him and introducing herself to the Amazon who stood hand in hand with her baby brother.

And as she spoke to the sweet-natured girl who handled her brother like an old pro, she fought off the feeling of dread that was rising within her.

She was home.

It was time to pay the piper.

Wade wasn't one for resolutions, but this year he'd decided to make one and had actually started well before the New Year even rolled around. It wasn't one he had any intention of breaking.

He had finally figured something out. Nikki had left her home to get away from him. She couldn't be around him, didn't want to be around him.

167

Whether it still hurt her too much, whether she no longer cared, he just didn't know.

Although part of him remembered the pain he saw all too often in her eyes and it made him think...it just hurt her too much. The girl he remembered would have happily danced on his grave for what he'd done to her, but obviously that wasn't how Nikki had spent the past five years.

She wanted him out of her life and he needed to let her go. He needed to move on with his life so she could move on with hers.

That was his resolution.

Leanne was a part of it.

She gazed at him over the golden glow of the candles, her eyes smiling shyly into his. Soft violin music played over discreetly hidden speakers and ubiquitous waiters answered every wish before it could even be spoken.

January was almost a memory now. He'd spent the month putting his resolution to the test. His past with Nikki needed to be put to rest.

She was back in town. Had been for nearly two weeks. He hadn't seen her yet but would eventually.

He had to convince her, and himself, that when he saw her, it was over. As though there was nothing between them.

Sooner or later he would convince himself it was over.

Sooner or later maybe Nikki would move on with her life.

And maybe sooner or later he could feel something for Leanne besides this vague affection. Abby loved her and Leanne adored Abby. Leanne wanted a family... Maybe in time...

Wade was giving himself a much repeated pep talk as they waited for their meal. He had just taken a sip of the wine Leanne had sweetly asked he try when he looked up and saw her.

His throat tightened. His stomach clenched as though he had just taken a particularly viscous sucker punch.

Nikki.

She walked past about twenty feet away, her head bent as she followed the hostess around the corner. His eyes landed on her family and he cursed the sense of relief that rushed through him when he realized she wasn't here with a date. Or a lover.

A cocky little beret sat atop curls shorn to chin length, her long leather coat swept her ankles as she disappeared from his sight.

Wade nearly choked on the excellent wine as he automatically inhaled at the sight of her. A fist closed around his heart and he could have sworn he smelled the subtle alluring scent of lotion-slicked flesh. Blood pounded in his head and muscles tensed.

He had been deluding himself.

Maybe he could let her out of his life but never out of his heart. And he could never let another woman take the position that should have been hers from the first, that would have been hers if he hadn't been such an ass.

She was his first love. His only love.

And if he couldn't have her at his side...he'd go it alone.

A gentle cough had him looking up to see Leanne studying him with sad, wise eyes. Thick lashes briefly shielded her dark blue eyes as she lowered her wineglass to the table with hands that shook slightly. Her mouth trembled once before firming as she asked, "Is she the one whose memory I'm competing with?"

Wade remained silent, closing his eyes as he tried to calm his racing heart. She was back. After more than four months she had really come back home.

"I wasn't sure if that was the Nikki that Abby kept talking about all the time, but I guess I have the answer to that now, don't I?" she murmured, crossing her hands in her lap. "I didn't know you two had met. Looks like you've done a little more than that."

Wade murmured something. What, he didn't know. He stared into his wineglass at the deep red liquid as his mind raced and chased itself in dizzying circles. The flickering candlelight only added to the effect, making his head spin as blood roared in his ears.

"Was it love at first sight?" Leanne asked, watching him. "Or did you know her from before she moved here?"

"Yes. And yes," he whispered, his voice slightly hoarse.

"I see," Leanne replied, her eyes stating clearly that she didn't see at all.

She wanted to know. It was written all over her face.

And he wanted, *needed*, to tell somebody. Five years had passed and nobody but him knew the whole of it. He had been ashamed to talk to any of his old friends, and Lord knew he couldn't talk it over with his best friend. That had been Nikki, and he had lost her. He had hurt her, broken her heart. His parents weren't viable candidates for purging his soul either.

Hadn't he kept quiet about it long enough? If nothing else, maybe telling it out loud would exorcise her from his heart and soul and he could let her go, the way he needed to.

"I...met Nikki before I got married. I've known her for years," he said, his voice sounding rusty. His hand clenched tightly around the fragile stem of the wineglass before he made it relax. He loosened the tie at his neck, released the top button of his shirt.

"How many years?" Leanne repeated.

"A little over eight years now," he said softly.

"She would have just been a kid."

Wade snorted and said, "I don't think she was ever really a kid, not like we were." He grabbed his wine and tossed it back and wished it were something stronger. The words started to pour from him. The meals were served but hardly touched as he told of the first few awkward dates and the furious fights. The final fight that caused Wade to destroy what was most important to him in the world.

"I don't even remember it," he whispered. "I lost everything that mattered to me because of that night and I don't remember it. I sure as hell don't know why I let it happen. I never thought of her like that, never. She was just...Jamie, this girl I had grown up with."

He told her about the last night when he had told Nikki about what he had done, how that had ripped his heart from his body. Of the months of depression that followed, depression that was relieved only by the arrival of his newborn daughter.

"I don't regret her. I couldn't. She's everything to me," Wade said, his harsh face softening as he thought of her, that sweet smile, the mischief that glinted in her eyes, her unfaltering love. "I didn't know it was possible to love somebody like that. But to get her, I had to lose Nikki. Had to hurt her."

Leanne listened in silence as he told her about Jamie, how his wife had slipped away and how he hadn't been able to help her, hadn't been able to care enough to do it.

"She killed herself, you know." His voice was conversational, his eyes bland, showing little emotion. He could have been discussing the weather. "Took a bottle of sleeping pills and never woke up. A few days before she did, I was napping in the lounge at the hospital. I dreamed it but didn't think anything of it. I was always having really odd dreams. But I came home one day after picking up our daughter and she was gone."

"And when all was said and done, I was *relieved*. I was tired of trying to help her, tired of listening to her cry about how rough she had it, sitting at home day after day. Tired of her pretending Abby didn't exist. I just didn't care."

It was late. Over an hour had passed since he had seen Nikki enter the restaurant. In halting tones he spoke of the fight that last day on her mountain, the one that had sent her away.

And when he finished, he sat back and looked at the woman he had hoped, had planned, would take Nikki's place. How in the hell had he even thought it would work? He'd been trapped in one loveless marriage already. And he had almost walked right into another one.

"I went to her house about a week later to apologize and see if I could salvage anything. But she was already gone. I kept waiting, certain she would come back. I had this little speech all laid out in my mind. I went up twice a week that first month, but she was never there. Her father wouldn't tell me a damn thing, and her brothers would just as soon rearrange my face as look at me."

He leaned back in his chair and rubbed the back of his neck, closing his eyes against the tension headache that had formed ages ago. "I kept waiting for her to show up so I could apologize. I had no right to demand a damn thing from her, no right to say anything I said. I had to apologize," he rasped, staring into the understanding eyes across from him. "I had to. It was eating me up inside. But I never got the chance."

Finally, he fell silent, staring at the melting candles. His untouched meal lay cold before him. The perfect night he had planned lay in shambles. But he should have known better.

Leanne opened her mouth to speak and then closed it, pursing her lips and staring blindly into her wineglass. Wade realized he had hurt another woman he cared about, but he didn't know what to do about it.

Finally, after eons of silence, Leanne looked up at him and forced a smile.

"Not much for the relationship thing, are you, Wade?"

"No." His eyes dropped, unable to look into that indigo gaze and see the hurt she was trying so hard to hide. "Leanne, I'm sorry. I never—"

"Wade," Leanne interrupted. "Don't, okay? No real harm done. And I was asking for it anyway. I could tell you had somebody else in your heart, but I just kept pushing it. I kept telling myself you'd get over whoever it was, but I ought to know better. Love isn't like the flu. It isn't something you can get over."

Morosely, rubbing his heart with the heel of his hand, Wade muttered, "It's more like cancer. The incurable kind."

Leanne chuckled softly. "I don't think it's always that bad, Wade. You've just had a couple of rough roads. Maybe it'll get better."

Yeah. And maybe there is a blizzard raging in hell right this moment, Wade thought dourly. But he didn't say anything.

Shortly after that, they were outside, heading to Wade's truck.

"I guess I'm kind of surprised to see her back here," he said as he helped Leanne into the truck. He remained at the open door, staring thoughtfully into the night. "She must like New York for her to stay there so long. I halfway expected her to stay there. There sure as hell isn't much to hold her here."

Frowning, Leanne shot him a look. "She's lived here for almost five years, Wade. She's made her home here. Her family's here. Her little boy is here." She wasn't looking at him as she fished around for her seatbelt. Her words were delivered in an almost offhand manner.

It might have been comical, the way he froze in mid-action. His hand hovered an inch from the door. The ground seemed to drop out from under him and time stood still. Frozen in place, he attempted several times to work his mouth but found his couldn't speak.

Little boy.

Little boy.

Wade hadn't heard her right. Before his vocal cords could relax enough for him to speak, Leanne gave him a questioning look.

"Are you okay?" she asked, but he couldn't hear, just saw her lips move.

"What..." His voice wasn't even a whisper. He cleared his throat and tried again. "What...did...you...say?"

Leanne stared at him, aghast. Her creamy complexion paled, twin flags of red riding high on her cheekbones. There was no way. He had to have known. But his pole-axed expression, the gray cast to his skin said otherwise. "You didn't know," she murmured, her eyes wide and confused.

"Didn't know what?" he asked, but before she could reply, voices intruded. Like a wolf scenting wounded prey, he whirled, eyes narrowing as a slim figure moved across the parking lot. "Didn't know what?" he repeated softly, staring at Nicole as if just that alone would tell him what he wanted to know.

Nicole came to a halt thirty feet away, her eyes colliding with his. They rested on him, then on Leanne for a brief moment before she turned away.

"If you aren't going to tell me, then I guess I'll go ask her," he said, his voice sharp.

"This isn't the right time, Wade. Damn it, I thought you knew. I'm not the person who should be telling you," Leanne said softly, her eyes locking on his as she caught his arm.

"You're right. The right time would have been *months* ago," he snarled, jerking his arm free. "And she should have told me." He started in the direction Nikki had headed.

"No," Leanne snarled, releasing the seatbelt and jumping from the car, forced into action as she remembered the desolate look on Nikki's face moments earlier. The look would haunt her until the day she died. Much like the look that had been on

Nicole's face when Leanne had revealed that Jason was gone. She caught up with him when he was halfway to where Nikki and her family had parked. Seizing his arm, she put all her weight into slowing him down.

"Damn it, Wade. Let her go."

"Tell me," he said once again, his voice whisper soft.

A car door slammed shut and Leanne's head whipped around, following the taillights of a classic Mustang. Gone. Nikki was gone. She breathed a sigh of relief and turned her head to Wade, wishing to God she had never laid eyes on him.

As she remained silent, shifting awkwardly from one foot to the other, Wade cupped her shoulders, drew her closer to him. Leaning down, he repeated a second time, "Tell me. Now, Leanne. Or I'll chase her down and have her tell me."

Leanne shrugged away his hands, turning away from him. The cold winter wind blew across the parking lot, cutting through her coat like it wasn't there. It settled deep inside her, making her feel as though she would never be warm again. The bitter hot taste of grief welled up in her throat until speech was nearly impossible. This wasn't her story to tell.

Finally, she softly said, "I met Nikki in the grocery store a couple of years ago. She had this little boy with her." Her voice trailed off as she remembered those wide, innocent brown eyes, that sweet laugh silenced forever.

Wade's eyes were sharper than shards of glass as he caught hold of her chin, forcing her to look at him. "I haven't seen that little boy. I've been here for *months* and I've never seen him."

Leanne closed her eyes, shook her head. "You aren't listening," she whispered, her voice breaking. "About two weeks after that, I saw her again. This time in the ER. She was comatose. One of her brothers was with her, and he was pretty banged up but nothing serious.

"And her little boy was in the morgue. He was killed when a drunk driver ran them off the road by her dad's home."

Wade wasn't even aware she was still speaking. The tragic story fell on unheeding ears. All he could think was that somebody else had touched her, held her in the night, loved her. While he had scorned the touch of his wife, clinging to his memories of Nikki, she had been with another man. She had given herself to somebody else, given what was *his*.

Had born another man's child, probably that faceless high-society bastard he had imagined her with. He could almost see it. Some rich New Yorker had met up with her when she hit it big, had wined and dined her, taken her to some penthouse, lain with her on silk sheets.

His stomach revolted at the thought, acid burning bitterly at the back of this throat. But somewhere inside, he clung to hope. Maybe...

His vision faded to gray before coming back into sharp focus, the edges gone eerily red. "You take me to the grave," he rasped, shoving Leanne toward the truck. "Now."

Chapter Fifteen

JASON CHRISTIAN KLINE
BORN MAY 11, 2006 DIED SEPTEMBER 2, 2007
Beloved Son
I'll Be With You Always, Until the End of Time.

The date was all wrong. Only by a month, a handful of weeks, but it might as well have been six months or a year. She hadn't even waited a damn month, if that. Wade ran it through his head, hoping against hope. But it wouldn't work out. Pregnancy lasted nine months. That last frantic coupling in the woods couldn't have done it.

It had happened after that. And that meant the boy couldn't have been his.

Not even a damn month.

Her voice hesitant, soft, Leanne asked, "When...when did you two break up?"

Bitterly, Wade replied, "Not soon enough. She didn't wait very long though, a month at most."

She had gone straight to another man and yet she had been punishing him all this time. "Bitch," he breathed out, hands clenching and unclenching, a vein throbbing at his right temple.

All the times she had pulled back, had thrown Jamie in his

face, rushed back at him. All this time he had thought she had been mourning what they had lost, had been too afraid to get involved and feared being hurt. She had been mourning all right, but not over him. She'd been mourning the loss of some other guy's kid.

And his little girl. She had done the unforgivable, had hurt Abby. The cool answers, the distance she had insisted on keeping between them, the reluctance to talk to her, touch her. It had all affected his baby, even though Abby had tried hard not to let it show.

In the back of his mind, a voice whispered, *She told you time and again to leave her alone. To let her go. Told you, warned you—she wasn't who she used to be.*

The memory of her voice echoed in his mind. *Sooner or later you'll figure out I'm not who I used to be and I'm not somebody you want to be around. Certainly not somebody you want your daughter around.* She had been warning him but he hadn't listened. Those words played over and over in his mind.

But they were drowned out by the louder refrain of his bruised heart and pride. It kept replaying other words she had spoken.

I can't look at you without thinking about Jamie. About what you did.

There was an aching, gaping hole inside him and a rage so hot, so burning, it all but incapacitated him.

How many times had she twisted the knife in his gut? Jerked the past up and stabbed him with it? His guilt had been choking him for months, and every time he looked at her, saw the shadow she'd become, it got worse. But Nikki wasn't still hurting over him. She was mourning a child...and using him as her fucking punching bag. Him, and Abby too.

She would pay, damn it. For every time she had twisted his heart inside his chest, for every time she had put even a flicker of hurt or disappointment in Abby's eyes, for every slur she had made against his wife.

He hadn't even realized he had spoken aloud until a palm smacked up against his chest. He almost didn't recognize the livid face practically nose to nose with his. Leanne's voice rang out in the quiet cemetery as she shouted, "Pay? *Pay?* Damn you, she has paid! She lost everything she held dear. That little boy was her entire life and he's gone."

"My little girl is my life," Wade rasped. "She hurt her. She called my wife a whore, treated me like shit and made me think she'd spent the past five years in hell because of what I'd done, but it *wasn't me.* She treated Abby like she had the plague, treated me like dirt."

Leanne was practically shaking with anger and with shock. She couldn't believe what she was hearing or what she was seeing. The man before her seemed like a stranger, someone she didn't know. Eyes wide with disappointment and disillusionment, she bitterly whispered, "You cold-hearted bastard. That little boy was her reason for living. I took care of her after the accident. She was in a coma for nearly a week. And when she woke up, she was empty inside. There was *nothing* there.

"You think about how you would feel if the reason you had for living was suddenly ripped away," she whispered, her own heart aching at the memory of those grief-stricken, desolate eyes she had faced, eyes that haunted Leanne day after day. "*Ripped* away, not stolen like you were. Jason didn't abandon her or leave, but was ripped away for no reason. Everything just suddenly gone, with no hope of ever getting it back.

"She's never completely healed from it. Her grief damn near killed her," Leanne said roughly, trembling inside from the force of her emotions. "She had to bury her own child, Wade. That is a price no parent should ever be asked to pay."

But he barely even registered her words. His fury, his

179

jealousy, his pain deafened and blinded him.

Blind fury fueled him, kept him running for the next few weeks. The house was placed on the market and he gave his two weeks notice. His old job back in Louisville had been promised to him and they would stay with his folks until he found a new home for him and Abby.

All the while, Wade tortured himself with images of Nikki and the father of the baby. He didn't think about the boy, didn't think of the tiny little grave on the hillside. Didn't think about the accident that should have killed her as well.

The accident report. He shouldn't have had an acquaintance in the police department track it down. It had almost lessened his resolve. It had been frank, brutal, frightening. Truck overturned twice, tumbled down a thirty-foot embankment. Snapped a little boy's neck and nearly blinded his mother. Both Nikki and Shawn had worn their seatbelts and Jason had been secured in his seat. None of that had mattered—the boy had died and the fact that Nikki and Shawn had survived was nothing short of a miracle.

Wade refused to think about that piece of paper. It was just words strung together. He didn't think about it or about what he was doing.

He wasn't sleeping much, but that was fine. When he slept, it gave his conscience a chance to argue with the less rational part of his mind. Plus, it gave his imagination plenty of time to cook up dreams that starred Nikki and some nameless, faceless fuck who'd planted a child in her and then walked away.

No, he was better off without sleeping.

Anger had a fuel all its own.

Chapter Sixteen

The house was silent save for the faint electronic hum of her computer.

She really needed to be working. She had revisions waiting. She had another book waiting and more email than she even wanted to think about. There was a slew of file-sharing sites she needed to deal with, but that task was more than she could handle just now.

The ache in her heart made working almost impossible.

There were some who seemed to think authors, artists and the like thrived on misery, but Nikki was realizing she wasn't one of them. She'd found solace in her writing when she'd lost Jason, but that wasn't happening this time around.

There was no solace.

The only thing that helped was keeping her mind blank. Carefully blank.

She was tired, exhausted-clear-to-the-bone tired, weak, bleary-minded tired. Her muscles ached from a two-hour wood chopping stint the day before. And the day before that she had ridden her bike over the cold, winding roads for several hours. Her face was chapped from the biting wind and it had taken hours to feel warm again.

The wood pile outside her house was unbelievably large. Nikki was stocked in enough wood to last through several winters. She had put more miles in on her bike the past four weeks than she normally did all summer.

Wade and Leanne. Together.

The night in the parking lot of Tonito's loomed large in her mind at the worst times.

Nikki forced herself to get up and walk into the kitchen. Conscious of the wisdom in Kirsten's words, she made herself eat a good meal at least once a day, even if she didn't want it. Though she had gained another four pounds, Nikki was aware she was still too thin. She'd been to see her doctor and he'd been so aggravated with her she wouldn't be surprised if he had found a picture of her to throw darts at once she was out of the office.

She was now on a high-calorie, high-protein diet. And that damned doctor had told her if she didn't put on at least a pound every week over the next month, he was putting her on a liquid dietary supplement.

Nikki's lip curled at the thought. No way was she drinking that crap.

So she ate the damned food. And hated every tasteless bite.

Later, as the sun rose to its zenith, shining down a thin, watery winter light, she sat at the table, staring outside without seeing anything, eating a sandwich piled high with ham and tomatoes. She ate the chili her dad had made and sent home with her.

It all tasted like sawdust to her. It had for weeks. Months.

Wade hadn't called. Hadn't spoken to her the one time she had seen him in the store. Not that this was a bad thing. Nikki wasn't sure she could handle it. She was far too fragile. Seeing him with another woman had hurt her even more than she expected. Part of her insisted once she recovered from the shock of that she would do what she had come home to do.

But another part knew that if she approached him and he

rebuffed her, it would destroy her stubborn determination to keep going. She knew she wasn't as strong as Kirsten said she was. She would, once again, lose the will to live. And she wouldn't have Jason to keep her going.

If for no other reason than just sheer stubbornness, Nikki didn't want to just fade away again. Maybe the pain would go away, but then again, so would she. She had never been a quitter, and she didn't want to start now.

But something would have to give, and soon. She couldn't keep going on in this limbo forever.

Chapter Seventeen

Nikki's black SUV came to an abrupt halt when she took the final curve to her house. Wade's truck sat blocking the road, and he was leaning against the hood, hands buried in the pockets of a beat-up leather jacket—one she had bought their second Christmas together.

He still has it.

Blinking away the tears, Nikki shifted the SUV into park and rolled the window down as Wade approached. She had been home nearly six weeks and this was the closest she had been to him since that awful day late last summer.

The cold wind blew through the window, whipping her hair, stinging her eyes. It was blocked when Wade leaned against the door, propping his elbows in the window frame. He was silent for a long time, studying her.

"Hey," Wade said quietly. The words he had rehearsed left him when he got his first good look at her. *Dear Lord. She looks like a war refugee.* She was thin, unbelievably so. Her cheeks were hollow and the hands that gripped the steering wheel were pale and fragile looking. Her eyes looked unnaturally dark in her wan face.

Sourly, Wade decided her high society boyfriend in New York must like his woman scrawny.

Angry as he was, it wasn't as hard as he would have liked to make his voice sound hesitant and uncertain. Pleading. "Nikki." He cursed himself when his voice faltered of its own accord. His throat was tight as he said, "How...how've you been?"

"Well enough," Nikki replied. Wade didn't like just how easy, how steady her voice was. How could she sound normal when he was a mass of fury and pain inside? "You?"

"Awful," he said bluntly, hating that it was true. Hated that just seeing her made his wounded heart feel better.

"Is there—"

"Will you—"

They both spoke at once, then fell silent.

"You first," she offered. A slight smile edging up the corners of her mouth.

Wade took the chance, not wanting to give her opening to slip up the hill, into her house, away from him where she could lock the rest of the world out and remain hidden in her fortress. He steeled himself and reminded himself he had a job to do. Something that had to be done before he could get on with his life.

"I want to talk with you. Can you come for a ride with me?" he asked. Half of him shouted, *Say yes!* The other half begged, *Say no. Don't let me do this to you.*

Nikki shrugged and looked away. "You're welcome to come on up," she said, reaching for the gear shift.

"I'd rather you come with me. I..." Letting his voice trail off, he gazed at her with hot eyes. "I really don't need to be alone in that house with you, Nik. Not just yet."

He didn't tell her he didn't want to be in that house. A house where she had raised her son. A house where she might have welcomed her son's father, her lover. A house where he had never been welcomed.

185

Blood rushed to her face as he stared at her, and he could all but feel the heat that was rushing through her body as she shifted on the seat. She was going to refuse. Wade could see it in her eyes. Telling himself he had to convince her, he gave in to the urge to touch her, just brush his hand across her cheek. He was just trying to get her to go with him. That was all. If he satisfied this crazy urge to touch her, so what?

So soft, he wondered. *So cool, silky.* "Please," he implored, willing to beg if that was what it took.

Her eyes widened before flickering shut. Without moving, she seemed to arch closer against his feather-light caress. And then as if somebody had turned off a light, she shut down, locked herself back in.

"All right," she said quietly. "I can't be gone long though. I've got a lot to get done."

He backed away without answering. "I'll follow you up," he said softly. And then he turned on his heel.

Soon. In a few more days she would be out of his life. And hopefully out of his heart.

He certainly would not be in hers. She was going to hate him, very shortly.

The very thought twisted his guts, tightened his throat until he could barely breathe. Scowling, he reminded himself it didn't matter if she hated him.

But he knew he was lying.

He frowned as she climbed out of the Explorer. His eyes locked on her slight figure, clearly outlined by navy jeans. Why in the hell had she lost so much weight? Whoever he was—and Wade had no doubt that there was a he—he must like his woman all skin and bone.

Wade couldn't help but wonder if it was the father of the baby. Maybe she had been in New York with him all this time. Maybe...

With a growl, Wade stopped that thought before it could fully form. Nikki had come to a halt outside his truck and was eyeing him uncertainly. Her purse was slung over one shoulder, hands tucked into the pockets of her trench coat. Wade forced a smile that felt as though it would crack his face as he swung out of the truck.

She moved slowly, tiredly. Probably wasn't eating enough to keep a bird alive.

Well, her appetite would be roused over the next few days. He would take her to bed until she couldn't take him any more. He intended to mark her, brand her as his, so that for the rest of her life, she would never be able to look at another man for want of him.

He would use that sleek body until he had her out of his system.

And then he was going to walk away.

Nikki eyed Wade, her uneasiness growing by leaps and bounds. It had merely been a seed when she had climbed into the truck. Wade wouldn't hurt her physically and she had taken everything else he had dished out. She would be fine.

But they had been driving for well over two hours. And Wade hadn't made a single sound other than a noncommittal grunt from time to time. As the highway sped on by, she forced herself to speak. "Wade," she said, striving for a light tone. "I know you are a man of few words, but this is a record even for you. How are we supposed to talk when you won't even open your mouth?"

Wade merely sent a sidelong look she couldn't decipher and drove on.

"Wade, what's going on?" she asked flatly, crossing her arms over her chest as he turned off the main highway onto a side road.

"I figured we needed to clear the air," he finally said.

Minutes passed and he said nothing else, so Nikki sighed and again spoke. "Is there some reason we can't do that in Monticello?" she prodded.

By now they were on a road that was little more than a gravel path and he didn't take his eyes off of her as he drove on. "I didn't want to do it in your house. Too easy for you to kick me out there," he said, shrugging his shoulders.

He fell back into silence without another word. But there was something in his eyes that bothered her, something that had her belly drawn into a tight knot, something that got tighter with every mile that passed. Silent, she stared out the window as he followed that country road, taking another one that spiraled upward.

They were in the mountains now. Through the occasional break in trees she could see the Smokies soaring into the sky, their peaks shrouded by low-hanging clouds.

Stifling a shiver, she leaned back in the seat, wishing she had listened to her gut when it had insisted she not go with him.

And fighting off the fear that she really hadn't had a choice.

Out of the corner of his eye nearly an hour later, Wade watched her shift in the seat. Her face had become paler and paler as they drove farther. They hadn't seen a car in nearly two hours. This rutted dirt road would eventually end some twenty miles ahead, if he was going the right way.

If she sat up much straighter, her spine was going to crack from the strain and she was as pale as death. Scared. Sighing, he edged his truck as far off the narrow road as he could. Scaring her wasn't what he wanted. He wanted some payback for all the guilt she'd laid on him, and he wanted to prove to himself he could get her out of his system...and shit, he just plain wanted her, a few days with her. But no, he didn't want to scare her.

As he turned to face her, he turned up the heat. It was twenty degrees out and the nearest town was more than seventy miles back. One thing was certain, she was stuck with him until he decided otherwise.

With one arm draped across the steering wheel, the other across the back of the bench seat, he looked at her. Again, it struck him how wan she looked. She looked weak, fragile. In all the time he had known her she had never looked like that. He hadn't thought she could look like that.

But she did. She looked as though a breeze would knock her down. The emptiness in her eyes pulled at his heart and the words seemed pulled from there as he whispered, "Damnation, I've missed you."

Startled, Nikki turned her head to look at him. Her wary eyes skittered away and she shrugged as she said softly, "I don't know why. You said yourself you were tired of waiting around for me."

It wasn't as hard as it should have been to summon up a sheepish, sorry look. "We need to talk about that," he muttered. Reaching out, he trailed his finger down her cheek before hooking the back of her neck and drawing her closer. He closed his eyes and breathed in her scent.

That unforgettable scent drew him, lured him closer, tempted and taunted him. He counted to ten, then twenty as he reached for control.

He buried his face against her neck, basking in her warmth, softness. Control never seemed further away. "But we'll talk later," he muttered and dragged her across the seat to drape awkwardly across his lap.

Expecting her to go rigid, to say no.

But she didn't. She went willingly, almost eagerly into his

arms, her body shuddering violently as it came in contact with his. He instinctively realized she wouldn't back away this time.

Slanting his mouth across hers, he released the frustration and yearning that had been building for weeks, months. Years.

Whimpering deep in her throat, Nikki arched upward, straining against him. Her arms locked around his neck, her hands dipped into his hair and fisted.

With a few quick, economical motions, Wade divested her of her jacket and flannel shirt. Her slight weight was ridiculously easy to maneuver as he shifted, repositioning her so that she sat astride him, the steering wheel at her back.

A gasp fell from her lips when he touched her, and he watched as her eyes lit from within. That sleek ivory flesh felt so soft under his hands, so warm.

Greedy, he buried his hands in the short curls at the nape of her neck, arching her mouth up to his.

Through the thick cotton of his sweater, he felt her nails biting into his skin. A hungry little whimper fell from her lips as he traced a line of kisses down her neck, raking the sensitive skin there with his teeth.

"Wade," she moaned, and he felt her entire body shiver under his hands. His cock ached and throbbed, and as she started to rock against him, he thought he'd leap right out of his skin.

"Damn it," he hissed, lifting her slightly, moving away from that sweet, hot heat between her thighs. Through the thin silk of her bra her nipples beckoned, hard dark little circles he was dying to have in his mouth again.

He was having a hard time focusing on his plans when she was plastered against him, her mouth hot on his, her tongue dancing in his mouth, her body wrapped around his like a kudzu vine. Cursing the tight confines of the cab, he twisted and shifted until she lay beneath him.

Her hands clutched at his shoulders. Her hips rocked against his. Wade swore he could feel the heat of her right through their clothes. Too many clothes. Wrenching away, he drew to his knees to remedy that.

The silk and lace of her bra opened at a flick of his hand, the cups falling aside to reveal round firm breasts with rose-brown nipples already erect. Rolling them between his fingers, he watched though slitted eyes as she arched up, panting. Giving in to the urge, Wade lowered his head to nip and suck and suckle until she was mewing beneath him, whimpering deep in her throat.

He tore at the laces of her hiking boots until he could tug them off, then he reached for the waist of the slim fitting jeans she wore, pulling them down with quick, impatient jerks of his hands.

As he revealed her sleek body to his eyes, he stopped and stared. The thin, pale woman before him was like nothing compared to the woman he remembered. Pale flesh, concave abdomen.

Wade gazed at her, torn between lust and disbelief. He could count her ribs.

Bitterly, he reminded himself that girl didn't exist anymore. Probably never did. Hooking his fingers in the lacy front panel of her panties, he jerked hard, shredding the fragile material, tossing it aside.

Levering himself fully clothed over her, Wade cupped her face in his hands, covered her mouth with his. He kissed her deeply, stroking the sweet hollow of her mouth as she wrapped her arms around him and held him close.

Closing her eyes, Nikki basked in the warmth of his body and shuddered at the slow, teasing touch of his hand as it stroked from armpit to waist and back again. On each stroke, his hand wandered lower, fingers searching, seeking, gentle. It was a direct contrast with his hard, determined mouth as it pressed one biting kiss after another to her mouth, her neck and her breasts. Her breath caught in her throat and her lids drifted partly shut when he caught one pearled nipple between his teeth, bit down gently, then swirled his tongue across, easing the slight hurt.

Stroke after teasing stroke, he circled around her nipple now, nipping at the underside, blowing a cool puff of air across it, nuzzled it while lower, his hand eased closer and closer.

His hands became greedy, demanding.

Rough denim rubbed against the tender flesh of her inner thighs, rasped sensitive nerves as he shifted slightly to give that roaming hand easy access. One long, callused finger parted her, slid across the damp portal while his thumb flickered across the hardened pebble of flesh.

"Wade," she gasped, her hands reaching for his, tugging. Her eyes were nearly blind with need, her weakened heart pounding in her chest, strong and sure.

Nikki's eyes fluttered open, locked on his intent face. His eyes glittered fiercely, his jaw tight. And she shivered. She recognized his touch. Her body recognized his, but she didn't know this man, this hard-faced, grim stranger.

Something cold settled low in her belly, warring with the heat. A flash of fear fluttered in her chest. She was deeply aware of the feeling that something wasn't right, something was off.

Unconsciously, she raised one arm to shield her body while the other went out, pressing to his chest, whether to stay him or drawn him close, she didn't know.

A muscle spasmed in his cheek and he slid his hands over her thighs, draped them over his.

"Wade," she whispered, distraught, nervous, almost afraid.

His eyes locked on hers, dark and relentless. And angry, she thought. Determination oozed from every pore of his body and she was certain he meant to do this, whether she was willing or not. He was intent on something he seemed to need.

He buried his face against her neck, held her tightly against him. His voice nearly breaking, he asked "Don't you want me anymore, Nikki?"

Wade didn't recognize his own voice, the need in it. He only knew he had to do this, had to have her. He couldn't live another minute if he didn't mark her, brand her as his and erase the touch of another man's with his. If he didn't ease the ache that had been building for five years... God, she had to want to him. He would die if she stopped him.

He didn't hear the need, but she did. It roared through her like a tornado, destroying all resistance.

Beneath him her arms closed around him, shielding him against something she couldn't see, but sensed. Her eyes closed. *Not want you?* she thought desperately. *My God. A day hasn't gone by that I haven't wanted you.*

She didn't even realize she had spoken out loud, but Wade heard her words, heard the truth in them, and shuddered. He stiffened, his eyes tightly closed as her words echoed in his mind. The absolute sincerity in her words, in her eyes, soothed a thousand hurts, and caused a million more to take their place.

She'd gone to another man... Like a freight train, one thought after another rammed into his head, a hard fist of nausea closing around his stomach until he thought he would vomit. Another man had seen this, had touched her like this, felt the wet tight embrace of her body.

Hands that had unconsciously gentled went hard as unspoken pleas turned to demands. Covering her body once more with his, Wade moved closer until his sex nudged her damp flesh. One hand moved to guide him in while he propped

193

his weight on the other elbow. With one heavy thrust, he buried himself inside her.

She flinched, arching up against him with a weak whimper, her eyes wide and dark as the sharp discomfort bordered on pain. Her body recoiled from the rough, sudden invasion.

The movement didn't slow him, didn't deter him. She was wet and hot, but his entry was difficult, for her tight flesh resisted him. She was wet, hot and hungry...but her sheath was so tight... He flexed his hips, pushing deeper until he was sheathed to the hilt.

Her flesh rippled around his, alternately clenching and relaxing. As her muscles worked to accommodate him, he wondered at it. *She's so tight.*

And one thing was certain. Whatever she had been doing in New York, she had not been with another man.

Her eyes opened slowly, her lips parted as she took rapid shallow breaths. She stared up at him, her face flushed with need.

"Are you okay?" he asked roughly, forcing his body to wait. At her nod he dipped his head, planted a sweet gentle kiss on her damp mouth. Weight braced on his elbows, he began rocking against her, his thrusts slow and gentle. With each steady thrust, her body opened, relaxed, welcoming his instead of resisting. Silky hot tissues gripped at his sex as he pulled away, hugging him tight as he buried his length back inside her.

Raining kisses over her face, he crooned against her ear, coaxing, praising, pleading. "You feel so damn good, baby," he whispered.

Beneath him she tossed her head back, staring at him. He shuddered as she wrapped her legs around him, holding him tight, as though she never intended to let go. And he was holding back. She held his eyes, arched up, trying to take him deeper, but he stilled her movements by pinning her hips with his own.

Wade's body tensed as she clamped those silken little muscles around his cock, released, then did it again. "Wade, please," she whispered.

"Easy," he crooned in her ear, using one hand to hold her still as he pulled back, nearly withdrawing. "We've got a lot of time to make up for."

And slowly he entered her. Gave her an inch, then pulled back. Slid a little deeper that time, not so deep next. All the way in this time, then so far back only the tip of his head remained within her. Clamping a tight rein on his lust, he filled his sight with the picture she presented. Eyes dark with passion and need, lips swollen and red from his, legs spread wide to receive him. Dipping his head, he asked, "Do you want me?"

"Yes," she gasped when he nipped at her neck.

"How much?" he demanded, shaking his head to clear his vision.

"More than anything," she whispered, reaching down to cup his buttocks, draw him more firmly against her, trying to keep him from pulling back, from pulling away.

He caught her hands, pinned them beside her head. Then he slowly rotated his hips against hers, ducking his head to suckle at her breast. His voice was muffled as he asked, "More than everything?"

"Yes," she whispered.

He stared into her eyes as she arched up, taking him in just the slightest bit deeper. "More than everything. It's always been like that."

"Always?" he repeated, lifting his head and resting his chin between her breasts as he stared at her.

She opened her heavy-lidded eyes, stared into his. Those soft hazel eyes were open and naked with her need. "Always,"

195

she whispered.

"Always," she repeated softly. "Even when you were no longer mine."

Shaking, he sank deep within her and hooked his arms under hers, cupping her face in his hands as he gently took her mouth. He held his body still within hers as he loved her mouth endlessly. Her inner muscles rippled around his shaft and he pulled back. His tongue stroked over hers, plunged deep, withdrew from her mouth to nip her lip, nuzzle her cheek, then he pulled back slowly, studying her with searching eyes.

His gaze landed on the faint scars at her left brow. And they reminded him. Deliberately, he dredged up hated thoughts of her with another.

It gave him strength, control, reminded him of why he was here. He wanted her to know, she had to know, what it felt like to have your heart shatter within your chest. She had to know. And he had to make her feel it.

But it wasn't easy. She flexed around him, her sheath like hot wet silk. He eased deeper, slowly inch by inch, until he rested against the mouth of her womb. Slowly, he withdrew, eased back, pulled back until they were nearly separated. He remembered how empty he felt, how his heart had fallen to pieces. Shattered.

He thrust hard and deep, held himself there and asked, "And what about when you were no longer mine?"

His heart froze within his chest as those beautiful eyes flooded with tears. It resumed beating, fast and furious as she reached up, cupping his cheek in her hand. Brokenly, she whispered, "I've always been yours."

He shuddered, unable to move as her words rippled over him. Wade felt his throat close, threatening to choke him. His heart swelled so that his chest ached as badly as his sex.

Instead of shattering her, she had shattered him.

Looking into those tear-drenched eyes, he saw the truth there. Whatever had happened in the weeks after she had left him hadn't changed how she felt in her heart.

In her heart she was and always had been his.

And this pointless game of domination seemed childish. Shamed, he hung his head as her words whispered over in his head and heart.

"You always will be," he promised, cupping her hips in his hands and driving himself home.

His hips pumped harder and harder until he was lifting her on the seat with each thrust. She pulsed around him. As her body arched up, her pebbled nipples came in contact with his chest, leaving trails of sensation. The base of his spine tingled and he felt his testicles drawing in tighter to his body.

Harder and harder he moved, tightening some coil deep within.

In a broken litany, Nikki whispered to him, "Not enough...please...love you...Wade..."

The words made little sense aloud, but he understood, adjusting his position so he could slide a hand between her thighs and circle his thumb around the tiny bud of nerves, He edged closer and closer until with one sudden movement, he pressed down hard, firm.

A sharp startled cry left her lips, echoing through his body like a jolt of lightning, while her snug channel clamped tight around his sex, her flesh becoming even hotter, wetter as she screamed out his name.

She convulsed around him, sinking her teeth into his shoulder just as he emptied within her. A low groan left him as her hips pumped against his, her body trembling. His body jerked as he withdrew and plunged deep one last time. Held himself there as her body milked his.

Damnation.

Chapter Eighteen

Nikki slept quietly, curled up against his side. The rough ride didn't disturb her, nor did the silence of the man next to her. She was unaware of his indecision, of his dilemma as she enjoyed the first sound sleep she'd had in months.

Wade felt her warmth against his side as he steered the truck over rough, uneven terrain. She slept as peacefully as Abby did at night. The way he hadn't slept in years.

What in the hell am I doing out here? he wondered.

His shattered heart and bruised pride were calling out for something. She had played him for a fool. She'd misled him, all but lied to him—that knife she'd twisted in his gut. Many times she'd thrown his past mistakes at him and let him think that was why she was so miserable, but it wasn't *him*... It was the loss of her son.

Shit. Her son.

Fuck, what was he doing?

What would he do if he'd lost Abby? It just might kill him.

The pain alone would drive him to the edge.

But she kept twisting the knife like everything wrong in her life was *his* fault, and it wasn't.

She'd played him for an idiot all this time, made him believe he was the reason she was so miserable. That was simply how he saw it. She had purposefully led him to believe there was no other man in her life, had claimed that even when her eyes had been black with passion just a short while ago in the cab of this very truck.

Hell, he could still smell the musky scent of sweat, sex and woman in the air. *Her* scent still clung to him, stirring his flesh even as he damned himself for wanting her so badly.

He hurt for what she'd lost, and at the same time he was so blind with jealousy, so pissed she'd lied, he couldn't see straight.

Could he live the rest of his life knowing she had given away what he felt was *his*?

But it wasn't... She wasn't, a voice inside him whispered. *You lost her. You lost any right to her.* Logically, that made sense.

But logic wasn't holding much weight here.

He couldn't get past it.

Did he want it to go unpunished, all the times he had seen the light in Abby's eyes extinguished by a cool word or look? Nikki hadn't ever been cruel, but Abby's sweet, childish attempts to befriend Nikki had all been ignored, and Abby had sensed in her heart that Nikki rejected her.

No. Steeling himself, locking his jaw, he told himself, *You have to do this.* He had to get her out of his system. Once and for all.

He pulled up in front of the cabin some twenty minutes later. It was cold out already and the sun hadn't even started to set. He shook the sleeping woman awake instead of kissing her awake the way he wanted to. He couldn't give in to the urge to cuddle her close, hold her tight.

Wade would learn to live without that. He would have to.

Nikki came awake slowly, reluctantly. Damn it all. She didn't want to wake up. Her sleep had been peaceful and dreamless. Her body was warm and relaxed, sated.

Her mind, however, was puzzled. Her eyes scanned over unfamiliar territory and a frown wrinkled her brow. She looked over to see Wade staring moodily at the front of a little cabin.

"Where are we?" she asked, her voice husky from sleep.

She barely heard his terse reply, for her eyes had fallen on the clock. It was nearly six. They had been driving for four hours. Well, not all of the time had been spent driving, she realized, a dull flush creeping up her neck.

It faded quickly as she climbed out of the truck. His answer had just sunk in enough for her to grasp what he had said. But she must have misheard.

"Exactly what are we doing in Gatlinburg?" she asked, pulling her coat closed over her chest. Damn it, it was cold.

He paused in the middle of unloading boxes from underneath the bed cover. His eyes were solemn, his mouth a tight narrow line.

"Settling things," he finally said after staring long and hard into her eyes for what seemed like an eternity.

"Why here?" she asked, baffled.

He didn't answer, but she didn't notice right away as her mind finally started functioning."Why here?" She held her hands out, palms up in the age-old gesture of confusion.

"Because here you can't kick me out of the house or walk away from me. Because here, your damn brothers can't interfere, nor can anybody else. We're on equal ground here and I'll have my say," Wade said, facing her over the bed of the truck.

"You did that a few months ago," she reminded quietly, remembered pain darkening her eyes.

"That was anger, not me." He took a box from the truck and shoved it into her arms.

Automatically, Nikki took it and dimly noted that it was full of food. She frowned at it while she studied him, trying to fit the pieces together in her head. It wasn't easy—her brain was still addled from sleep and sex. She realized he had planned this. Very thoroughly planned it. Finally, she asked, "Are you saying you're not angry now?"

Unreadable brown eyes met hers. Softly, truthfully, he said, "No. I am not angry." He was hurting. He was desperate. He was unbelievably confused, he was insanely jealous and he was furious. Anger didn't come close to describing what he was feeling now.

He took the box from her, dropped it to the ground, then moved closer until his toes nudged hers and she had to tip her head back to meet his eyes. He cupped her chin in his hand, studying her face.

She stiffened when his fingers traced over the scars nearly hidden at her hairline, but the questions didn't come. His mouth spasmed once before it drew tight into a frown. "We're going to settle this," he repeated, his voice firm. Then he released her, took up a couple of boxes and walked away.

She shivered deep inside.

Why had that sounded so much like "end this"?

She cast a look around the isolated cabin, then glanced at her purse and checked the time. As far as being kidnapped went, she actually had luck on her side. She'd gone into town because she needed to get her prescription refilled—she had her medicine with her, thank God.

She could get Wade to drive her back home if she had to, just by explaining she needed the drugs. But she didn't want him knowing about it yet. Or why.

In her gut though, she realized she was probably running out of time.

He was going to find out soon.

She needed to lay things out for him.

Just tell him, all of it.

Canned stew and biscuits were on the menu for that night. Nikki sat in her chair, quiet. Wade frowned as she continued to push the food around on her plate. She had eaten exactly four small bites. Three minutes passed and he watched as she took another four small bites. Three more minutes passed and she ate four more bites.

The last bite had been ten minutes ago and he watched as she pushed the food around on the plate with her fork.

She glanced up at him, caught him watching her. She attempted a smile, but it fell short of being successful as she said, "Dad bought a cabin up here a few years ago. I've never gone to it, but my brothers come out a lot in the winter to go ice fishing or hunting. And Dad practically lives there during the summer."

Wade's only answer was an unintelligible grunt. He continued to stare at her, scowling when she laid her fork down and closed her hands around her glass, staring into it as though the sweetened iced tea held the answers to all of life's problems.

Wade's own appetite was somewhat diminished. Guilt was a living breathing thing. It had a taste, a feel, a smell to it all its own. It filled his belly until there was no room for food.

He insisted to himself once more that he had nothing to feel guilty about. He was simply settling the score. She was the one who had lied and betrayed.

She's also the one who had to bury her baby, his conscience whispered.

She lied to me, led me to believe one thing while something else was the truth. She betrayed me.

Didn't you betray her first? What did you expect her to do? Join a convent?

Wade forced himself to take deep, slow, steadying breath. Now he was arguing with himself. A sure sign of impending mental breakdown. He forced his normally rigid self-discipline into place as he reminded himself he had a job to do.

Forcing the guilt aside, swallowing its bitter taste, he studied her skinny frame.

"You need to eat more," he told her as he popped the last piece of biscuit in his mouth. He chewed and swallowed, drank some tea, staring at her the entire time.

A disinterested shrug was his only answer, so he repeated himself.

Her eyes met his and she calmly said, "I'm not hungry."

No. He didn't imagine she was. After damn near starving herself, food probably wasn't even an afterthought for her anymore. She looked so pale and tired. Her cheeks were hollow, large half-moons bruising the delicate skin under her eyes. The bones of wrists and elbows pushed sharply against soft flesh.

And he'd be damned if he would let her go to waste all because some fancy suit in New York wanted her looking like a scarecrow.

"You can either eat, or I'll shove it down your throat," he offered.

She merely arched an eloquent eyebrow at him. "You do that and I'll just throw it back up. And assuming I don't beat you bloody while you attempt it, you can rest assured I'll do it when I'm done puking. I told you I'm not hungry."

Bluntly, he informed her, "You look like hell. You're pale, exhausted. Your cheekbones stick out so much it is a wonder they don't cut right through your skin. You look like the poster child for world hunger."

She smiled slightly and shrugged yet again. "I doubt I look

all that bad. I eat a good meal on a regular basis."

"Regular as in regularly once a week?" he bit out.

"Regularly as in three times a day. I just don't eat as much as I should. I was just eating about once a day, but I got fussed at. So I eat three times a day, just like a normal person."

Once a day? Wade thought incredulously. *Once a day?*

Narrowing his eyes, he asked, "How often do you ride?"

"Generally three or four times a week," she said, shrugging.

"How long?"

"Depends. Sometimes I'll just do four or five miles, sometimes ten or twelve. Rarely, I'll go longer."

"So you spend a minimum of thirty minutes, on average, riding three or four times a week, sometimes longer, and you think eating once *a fucking day* is enough?"

"I said I *was* eating about once day. I eat three times a day usually. I had breakfast and I had lunch." She glanced at the plate and said, "And that counts as dinner."

Wade snorted. "That barely counts as a snack. You ate twelve damn bites of food. That is *not* a meal."

Nikki just stared at him.

"Why are you doing this to yourself?" he demanded, shoving his chair from the table. "You have no spare flesh on you. You're nothing more than skin and bone. Hell, I can practically see right through you."

Her shoulders moved restlessly as her eyes roamed around the room. "I'm taking care of myself. I just don't ever have an appetite anymore. I'm only a few pounds under my ideal body weight. I can't help it that I'm not hungry anymore."

A few pounds my ass, Wade thought. Though she wasn't at all tall, her frame was hardly a delicate one. She had broad shoulders, broad hips. Sturdy muscle and strong bones made up her body. He'd bet his next paycheck she was at least twenty pounds under what she should be.

And it sickened him to think she might be doing this to herself to please some man. It made him furious to see that damn blank look on her face, as though she were staring through him. As though they hadn't just had explosive sex in the front seat of his truck a few hours earlier.

Narrowing his eyes, he decided maybe she needed a reminder. Damn it to hell, she wouldn't look through him. Not anymore. His eyes focused on her face, then her mouth as he said, "You always used to be...hungry."

Her eyes darted to his, then skittered away as he rose. This cabin, Nikki realized, was damn small. Climbing to her feet, she circled the table, eying the space around her.

The cabin consisted of one room that was for eating, cooking and sleeping. A large king-size bed took up a good portion of space. Only one bed. A lumpy looking sofa. The tiny little bathroom didn't even have a lock on the door.

He closed in on her, lessening the space between them even as she tried desperately to widen it. His eyes ran over her, mentally removing every stitch of clothing from her hide as he offered, "Let's see what I can do about whetting your appetite. Maybe all you need is some strenuous activity."

"Wade, this isn't exactly what I would call settling things," she said, her voice placating even as her eyes darted about, looking for an escape route that didn't exist. "I thought we were here to talk."

"We've talked. We've settled nothing. Let's try a different sort of communication," he whispered as he walked her up against the wall. "You've run out of room, Nikki. No place left to go." His eyes lit with unholy glee as he added, "No place left to hide."

His voice rasped like a callused hand over smooth silk. A shudder racked her from head to toe as his arms came up to rest beside her head, bracketing her between the wall and his body. She swallowed and hoped her voice would be steady. "I'm not hiding from you, Wade. If I wanted to hide, I wouldn't have gotten into the truck with you."

"Why did you?" he asked, lowering his head until they were nose to nose, mouth to mouth, his body heat reaching out to warm her from only inches away.

"I thought we were going to talk," she said faintly, arching her head back, trying to maintain a little bit of distance.

"We will. Eventually," Wade whispered, following her retreating mouth with his own.

"Wade—"

He cut her off with a soft, slow kiss that had her blood sizzling its way throughout her body. "We've always communicated so much better when we didn't use our mouths to talk," he murmured as he pulled his mouth from hers, lowering his head to nuzzle at her neck.

As his hot mouth blazed a trail down her neck, Nikki stifled a whimper by biting the inside of her cheek. He moved closer and closer until she was caught between a hard male body and the rough wooden wall at her back.

"Wade," she said shakily. Squirming weakly, she tried to loosen his hold. "Wade, this is not going to solve anything." The last word ended on a gasp as she tried to suck in much needed air.

"Yes," he countered, his voice guttural. "It will. Damn it, woman. I should have done this from the beginning. We get along fine as long as you aren't thinking." His dark head dipped as he spoke, so that the final words were spoken against her mouth. His tongue thrust between her lips, past her teeth, to steal the air from her body.

Hot hands moved down her torso, to her hips, sliding beneath the waistband of her jeans, shoving the material out of the way. Her boots, never tied from the first time in the truck, fell easily from her feet as he lifted her, pinning her body to the wall with his own. One jean-clad leg came between hers and he bent his knee, bringing it in contact with her exposed flesh.

Planting his foot in the crotch of her jeans, he shoved them the rest of the way down, kicking them away in a tangle. His hand came up between them, hooked in the neck of her sturdy button down flannel. Nikki felt a hard jerk as he rent it down the middle. Buttons went flying as he lifted her up, moved between her dangling legs and closed his mouth around a lace-covered nipple.

Slowly, oh, so slowly, he eased his hold until her weight came down. Nikki gasped as it brought her up against his groin. The rough material of his jeans chafed against the inside of her thighs as she arched her hips and shuddered, trying desperately to get closer.

And then she was. He freed his erection from the confines of his jeans and then adjusted her position. Wade slowed his hands as one hand strayed to the juncture of her thighs, tested her flesh. "I don't want to hurt you," he murmured.

"Wade," she whimpered, rubbing against him, pleading.

Moisture flooded his hand and hot satisfaction gleamed in his eyes as he petted the slick flesh with a feathery light touch. He shifted, grasped her hips and filled her as his name fell from her mouth in a rippling gasp. She was still so tight. His hands went to her buttocks and cupped them as he worked her up and down.

Her legs closed around his hips like a vise while she panted and twisted her hips until he buried himself to the hilt with a groan.

Flesh slid against flesh. Stifled mews of pleasure and whispered exclamations filled the air. His hips hammered against hers, her hot tight flesh rippling around him. She arched back with a gasp as inner convulsions started, caressing his shaft until he thought he would go mad with the pleasure of it.

With a muttered oath, he pushed away from the wall and stumbled the three feet to the bed. He came down on top of her and thrust violently into her once before pulling out, away from her clinging hands.

Wade put his mouth against her, tasting the spicy sweet tang of her as she climaxed against his mouth and hands. He rose and stared down at her, his chest heaving, while he waited for her to calm.

Her breathing started to slow and sense began to gather within her eyes. He wanted to watch her eyes go blind again. He stripped off his shirt, came down on her and drove in. He pushed her quickly toward another orgasm, had her hovering on the brink, then changed his rhythm and withheld it from her. He shuddered when she locked her arms around his neck, gasped his name and pleaded with him.

Beneath him Nikki clenched tightly around his cock, her flesh convulsing, her nails digging into the ridge of muscles at his shoulders. "Wade, oh, Wade, please," she whimpered, her head thrashing back and forth.

"Nobody else can make you feel like this," he rasped against her ear, settling into a hard driving rhythm.

Her hips bucked against his as he thrust against her, driving deep within the wet well of her body. One hand raced down, cupped her buttocks and squeezed, his fingers digging into the soft flesh, the dark crevice. "Nobody," he repeated, thickly.

She screamed, her eyes blank as a massive orgasm ripped through her, leaving her weak and shuddering as Wade, savagely triumphant, found his own release. Closing his eyes, he anchored her hips against his, rode it through to the very end as her body milked his, demanding everything he had to give.

With a shudder, Wade collapsed against her, body numb from pleasure. Mind numb from shock. And his heart was aching.

His name. She had screamed and whispered his name as her flesh had shuddered and heaved around his. And right before a sob had torn through her, Nikki had gasped out, "I love you."

Ragged breaths sawing in and out of him, Wade closed his eyes, now in despair.

Because Wade Lightfoot had finally realized that no matter what he did, or what she did, it wasn't the end of things. Nothing would ever completely end things.

Because he would never be free of her.

She wore a wristwatch that had a damned annoying alarm, Wade realized. It went off at ten o'clock, and he watched as a dull blush stained her cheeks red, watched as she clambered out of his bed and fumbled with the watch, silencing the alarm.

"What's that for?" he asked.

"A reminder," she said, forcing a smile. She grabbed her purse and disappeared into the bathroom while he sat in the bed brooding.

When she returned to the bed, sans the watch and wearing nothing but the rather battered shirt from earlier, he took her in his arms, held her close. His mind raced and spun in dizzying circles.

Damn it.

What in the hell was he supposed do now?

The cabin was dark, lit only by the fire. She was cuddled close to him, warm, soft, everything he held dear. Turning lambent eyes to his, she smiled and her lids lowered slowly, closing, before opening to reveal something that made his blood run hot. As he struggled to find his tongue, Nikki shifted and straddled him.

Her shirt fell away with a graceful shrug of her shoulders, revealing skin made golden by the firelight. As it flickered and danced, highlighting hollows and curves, Nikki skimmed hands up her sides, licked her lips and whispered against his mouth, "I'm feeling...hungry."

He cracked a smile and found his voice as his hands reached up to close around her waist. "I've made a monster," he whispered. "You'll be the death of me." His eyes nearly crossed with pleasure when her talented fingers slipped below his waist, inside his jeans after making quick work of the zipper.

"I can't think of a better way to go," he admitted weakly as she closed her hand around him and she sank to her knees before him, lowering her head until the soft heat of her mouth enclosed the head of his cock.

Hours later Wade lay wide awake while she slept curled against his side.

What kind of monster have I become? he wondered.

The red haze that had clouded his mind and fogged his vision for weeks had suddenly and completely cleared, leaving him sick with guilt.

Wade had no claim on her, had lost all rights the minute he had gone to bed with Jamie.

God above, she had lost her baby. It bore too much pain to think of—he couldn't imagine losing his little girl. He wouldn't have wanted to live.

Who in the hell was he to blame her for anything? To want any kind of retribution. Any imagined slight was nothing compared to the agony she must have gone through. Yeah, she might have used him as a punching bag, lashing out at him, but so fucking what? She'd told him to keep his distance and when that hadn't worked she'd used whatever weapons she had—the most efficient being the guilt he still had over what he'd done to her.

Slowly, carefully, Wade rose, slipping from the bed, not wanting to disturb her. She looked so exhausted, needed her rest so badly. He got dressed and headed for the door, pausing long enough to slip his feet in battered work boots. Cold air hit his face and chest as he headed for the railing of the tiny porch deck.

What in the hell was I thinking?

If he could reach his own ass he would kick it from here to Tokyo. Slumping against the rail, he called himself every name he knew, berated himself for being such a fool. Then he repeated himself. Twice.

Nikki had lied to him by omission, and she had misled him all these weeks, not telling him about her son, letting him think he was the reason she'd been so miserable all these years. But considering the grief she lived with he couldn't blame her for not wanting to talk about it.

Plus, she'd warned him. More than once, she'd told him to leave her alone. To leave her be. And she had meant it. It had all been done out of self-defense in effort to protect herself from further pain. From letting him cause her any more pain. From letting *life* cause her any more pain.

It kept kicking her anyway.

When he'd first seen her, all those months ago, the last thing he'd thought he'd ever do was hurt her again...and look at him. Look where he was, what he'd done.

He remembered how she flinched, how her body had tried to retreat from his, and he could still see the flash of pain in her dark eyes when he had entered her that first time.

And then his thoughts turned inward as he thought of the

hill by her family's home.

He knew exactly where the crash had happened. Had driven there, climbed from his truck and looked around, not expecting to see anything. But more than three years after it had happened, one could still see the path her truck had taken down the incline. Patches of bareness, branches broken off long ago due to impact with a large object. Metal, steel and earth weren't a pretty combination. He would know, considering how many accident victims he'd tried to keep alive over the years. Most often he succeeded, but often enough he failed.

She could have been killed. It was a miracle she and Shawn had escaped with their lives.

Nikki was so lucky to be alive.

And so miserable for being so. She had been grieving for far too long. Hurting over what he had done to her, then hurting because life had ripped her only child from her. She had told him, time after time, that she wasn't strong enough to handle it.

What had she said?

You can't make it up to me, her voice whispered in his mind as he remembered. *You have no idea how badly I was hurt, how much I lost.*

Nikki was right. He was completely clueless.

They were finished. He knew that. There was no way they could have a life together, not with all the anger and resentment that swirled in him, despite all his attempts to drown them. She may not know it, would not be expecting it because he had just told her in graphic detail that he wanted her back.

But there was no way he could stay.

Wade was selfish. He was a bastard, a Neanderthal, and he knew it. But it would eat him alive to stay here, trying to make it work, knowing she had been with another man. His jealousy would be like acid, eating away at him until one day when the poison would erupt and destroy everything in its path.

He wouldn't let his own anger, his own jealousy, hurt her again.

Never again.

His emotions were illogical, unjustified. But he knew it was a fact. Not liking it didn't make it any less true. Wishing it were otherwise couldn't change how he felt.

A numbness settled around his heart, growing until it encased his entire body. He could not possibly stay with her now. God only knew he'd hurt her enough already. What else was there left to do but leave her in peace? That was what she wanted to begin with.

Nikki came awake slowly, stretching her body and smiling at the pleasant aches that made themselves known. She didn't know exactly what was going on, but it was looking fairly promising.

Maybe they were going to get that second chance after all.

She hummed deep in her throat as she rolled to her back, hugging the pillow to her chest. Her eyes caught a motion outside and she turned her head.

Wade.

He stood outside, staring off into the distance, his head bent, shoulders slumped, looking utterly defeated. She had only seen him look like that two other times. That day he had come to her home after that fight in the grocery store parking lot over a boy whose face she barely remembered. And that day when she had learned about Jamie and the baby.

Dread filled her.

Nikki sat up slowly, tugging the blanket around her.

Maybe they were going to get a second chance.

But they were going to have to be honest with each other

first. Starting with her. Eventually Wade would find out about Jason. And if he found out from somebody other than her, it would ruin whatever they had made.

Her pleasure faded to a dim glow as she drew in a shuddering breath. How did one go about telling a man he had a child he had never known, and never would know? That the child had been killed in an accident years earlier?

Clutching the blanket tighter, Nikki was amazed to discover she felt relief beneath the dread. She was scared about his reaction, hated the pain she knew this would cause, but deep inside, she wanted to do this, had to do this. She wanted to tell Wade all about his little boy and she wanted to grieve with him.

But how did she tell him? How did she explain why she didn't tell him before now?

You're a writer. Finding the right words is what you do, Nikki reminded herself as she slid from the bed and stood.

Hopefully, when it was most important, she would be able to do just that.

"Wade?"

Her voice, soft and sleepy, came to him over the roaring in his ears. Unbelievably weary, he turned his head to see her standing in the doorway, the blanket clutched around her naked shoulders by a thin hand.

His voice rough, he said, "It's too cold out. You ought to be inside."

With a slight smile, Nikki glanced at him, from the bare feet tucked inside boots, to the naked chest revealed by his open shirt. "You're one to talk," she said, smiling at him. Then she held out her hand. "Come inside."

Slowly, his cold hand came up and closed over her warm one. Despising himself, hating himself, but unable to deny the need to be close to her, to be warm, for just a little while longer.

214

He was going to have to be without her soon enough.

He would need this time to get through the empty years ahead.

Nikki silently urged him onto the sofa, curling her body next to his. Wade buried his face in her hair, breathing her in, his arms locked tightly around her. It wasn't right. How could he have found her again, only to have barriers come between them that would be impossible to break? Barriers of *his* making, damn it all to hell.

"Wade, I think it's time we had that talk," Nikki said, breaking into his thoughts.

He raised his head automatically when she spoke but quickly lowered it again, mumbling something under his breath. Even he wasn't sure what it was he had said.

Quietly, Nikki told him, "There's some things you need to know, Wade. Things I should have told you months ago."

His body went rigid. *Now? Why is she going to tell me now?*

Over the pounding of his heart he realized she was speaking to him, and her words were slow, almost awkward. "I was in pretty rough shape after you told me about Jamie. A part of me died that day and I just lost interest in life. I wasn't interested in eating or writing or reading. All I wanted to do was sleep. So that's all I did for the longest time. I never went back to school, never did anything.

"I ended up selling my book, but Dylan kind of helped me through that. Got me through the mess of contracts, talked to a couple of agents, helped with everything. Hell, he could probably *be* an agent at this point. He handled so much for me.

"He was so damn proud of me. I wasn't all that concerned about it. When they read the third book I'd written in the *Chronicles* line, they offered me contracts and money on the spot. So I was able to buy Dad and them the house I'd always promised. I didn't much care, but I wanted to keep my

215

promises. Once we moved, all I did was wander around inside those four walls day in and day out." Her voice faded, growing distant as her eyes turned inward. "I was sort of fading away, losing weight, losing myself.

"You had married Jamie and I thought my life was over." She straightened, gently shrugging his arms away. Clutching the blanket around her shoulders, she rose and walked to stare out the window.

Wade could picture all too well what she was describing. It was the shadow of the woman he had found on the road several hours ago. Had somebody come along and taken away the loneliness for a little while?

Or God, no, had something else happened? Why in the hell hadn't he thought of that before now? Anything was possible, especially in that hellhole she had lived in. She was so small, and while she could most likely hold her own against a lone man, what could she do about a number of *men*?

He shook his head to clear his thoughts as she started to speak again.

"I was probably just a few months away from my own funeral. I had stopped eating. I hadn't taken a bath in God only knows how long," Nikki continued, one hand straying up to touch shiny strands of hair. "My hair was so filthy, so matted. I wonder how anybody was even able to tolerate being in the same room with me."

Eyes full of bemusement, Nikki turned to look at him. "And then I passed out. Right in front of my dad. He had been standing there, griping about what a mess his life was, how he couldn't find a job he liked, blah, blah, blah... The next thing I remember I was in the emergency department. I'd passed out and I woke up with needles in my arms, doctors all over me, monitors, and my dad is looking at me like he doesn't even recognize me."

She licked her lips and took another breath. "When he

finally got me home, he poured every drop of liquor he had down the drain and never touched another drop. I think he figured he was going to need to be sober just to keep me alive."

"What do you mean?" he asked.

She swallowed. "I was in bad shape. Really bad."

A grim look entered her eyes as she described just how bad. And slowly Wade began to realize that if she was telling the truth, and he knew she was, she couldn't have been out carousing with another man, erasing him with another man's touch.

A niggling little doubt was making itself at home in his mind, darting out of reach any time he tried to latch on to it.

"They did tests at the hospital—lots of them. I had to go see specialists. At first they thought I was anorexic and they were talking about counseling and various pharmaceutical treatments for depression.

"I had starved myself so badly my body was no longer doing what it was supposed to do. I'd developed an arrhythmia because my electrolyte levels were so badly out of whack. My blood pressure was erratic. My stomach had started to atrophy and I had to learn how to eat all over again. The doctor very bluntly told me that if I hadn't collapsed, if I hadn't somehow ended up in the emergency department when I did, it might have been too late."

A soft, shuddering sigh escaped her. "Another few weeks, I might have been dead, probably from a heart attack. I had damn near destroyed my heart. As it is, it can't function on its own any more." She wandered over and picked up her purse, pulling out a brown prescription bottle.

She tossed it to him and he caught it automatically.

He read the bottle and the bottom of his stomach fell out.

Lanoxin. Standard medicine...and the sort of medicine somebody could die without. Oh, God.

217

"I'll probably be on heart medication for the rest of my life."

Wade had long since gone cold, was staring at her in some numb kind of shock. She wouldn't have let that happen, not over what he had done.

"You were stronger than that," he said, his voice harsh, half-broken. "You were always stronger than that. You wouldn't have done that to yourself. Not over *me*, damn it."

"You don't get it, Wade." Sadly, Nikki just stared at him and shook her head. "I wasn't *me* anymore. The girl you knew wasn't there anymore. I had let her go, and ended up getting lost inside myself. I couldn't find my way back."

She paused long enough to take a deep, shaking breath before meeting his eyes. "And that wasn't all. Bad enough that my heart was a wreck and my body was about ready to shut down. A complete physical for a woman of child bearing age includes a pregnancy test. They had almost forgotten it since it was so highly unlikely considering my condition. But...but they were wrong. I was four months pregnant, Wade."

January... She said January... Four months pregnant... It had happened in August. His heart simply stopped beating. He stared at her, dismayed and deeply shocked for the longest time. Pregnant. Four months pregnant. "How?"

"That last time in the woods." She turned away now, resting her forehead against the cold pane of glass while she struggled to speak around the knot in her throat. "By all things logical, there was no reason for me to have carried the baby that long. It was deprived of everything that was so important during the first few months. A miracle from God is the only way I can explain it. I'd lost you, but He had given me something else to hold onto. And that saved my life."

Nikki dashed away a tear with the back of her hand, started to drop her hand and then she paused, studying it, seeing how thin and pale it was, realizing how very weak she had become. How tired. She was doing it to herself again. Grimly, she swore to herself, *No more.* She was nowhere near as far gone as she had once been, but this wouldn't happen to her again. No matter what. She was doing better, but it wasn't enough. No matter what, she had to do more than this. Had to do better.

"The doctor strongly advised me to abort the baby. Told me I'd never make it to full term, and if by some slight chance I did, the baby would be severely handicapped and may not survive delivery. He had been starved and neglected when he needed the most care. He was so small. I didn't even weigh a hundred pounds, but somehow, this little life was inside me and trying to live.

"A part of you," she whispered, her voice hot and intense. "And that was all that mattered. I think the doctor thought I was crazy—thought maybe it was a way of committing suicide or something. He did everything he could to make me understand how dangerous it was. He tried to make Dad see his side. Neither one of us would listen. Dad was ready to support whatever decision I made. We found a doctor who was willing to try.

"Dr. Gray said from the beginning it was likely I would miscarry at any given time. And I might not survive the pregnancy. I was unbelievably weak. He wanted to make sure I knew what I was saying, what I was up against. I told him I wouldn't give up my baby. I wouldn't... I couldn't.

"So he put me in the hospital right away. Rode with me in the ambulance, walked me through the admission process. He wasn't leaving anything to chance. I think he spent more time with me than he spent with most of his other patients combined."

She sighed and turned around to face Wade. So far he hadn't said anything. Hadn't spoken. The look on his face was dark, unreadable. Unable to keep looking at him, she lowered her gaze to the floor.

"I was in the hospital two weeks. I gained back four pounds and my heart rate returned to normal. I had to stay on the medicine though, throughout the pregnancy. I was out of the danger zone, gaining weight and eating regular meals. But...but my baby wasn't doing so well. He had been neglected during the most important time and he wasn't growing or moving around the way he was supposed to. The ultrasound showed him to be half the size he should have been." Her mouth trembled briefly before firming.

Her next words were cut off with a yelp when hard arms closed tightly around her, like bands of iron. Wade buried his face against her neck, shuddering, rocking her back and forth. His baby. Not another man's. His. She had been too busy grieving herself to death to go to another man.

Wade didn't even realize she was speaking until he raised his head, his eyes diamond bright with unshed tears, and saw her mouth moving. *Sorry.* She whispered it, over and over. "I am so sorry."

Sorry...?

Wade shook her slightly, his voice low and rough. "Don't you apologize to me. I'm the one who screwed up. It was my fault—"

She covered his mouth with her hand and shook her head. "No, Wade." Her voice was determined and firm. "No. It was my fault. I put myself in the hospital and I let myself wither away. I almost killed our baby. I had screwed up and I was going to fix it."

She leaned forward then, settling into his arms briefly, steadying herself. "We pulled through somehow. He was born normal and healthy, just a little small for his age. I went overdue almost a month while his body played catch up." She grimaced and added, "I had to spend the final three weeks in

220

the hospital, hooked up to monitors, just in case."

"But then, like he had decided he was ready, I went into labor and he came along just fine on his own. He was so beautiful," she whispered, her voice soft and lost in thought.

Nikki shifted, turning around so that her back was against Wade's front. He remained wrapped around her, his face buried against her hair, while she continued to speak. "He looked just like you. He was the light of my life. Everything was going to work out okay for me. I bought my own house, and we moved into it the day after he turned six months. Spent our first Christmas there."

Wade closed his eyes, not wanting to hear any more. He knew the rest of the story, vividly, had a nightmare or two of his own about it. But she was determined to finish telling it.

"He would have been just four months younger than Abby," she whispered. "Would have started school next year."

A shudder racked her body from head to toe. Anger edged her voice as she started to speak of the stormy day three and a half years earlier. "Shawn was staying up at the house for a few days. He'd been fighting with Dad a lot, needed to get away from it. We had gone into town for some groceries and we were on our way out. This storm came up. We were going to Dad's. I knew better than to drive home in that kind of weather. We were less than a mile away and this car came out of nowhere. I heard this horrible noise, this loud crash and there was this terrible jolt. Then the world started to spin. I had tried to jerk the wheel to the right, away from the drop off.

"I wasn't able to." Her voice shuddered and broke, hands clenched into fists. "The bastard hit us again, trying to go around us on the side of the shoulder. The safe side. I lost control and we went tumbling over the hill, broke through the guard rail. When I came to the rain had stopped. And my little boy was gone."

She fell silent once she finished talking, and Wade just sat there while his eyes burned and his throat ached from the knot inside it. A hot, greasy ball of shame settled low in his gut. *My son.* Already dead and buried and Wade hadn't even known he existed. He was shaken and confused, angry at both himself and at her. Why hadn't she told him?

It was ironic. He had married a woman he didn't love because she had been pregnant, and years later he learns the woman he did love had been pregnant as well. It sounded like something that belonged on a talk show.

Do you know a man who left his fiancée to marry a woman he didn't love because she was pregnant with his child? Did this man unknowingly leave his fiancée pregnant?

Wade carefully shifted Nikki aside, not trusting himself to speak. He got to his feet and walked to stare out the window, hands tucked into the back pockets of his jeans. Damn it all to hell.

What am I supposed to do now? he wondered. He closed his eyes and rested his forehead against the cold pane of glass, a weary sigh escaping him. Grief, black as night, swirled within his heart, mixed with impotent anger. What was he supposed to say?

And beneath it all, the anger, the grief, the confusion and the guilt, he felt relief. It hadn't been another man. He wouldn't have to let her go in order to save her from his own anger.

The grief mingled with happiness, making it bittersweet. He had lost a son he had never known existed. But he would be able to keep her. They could make more children, other sons.

He'd never know this one.

There can be others though, he thought, his mind racing from one thought to the next.

Why hadn't she told him before now?

Why hadn't she come to him when she had learned about the baby? He would have helped her.

Do you really think she would have wanted your help?

No. Probably not.

But why hadn't she told him before now? There had been plenty of times she could have mentioned. *Wade, by the way, a few months after Jamie had Abby, I had a baby myself. He looked just like you.*

He heard the brush of fabric across fabric, then the shift of wooden planks being walked on. Turning, he stared into her eyes, seeing his own torment reflected there.

"Why didn't you tell me before now?" he asked quietly, keeping tight control of his own anger. It was, after all, rather poetic justice. He had come seeking retribution and had ended up finding out he was his own worst enemy. He was the nameless, faceless bastard that had haunted his dreams.

Her shoulders lifted and fell in a weak shrug, the corners of her full mouth turned down in an unhappy frown. "I didn't want you back in my life. I was determined to keep you out of it. I told myself you didn't have the right to know, even though I knew it wasn't true." Nikki moved away as she spoke, snagging his shirt from the floor and pulling it over her head. It fell quickly to cover her pale flesh and fragile body. "And I try not to think about it much. It hurts too much. Telling you wasn't going to bring him back, so I told myself there was no reason to put myself through it."

Slowly, Wade nodded, accepting that. He could understand that, even if he didn't like it. He couldn't even imagine how he would have felt if Abby—

He shied away from that thought, focusing on the matter at hand. "I had a right to know," he said quietly, his voice intense. "Regardless of how you felt about me, I had a right to know."

Nikki turned to stare at him, her head cocked, her shiny sweep of chestnut hair falling across her brow. "Did you really? Legally, yes, you did. But I have to wonder, if I had told you from the beginning, what would have happened? You would have insisted on having rights, visiting privileges. I would have been forced to see you with your wife and your daughter. I was already in bad shape. How right would it have been to put me through that, especially when I did nothing wrong, nothing to deserve what happened to me? I lost everything, Wade. He was all I had. Why should I have shared him with you?"

"Because he was mine," Wade rasped, his eyes narrowing as he moved closer.

"And you were mine. I shouldn't have had to share you with Jamie. It would have killed me to see you with her. Can't you understand that?" she demanded, her eyes flashing angrily at him.

"Yeah, well, if you had been forced to share your son, maybe you wouldn't have left Louisville, and maybe he'd still be alive," Wade snapped, catching hold of her and jerking her up against him.

It was a good thing he had hold of her arms, because she wilted at his words, her body going lax while she stared up at him out of huge anguished eyes.

Wade could have kicked himself the minute the words left his mouth. There was no way to take them back. Staring down at her, he damned himself to hell and back, but he didn't release his hold on her. She was as limp in his hands as a rag doll, absolutely no strength in her body. Her eyes were dark and wounded.

Carefully, he scooped her limp body up and deposited her on the couch before moving away, regret burning in the back of his mouth like acid. "I shouldn't have said that," he finally said, resuming his spot back at the window. "I'm sorry."

The silence reigned for what seemed like an eternity. Wade tried to find a way to soothe the most recent pain he had inflicted on this woman but could think of nothing. How could he have said that? He didn't blame her, so why did he say something that would make her think he did?

Wade had to figure out a way to make this better. They had so much they needed to talk about, so many important things, and he had gone and totally bungled things before they could even begin.

He was formulating what he would say and how to say it when the quiet noise behind him began.

When he worked up the nerve to turn around, she stood before him dressed in his shirt and her jeans, her boots laced up. Her jacket was in her arms and she held it to her breast like a shield. "I'd like to go home now," she said woodenly through stiff lips.

"No." The panic that rose was swift and thick, enveloping his mind and freezing any apologies he had been about to make. Panic fueled the simmering frustration and he lost the ability to think clearly.

"I would like to go home now," she repeated.

Wade shook his head, moving to grab her arms. She stood rigidly under his hands, staring at a point past his shoulder. "Damn it, Nikki. Don't you think it's time we settled this?" he insisted, wishing desperately he could take back the past few minutes. Hell, the past few weeks.

"It is settled, Wade."

"It's not," he argued, tipping her head back, forcing her eyes to meet his. They were empty, blank. Her skin was pale, her face smooth. Under his hands, she trembled slightly, minutely, as though frozen from within. "Don't you think I'm entitled to a little bit of anger here? Maybe one could even expect me to be a bit of a jackass. This is one hell of a piece of news you handed me."

Her lids lowered slowly, shielding her eyes from him while she studied him from under the fringe of her lashes. "I lost my fiancé. That damn near destroyed me. If it wasn't for my little

225

boy, I would have given up. Then I lost him. Again, I had to rebuild a life for myself, this time alone. The past few years have been a bit traumatic for me, Wade. If anybody is entitled to be a bit of a jackass, it would be me."

Now her eyes rose, locked on his. Hot, angry. Softly, she asked, "Tell me something, Wade, what have you lost?"

"I lost you," he whispered, his own eyes dark and haunted.

"Through nobody's fault but your own," she reminded. "That was your doing, nobody else's. I think I've had more than my fair share of heartache. I certainly don't need you to add to it. I told you this because I thought we were going to give this one more shot. I felt it was past time you knew. I made a mistake and I admit that. However, it has become clear to me that you blame me for making what most would agree was the right decision. You appear to blame me for wanting to raise my son in a place a little safer than where I lived. He could have easily been killed crossing the street or in a drive-by shooting. He could have been kidnapped and murdered or any number of things. Would that have been my fault? If it had happened in Louisville, would I still be to blame?"

Exasperated, frustrated, he shook her. "I don't blame you. I shouldn't have said that, but damn it, you threw me off track. How can I be expected to be logical?"

She merely stared at him, through him. From the way she was looking at him, he realized she had already dismissed him from her mind. *Not if I have anything to do with it, you haven't,* Wade thought angrily. She wasn't going to spring a surprise like this on him, and then stomp off because he had reacted in a less than admirable manner.

"You can't just leave things like this, damn it. It's unfinished."

"Is it?" She turned her head, looking at him this time instead of through him. "And how would you propose that we finish this? What would be an appropriate ending? Are we going to kiss and make up, act like we weren't the biggest mistake on God's green earth? Or maybe we should just shake hands and be friends. How should this story end, Wade? God knows I've tried to figure that out, but I'll have to admit I'm stumped."

"I...I don't know," he answered helplessly.

Nikki turned away, tossed her jacket down on the couch as she paced the floor. *Damn it all. When are things ever going to be easy for me?* she wondered with resignation. Nothing in her life was ever easy. She stopped at the back door, her eyes roaming sightlessly over the landscape.

She had to admit...it was lovely here, even in the desolate winter light.

Maybe this summer she would take a few weeks and go stay at her dad's cabin, wherever in the hell that was. If he didn't go and put it on the market like he had mentioned off and on the past two years.

On the market.

And Nikki remembered a For Sale sign that graced the yard of a little ranch house in Monticello.

Slowly, she turned on her heel. She remembered her feeling in the truck on the way up here that there was something odd going on behind those dark eyes. Remembered the odd shuttered look in his eyes as he braced himself above her. For a moment then, she hadn't known this man.

What in the hell is going on here? she wondered.

"Why did you bring me up here, Wade?" she inquired calmly, even though there was a burning in her chest. Even though deep inside, she already knew what was going on. Anger, the kind she hadn't felt in years, was building. She tried to rein it in, but she wasn't having much luck.

He stared at her, his dark eyes blank. She knew. She had figured it out. "I think you know why I brought you up here," he finally said, turning away.

"Why is your house for sale?"

He stared out the window, his eyes not really seeing the beautiful cold winter morning. "I'm moving back to Indiana. Abby's not happy here. I'm not happy."

His answer fanned the hot flames that were spreading to engulf her body. "So," she said coldly, glaring at him. "This was...what? One last trip down memory lane?"

"More or less," he replied.

"You went to an awful lot of trouble for a roll in the sack, Wade," Nikki said, her voice ice cold. As she spoke, she turned back to stare out the window. She struggled to regulate her breathing, to rein in the anger. *Stay calm about this, Nik,* she told herself. *Getting mad isn't going to solve anything.*

She was silent a moment longer and then she whirled, her eyes locking on his.

"*You son of a bitch!*" she shouted, advancing on him until she stood toe-to-toe with him. Small hands planted against his chest and she shoved with all her strength, but was unsatisfied when all he did was stumble backward a step before coming up against the wall.

"I never thought you were a cruel man, Wade, but that was before this little stunt. Did it ever occur to you what might be going on in my head if I were to give in to you?" she demanded, thumping his chest with a clenched fist. "You have been after me for months to give you a second chance. I wanted *us* to have a second chance. That's why I came back from New York. Hell, if I'd wanted some quick and easy sex, I could have gotten that *there*. I come back here. I give in, against my better judgment, only to find out you just wanted a private farewell party."

"Nikki—"

"Shut up," she said softly, baring her teeth at him in a snarl. "Just shut up." She spun on her heel, pacing back and forth. "You barged into my life just when I was finally able to think about living again," she muttered. Then she stomped back and rose up on her toes until they were nose-to-nose. "You tore it apart all over again. You intruded on my privacy for weeks. You interfered with my personal life. You went out of your way to cause me more pain. You brought me here under false pretenses."

She paused to suck in air, lower her voice. "I could have handled that. I didn't protest or tell you no when that's all it would have taken to make you stop. I didn't do that, because I wanted you. I wanted to make love with you. But this wasn't about making love. It was about adding one more memory to your hope chest."

Nikki moved away from him, cupping her elbows in her hands and hugging herself. "Well," she said hollowly, the anger draining out of her as quickly as it had risen. "I hope you enjoyed getting your rocks off. Did you get everything you wanted or is there something we missed?"

"Nikki—"

She held up her hand, cutting him off. Shutting him out. "Just take me home now, Wade. We're done."

Wade jammed his fists in his pockets, staring at her closed face. She had shut down and locked up, he realized. He wasn't going to be able to talk to her now. He relented with a slight nod, gathering his gear, dragging the rest of his clothes on as she stood and stared out the windows.

He knew she wasn't seeing anything. Her soulful eyes were as cold as the air outside, and empty.

Where do we go from here? he wondered wearily, shoving his arms into the sleeves of his coat, pocketing his keys.

This trip had definitely deviated from his plan.

I had a son, he thought bleakly.

And he wondered what the little boy had looked like, how his laugh had sounded.

Grief for the child he had never known, and never would know, ripped through him. He paused outside the door of the cabin. Behind him, Nikki was settling in the truck. He pressed his palms to his eyes and dragged a deep, cold draught of air into his lungs. *How in the hell am I supposed to deal with this?*

Hours later he pulled up in front of her house. "How much longer are you going to keep running from yourself, Nikki?" Wade asked, killing the engine as he stared up at her silent house. Moonlight gilded his features with a silvery glow, casting one half of his face into shadow.

"I'm not running from anything," she stated coldly. "I just want to lead my life the way I choose to do so. I don't want to have to live my life weighing every decision I make, wondering what next you'll find to blame me for."

She tugged on the door handle, only to discover it was still locked. "Let me out, Wade."

He ignored her as he quietly said, "The only thing I do blame you for is choosing to spend your life alone, miserable, instead of taking a chance. I'm sorry, Nicole. I don't know how many more times I'll have to say that before you can forgive me."

Tossing him an angry glare, she said, "I had forgiven you. More the fool me. I came back here to try to give things a second chance. If I wanted to be alone, I would have stayed in New York. And that's exactly what I should have done. Maybe I should thank you for that little trip to Smokies. It certainly brought me back to my senses."

"Is there anything I could say that would explain that?" he muttered, speaking more to himself than to her. "If you came back to try this again, then why not go ahead and try?"

"Because you proved to me it would be a waste of my time,

Wade. You're not worth wasting any more time on. You were right about that, after all. You are not worth it. No man who does what you just did is."

"What in the hell did I do that was so terrible?" he asked, refusing to think of what he had been planning to do, get her to admit how she felt and then walk away. "I didn't make you any promises. And you knew my house had been sold. You should have assumed what I was up to." Snagging her chin, he made her face him. "And you can't say you weren't willing."

"Why should I lie?" she asked, shrugging her shoulders. "You're right. I was willing. And I should have known better than to think it was all going to end happily ever after. But this is a better ending anyway. Now we both know where the other stands. I know you've turned into a using, lying, womanizing bastard. You know I've turned into the bitch who only looks out for number one." With an icy glare, she said, "Now, let me out of this damn truck, get off my damn mountain and out of this damn town. I don't ever want to see you again."

Silently, he thumbed the lock mechanism, all the while staring at her with sad eyes. As she started to slide out of the truck, he spoke. Unable to stop herself, she froze and listened.

"We didn't have a choice last time. I took that away from us with my stupidity. We had a choice this time. And it looks like you've made yours." He stretched out his arm, brushed his thumb across her lip.

"Find a way to be happy, Nikki. Believe it or not, I want that for you."

Moments later, her back pressed against the door to her house, Nikki started to shake. Gravel crunched outside as Wade turned his truck around and headed down the mountain. And out of her life.

Be happy.

Did he have to go and say things like that? Things that

made her think? Made her doubt her decisions?

Was she doing what was right? What was best?

When was the last time she had ever really been happy?

Chapter Nineteen

Three months later

A warm early summer breeze drifted past, catching the ends of her hair and tugging at them playfully. As she sat next to the grave, knees drawn up to her chest, Nikki stared at the pale gray headstone.

This was the first time she had come here in over a month. Slowly, she had come to realize it had become an obsession with her. Forcing herself to stay away had been her therapy. It had been harder than she had expected at first, and then it had been so much easier than she could ever have hoped. The grief that weighed upon her like a stone was lessening, bit by bit, day by day.

Running a hand over the closely cropped grass, she closed her eyes.

Her baby wasn't here. Not anymore. He was beyond where she could reach him and in a better place than this. A place where broken hearts and broken families were unknown. A place where rage, misery and betrayal didn't exist.

With her eyes still closed, she pulled up an image of him, his sweet laughing face as he had toddled though the stream not very far from where she sat, tiny fish darting between his little feet.

Over the past few months, since Wade and his little girl had packed up and left, she had come to realize a person didn't have to be there physically. Jason was still with her, tucked safely inside her soul where he couldn't be hurt.

The memories of his father and sister he had never known were with him.

With a sigh, she rose to her knees, pressed her hand flat to the headstone. Silently, she said her goodbyes.

It was time to let go.

And it was time to get on with her own life.

She made her way to the little church. Her SUV sat parked in front, black paint gleaming under the sun. She paused, one hand resting on the hood as she stared back at the cemetery. A breeze drifted by, bringing with it the unmistakable scent of honeysuckle. Tipping her head back, she drew the air in and smiled.

Saying goodbye didn't hurt as much as she had thought it would.

Something tickled her hand and she looked down. Perched there, on her index finger, was a tiny butterfly. Pale yellow wings marked with traces of blue.

Cautiously, she lifted her hand, waiting for it fly off.

It didn't. She held it up to her face as her smile bloomed.

Jason.

Vividly, she remembered the picnic. How her little boy had chased after butterflies and found a dead one, one with wings the color of the sun and the sky. The scent of honeysuckle on the air. The pleasure of the early summer sun shining down on them.

He had come back to say goodbye.

Sometimes she had thought his loss had been so devastating partially because she hadn't been able to say goodbye, had never been able to find the closure she so badly needed. Maybe she had spent all these hours by the graveside searching for him just so she could say goodbye.

But he had never been there.

Until now.

She could feel him all around her. Maybe it was her imagination, but at this moment she heard a deep baby chuckle, smelled the soft scent of his skin.

Suddenly the butterfly fluttered its wings and took off. As it flew away from her, the dragging, heavy weight of grief fell from her shoulders.

And Nikki understood what it was like to be free.

If only she'd been able to do this months ago, she might not have lost Wade.

Smiling a sad little smile, she climbed into her car. She had come to grips with the pain, the way she had so desperately needed. It had finally eased. It was still there, but it had distanced itself from her, become more bearable.

She had come to grips with losing Wade.

You simply couldn't have everything in life you wanted. You just had to make do with what you had.

Shrugging off the memories, she started the SUV and headed for home.

The little red light on her machine was blinking. For once it didn't occur to her to ignore it until the poor machine could hold no more messages. She hit the play button as she kicked off her sandals.

The voice that filled the room was unfamiliar.

At first.

"Hello. I'm trying to reach a Nicole Kline. I'm not sure if I have the right number." Silence. "This is Louise Lightfoot. I was asked to try and contact you." There was more silence, followed by a deep shuddering breath. As she waited, frozen in dread, listening to that voice from the past, Nikki prayed. Like she had never prayed before. "My son...Wade... There's been...an accident, Ms. Kline. He was asking for you. He's in..."

Nikki's legs folded beneath her as the woman named off the largest trauma hospital in Louisville. "Please, God," she whispered softly, weakly. "Please, God. Not again." For a few moments longer she knelt on the floor folded over, her face buried in her hands as her all-too-vivid imagination painted the worst possible pictures.

Then she saw Abby's little face.

And shot to her feet.

In less than ten minutes she was on the road to Louisville, speaking rapidly into a cellular phone she rarely used. It was several years old and dusty. She kept it out of habit more than anything else. This was the first time she'd used it in months, if not longer.

She listened to the standard tripe handed out to non-family members. She hung up on the bored nurse, called again, listened to the same crap from a more understanding nurse who offered to get a family member.

The voice that came on the phone was another blast from the past. Wade's older brother Joe. "He was working—trying to patch somebody up and some idiot ran the red light, didn't see the ambulance, bunch of stupid, lame-ass *shit* and he's in a coma. We've been trying to track you down ever since. He was...he was asking for you when they brought him in. It was touch and go that first night. They didn't think he would make it. Mom finally got in touch with your dad earlier today, but he wouldn't give her your number. She called back again later and your brother gave her your home phone number."

Nikki stored that little piece of information to deal with later and asked the question she hated to ask. "How is he?"

"Unresponsive," Joe said quietly. "Swelling on the brain. More medical crap than I can understand. We, ah, we don't know...we don't know if he's going to come out of it or not."

"The doctors?"

"They keep saying we have to keep hoping for the best, but you can tell they're losing faith that anything will happen. There's no physical reason for the coma. It's been a week, Nik."

"He's gonna be fine," Nikki said, her voice rough. "Talk to him, okay? He will hear you. Tell him...tell him I'm coming."

She could only hope he really wanted her there.

Wade was floating in darkness. Occasionally a familiar voice would break past the thick cloud that seemed to envelope him. Mom, Dad and Joe. Lori and Zack. It was funny those two being married. Most often it was Abby's sweet little voice that called to him, telling him stories the best she could remember. The longer she spoke the closer he came to getting out of the dark well, but always, her voice would start to falter, then tremble and break, and then she was gone and he was adrift again.

The one voice he wanted to hear, kept waiting for, never came. He thought he remembered calling out for her after... After what?

Had he been in an accident? He didn't feel like it. But then again, he couldn't feel much of anything.

Occasionally the darkness was relieved by lights. Two different lights. Confused, he would freeze where he was, afraid to move toward either one. He knew what those lights meant, but why would there be two of them? He didn't want to die. He wasn't ready.

Why were there two lights?

Another voice floated to him, soft, female, familiar, but then Wade recognized his mother's voice, her scent. Losing interest, he withdrew.

Nikki stood at the foot of the bed, staring at the figure lying limply under white sheets. Not so long ago she had lain in a bed much like this in a small country hospital, tubes running this way and that. A thin tube had been inserted through his nose to feed him and the faint outline of another tube led toward a catheter bag. Yeah. She had been there before.

One arm was turned up, exposing his inner elbow where an IV line was secured. Clear fluid fed into the line from a bag hanging at the bedside.

He was thinner, paler. Weaker.

"Are you going to talk to him?"

Slowly, she turned. Standing in the doorway was Abby, clad in a pink top and blue jeans. She had grown quite a bit from when Nikki had last seen her. With a start Nikki realized it had been almost a year.

"Yeah," she answered, her voice tight and rusty sounding. "I'm going to talk to him." She nodded politely at Louise, feeling vaguely uncomfortable and ashamed. Wade's mother had always made her feel that way. She held her hand out to Abby and offered, "Why don't we both talk to him?"

Slowly, Abby reached out her hand, leaving her grandmother's side. In her oddly adult way, she said, "I think my dad loves you. He was so sad when we left."

"I was sad too," Nikki admitted, passing a gentle hand down the inky black hair. Why did adults always think they were hiding their problems from children? The little kids always knew.

"Then why did you let us leave? We could have stayed if you'd asked him," Abby whispered, her large brown eyes filling with tears. "We could have stayed."

"Maybe we both needed some time to figure out what we really wanted," Nikki said.

"I know what he wanted. I know what I wanted. We wanted you to be our family," Abby said, her eyes straying to the figure in the bed. "Was it because of me? Didn't you like me enough to be my mom?"

Nikki didn't think her heart could hurt any more than it already did, but she was wrong. "Oh, sweetie," she murmured, pulling the little girl into her arms. "Baby, it wasn't you. It was me. I've been all messed up inside and I'm just now starting to get myself straightened out."

Over Abby's small shoulder, Nikki saw Louise Lightfoot standing guard. Protecting son and grandchild. Seeing the woman in front of her as someone who hadn't measured up, hadn't been good enough for her son. Nikki reckoned Louise blamed her for Wade's indiscretion with Jamie. If she had been the type of girl she should have been, Wade wouldn't have strayed. Nikki also knew she certainly wasn't what the older woman had pictured her future daughter-in-law to be. From the wrong side of town, a broken family, hoodlums for brothers, an alcoholic for a father, the daughter of a woman who had killed herself rather than deal with the problems in her life.

None of that counted now. Her hoodlum brothers were reformed for the most part. Her father was sober and had been for years. Nikki had stumbled a few times, but she had proven to be stronger than her mother. They lived in a small town where people liked and respected them.

But even if that hadn't been the case, Nikki knew it wouldn't have mattered.

Wade thought she was good enough. He had wanted her, and God willing, hopefully, he still did. The little girl clinging desperately to her shoulders definitely wanted her. That was what mattered.

Rubbing a soothing hand over Abby's back, she rose, cradling the little girl against her. Carefully, she settled in the chair by the bed and reached out and took Wade's hand.

239

"What should we say?" Abby whispered.

"I don't know. What do you think we should say?" Nikki asked.

With the hope of the young, Abby cocked her head and said, "Maybe we should tell him how little girls ought to have a dog. A real one."

"Wise choice," Nikki decided.

Side by side, they talked until their throats were raw and their voices hoarse. Twilight was settling in when they fell silent. Sleepily, Abby asked, "Do you think he heard?"

"I know he did, honey," Nikki said with a smile as she brushed back silky black locks of hair from Abby's face.

"Why doesn't he wake up?"

"I think he's kind of lost. It's like he's in a place he doesn't know and somebody went and turned out the lights. He's just got to find his way out. That's why we need to keep talking to him. If he hears us, he'll know which way to go."

With a sleepy smile, Abby said, "He gets lost a lot. He always finds his way back though."

"He will this time too," Nikki promised. She hoped she wasn't lying.

Abby fell asleep on her lap, her face pressed against Nikki's breast, small arms locked around her neck.

From the chair in the corner Louise sighed and said, "I wished we could have explained it to her like that. We didn't know what to tell her." Silence fell again as Louise came and collected her sleeping granddaughter. "I need to get her home. Do you really think he heard?" Louise asked, her voice breaking.

"Yes."

"How can you be so certain?"

With a sad smile, Nikki replied, "Because nothing else is

acceptable."

Moments later, quiet footsteps were followed by the soft click of the door and then Nikki was alone with Wade. Pressing her lips together, Nikki reached once again for his hand.

"Wade, it's me," she said, forcing her voice to be level. "Buddy, you need to wake up. There's people here who need you. Your little girl. Your folks." In a whisper, she added, "Me.

"We went and messed things up real good, Wade. But that doesn't mean we can't straighten them out." Her voice broke and she clenched her hand tightly around his. "Damn it, Wade. Don't do this. I can't lose somebody else. You've got to come out of this." Tears fell down her cheeks and she leaned forward, laying one arm around his waist, resting her face against his belly. "I love you. I always did. Sometimes I hated myself because I couldn't stop. But it's a part of me, like breathing, like writing. I can't live without you. I can live with you not wanting me, but I can't do it unless you're out there somewhere."

His face remained still, his eyes closed, as she continued to cry against his chest. "Damn you, Wade. Wake up."

Her voice faltered and then strengthened as she started to talk to him. She told him about Jason, about the pregnancy, about the short time she'd had with him before she lost him. "He looked just like you. He was smart and sweet and funny."

She told him about her books, the ones she had written. The ideas that brewed and simmered in her head before she was able to get them down on paper. She told him about her family, how they had straightened out and actually started acting like a family. How Dylan and Shawn had gone from troubled street punks to hotheaded but decent young men.

He was silent through it all.

Shifts changed. New nurses came and went. One quietly offered to get her a drink, some food, and was told no. Another suggested she get some rest and was ignored. Some of Wade's old friends had pulled strings, talked to a couple of doctors, and Nikki could stay around the clock. She wasn't leaving until he woke up.

Sometime near dawn, eyes dry and burning, Nikki released his hand and rose. She wandered over to the window and stared out at the sleeping city. In the distance she could see the Kennedy Bridge and the distant lights of southern Indiana.

She was back here. Again. Not exactly the way she'd wanted to return home. Restless, she paced the room. Why wouldn't he wake up?

Silence swarmed all around him and Wade wanted to scream with frustration. Where had she gone? Nikki?

He couldn't talk, couldn't move... *Damn it!* Was she going to walk away again? If she did, he wouldn't even be able to stop her. He should have tried harder last time, should have kept pushing her.

Damn it, where had she gone?

He floundered, hesitating. Two different lights. Which one led the way home, to Abby, to Nikki?

He paused, turning from one to the other. As the silence continued, he made a choice.

Soft sobs filled the room. Nikki still sat at the bedside, her face buried in the sheets by Wade's side. It had been three days. Three days since she had first entered this quiet room. Since that first day, she hadn't cried. Until now. Sheer exhaustion and fear had eaten away at her and sometime after Louise had taken Abby home she had simply broken.

"Oh, God, Wade," she whispered raggedly. "You have to come back." One hand clutched desperately at his.

"Cry..."

Startled, she jerked upright, one hand pressing against her

mouth. His face was pale, his hand limp in hers. But his sculpted mouth parted. "Wade?" she whispered, almost afraid to speak.

"Don't cry."

"Wade," she gasped, leaning forward as his eyelids slowly lifted. Then he was staring up at her. "Please don't...cry," he repeated, his voice a weak whisper.

"I can't help it," she wailed as more sobs built in her throat. Tears of relief this time, as she huddled at the bedside, his hand clutching hers tightly.

"Did you mean it?"

A day later Nikki raised her head to look him. Gritty-eyed from lack of sleep, her mind bleary, she asked, "Mean what?"

"What you said."

"You heard me?"

He frowned at her over the tray of hospital food, broth and jello. *Yum.* "I heard you say you loved me. Did you mean it?"

Locking her gaze on his, she simply said, "Yes."

"What do you plan do about it?"

"What do you think we should do?"

It was almost night again. His parents had finally headed out, leaving them alone. She was nervous and scared and hopeful. He had clutched her hand most of the day, as though he feared she would disappear if he let go.

"I think you should marry me," he decided, his voice hoarse, both from lack of use and from the feeding tube that been removed the past night. But his tone was firm, almost belligerent.

"Is that a proposal?" she asked, cocking her head as she lazily swung one foot back and forth. She looked casual and relaxed, but her insides were jumping with happiness and hope.

"No," he snapped. "I'm telling you. I proposed once and that was a damn disaster. This time I'm telling you."

"Telling me?" she asked archly, raising that arrogant eyebrow and staring at him. "Don't you think this is something we should talk about?"

Catching the teasing twinkle in her eye, he tugged her hand. Willingly, she came down to cuddle against his side. He covered her mouth with a rough, almost desperate kiss. Then he buried his face in her hair as he replied, "No. You spend too much time talking. Haven't I already told you we get along much better if we don't use our mouths to talk?"

She smiled and whispered, "I have just one more thing to say."

"What?" He scowled.

Nikki lowered her head, nipped his lip gently before turning her head to whisper into his ear, "Yes..."

Author's Note

Sometimes an author gets asked which of their characters they identify with the most. Without a doubt, for me it would be Nikki.

Both of us are writers and both of us fell for a guy in our teens, although my road was a lot smoother than Nikki's. I married my high school sweetheart without any of this drama and angst. I also, thank God, never had to deal with any of the relationship mishaps Nikki did—and that's good for my guy as well, because I might have skinned him.

We both deal with the same frustrations as writers—and there are many. The writing part is very often hard and a pain in the butt—it's also only part of an actual writer's job. Neither Nikki nor I realized that starting out.

We both suffered a similar loss.

Nikki's loss of her son was a pivotal point in her life and that loss was part of the reason I was leery to consider putting this book back out on the market.

In 2005, I miscarried. While the losses weren't identical, the pain of losing my baby was too close, and for too long I couldn't even think of this book without hurting.

When I first considered releasing this book again in late 2009, the first thing I had to consider was whether I could read the book without breaking apart. I managed. Since I could get through it, I decided maybe it was time to do some revisions.

So many people kept asking for the book. I hope you've enjoyed it. It's not one of my best, I know, but trust me, in ways you may never understand—and hopefully you won't have to—it's one of the hardest.

Shiloh Walker

About the Author

To learn more about Shiloh, please visit www.shilohwalker.com. Send an email to Shiloh at shiloh_@shilohwalker.com or join her Yahoo! group to join in the fun with other readers as well as Shiloh. http://groups.yahoo.com/group/SHI_nenigans/

LaVergne, TN USA
18 January 2011
212951LV00007B/16/P